M

 ROMANCING

D1013559

**Murder at the palace! Was this royal demise
carefully planned or strictly a crime of passion?
The search for the killer heats up as the king's
investigator is ordered to work with the victim's
beautifully distracting sister.**

**Meet the major players
in this royal mystery....**

Nina Caruso: Her brother's murder sweeps
her into a royal world of power and desire. Now
she must put her life in the hands of a brooding
investigator who isn't so sure of her brother's
innocence—or hers.

Ryan McDonough: His tragic past has made
him love-shy, but even this cagey investigator
can't ignore a royal order to learn one beautiful
woman's secrets.

Duke Lorenzo Sebastiani: A happy newlywed
with the power to bring together two seemingly
opposite people is a dangerous thing in a kingdom
suddenly bursting with romance and intrigue....

King Marcus of Montebello: As the eve of his
son's installation as heir to the throne approaches,
the king makes palace safety paramount. And if he
knows more about Lorenzo's reasons for allowing
a lovely woman to work with his head investigator,
this wise monarch is keeping his own counsel....

Dear Reader,

It's always cause for celebration when Sharon Sala writes a new book, so prepare to cheer for *The Way to Yesterday*. How many times have you wished for a chance to go back in time and get a second chance at something? Heroine Mary O'Rourke gets that chance, and you'll find yourself caught up in her story as she tries to make things right with the only man she'll ever love.

ROMANCING THE CROWN continues with Lyn Stone's *A Royal Murder*. The suspense—and passion—never flag in this exciting continuity series. Catherine Mann has only just begun her Intimate Moments career, but already she's created a page-turning military miniseries in WINGMEN WARRIORS. *Grayson's Surrender* is the first of three "don't miss" books. Look for the next, *Taking Cover,* in November.

The rest of the month unites two talented veterans—Beverly Bird, with *All the Way,* and Shelley Cooper, with *Laura and the Lawman*—with exciting newcomer Cindy Dees, who debuts with *Behind Enemy Lines*. Enjoy them all—and join us again next month, when we once again bring you an irresistible mix of excitement and romance in six new titles by the best authors in the business.

Leslie J. Wainger
Executive Senior Editor

Please address questions and book requests to:
Silhouette Reader Service
U.S.: 3010 Walden Ave., P.O. Box 1325, Buffalo, NY 14269
Canadian: P.O. Box 609, Fort Erie, Ont. L2A 5X3

A Royal Murder
LYN STONE

INTIMATE MOMENTS™

Published by Silhouette Books

America's Publisher of Contemporary Romance

Special thanks and acknowledgment are given to Lyn Stone for
her contribution to the ROMANCING THE CROWN series.

This book is dedicated to my grandmothers,
Dolly Pauline Cato, who treasured home and
family togetherness, and Jessie Herron Perkins,
who loved travel, adventure and making up stories.

 SILHOUETTE BOOKS

ISBN 0-373-27242-1

A ROYAL MURDER

Copyright © 2002 by Harlequin Books S.A.

Visit Silhouette at www.eHarlequin.com

Printed in U.S.A.

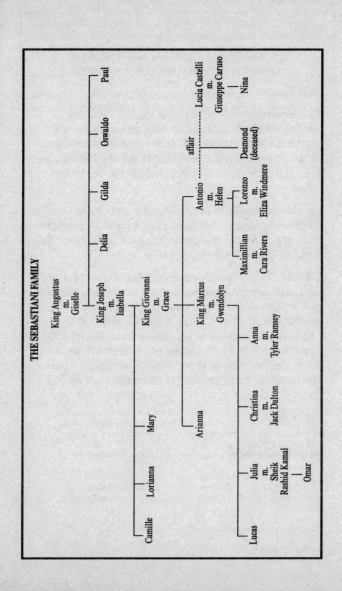

THE SEBASTIANI FAMILY

A note from Lyn Stone, author of both contemporary and historical romance!

Dear Reader,

The opportunity to interact with the other authors in this ROMANCING THE CROWN series has been a joy. Montebello, Tamir and all the inhabitants of these locations have become quite real to me after visiting them and their creators so regularly in the books and online.

My sincere thanks to Leslie Wainger and Lynda Curnyn for offering me the chance to participate in this unique project, and for the wonderful guidance and editing that made all the books tie in so well.

A Royal Murder introduces Ryan McDonough, former Savannah detective and present private investigator hired by the Montebellan royal family, to the sister of the murder victim, Nina Caruso, a graphic designer from California determined to see justice done. Not exactly a match made in heaven when it comes to solving a homicide, but they do strike a match of another kind. The resulting blaze flames out of control even as they dodge the danger of a killer tying up loose ends.

Enjoy the heat!

Lyn Stone

Chapter 1

Ryan McDonough gave the woman the once-over, noting the thinly concealed frustration in her sin-dark eyes and her subtly defensive stance. "I'm sorry for your loss, Ms. Caruso," he said automatically, words repeated countless times to families of countless victims. "I understand your offer to help, but what you want is not possible."

He was sorry to see anyone grieve. God knows he knew what it was like. Grief in this instance must already have passed beyond tears to the second phase. Anger. She was gritting her teeth.

The Caruso woman inclined her head and said, "Thank you for your condolences, but I must insist." Very proper. But still not acceptable.

Ryan turned to Vincente Pavelli, the royal messenger, or crown gofer, or whatever the hell the man's title was. "Tell His Majesty I said thank you, but no dice. Phrase it however you want to, just get the message across."

"But Mr. McDonough…" Pavelli's swarthy face fell and he started to hyperventilate. Sweat popped out in little beads on the forehead that extended to the back of his head as he slid a shaking finger beneath his collar to loosen it.

"Hey, it's not like he shoots the bearer of bad tidings, man. Lighten up." Ryan came around his desk to usher them out. He clapped the man on his skinny, expensively padded shoulder. "Tell him I make it a policy never to include civilians while conducting an investigation. Hard and fast rule. *Capisce?*"

The gofer took several jerky steps toward the door, still looking as if he wanted to argue about it.

"Wait just a minute," Ryan said, his voice a warning growl. "You forgot something." He turned and gestured at the woman, who seemed determined to hold her ground.

She ignored him. "Go ahead and wait in the car, Mr. Pavelli. I need to speak with Mr. McDonough alone."

Pavelli left hurriedly, closing the door, leaving them alone.

Ryan kept a cool head. It usually gave him the advantage. Neither the Montebellans nor the Italians passed on many even-tempered genes to their progeny. Nina Caruso was descended from both. Being raised in America obviously hadn't altered her temperament much. While all that fire just beneath her surface intrigued him, he didn't need to deal with it right now.

"We have nothing to discuss, ma'am," he told her calmly. "The king will have my preliminary report on your brother's death first thing in the morning and any further information as soon as I discover it. His Majesty's advisors will keep you up to date."

She sighed, walked around his desk and sat down in his chair, bold as you please. *His* chair. Propping her elbows on the arms of it, she steepled her fingers under her chin. She had great hands. Long, supple fingers tipped with fairly short nails, painted wine red to match her lips. He tried not to look at the lips, but they kept drawing his attention even when she wasn't speaking.

Ryan shook off his fascination, disgruntled with himself for noticing her looks and with her for provoking him to notice.

"I didn't come halfway around the world to sit somewhere and wait," she declared, her voice clipped and precise, totally devoid of an accent. "My brother's been killed and I'm sticking to you like Super Glue until we find out who did it. Get used to it."

Ryan fought hard for patience. She might be rude, but he hated to be sharp with her. That wasn't his way, especially when she was probably just upset about her half brother's violent death.

Probably being the key word here. Now that he looked at her more objectively, she didn't appear to be all that grief stricken. And she was dangerously close to pushing the wrong button on his control panel, barging in here demanding to know what he'd been doing on the case.

Hell, he was tired. Clearing out all his most urgent cases had eaten up most of yesterday and last night. Since the prime suspect had been cleared, Ryan had yet to decide where he'd go first with the investigation he'd just been assigned. There were forensics reports to go over. He'd only thumbed through the prelims, knowing they weren't yet complete.

Also, he needed to plan interviews, conduct them, talk with the coroner and also do an additional forensics sweep. The police had done the initial investigation of the scene, but he wanted to be thorough now that he was in charge.

First things first. He needed to unload the little baggage who had just arrived.

He sat on the corner of his desk and assumed a relaxed pose, wishing he felt relaxed. "Look, Ms. Caruso—"

"Nina," she said curtly. "We might as well use first names since we'll be spending a great deal of time together. Why don't you begin by listing what you've found out so far. You've had two full days and part of this one." She paused for a second, then added, "Ryan."

Ryan bit his tongue and unclenched his fist, deliberately projecting benevolence and goodwill. She didn't react as expected to outright dismissal. He'd try manners. Not usually his *last* resort and shouldn't be now, but they had gotten off on the wrong foot the minute she'd walked in.

Empathize first, he thought. "Of course you want to know what's going on and I understand that completely. You may read copies of the reports tomorrow if His Majesty sees fit to share them with you. Until then, I must ask you to excuse me so that I can continue to do my job." There. Polite and to the point. *Get lost, cookie.*

"Exactly what is your job?" she asked, not moving a hair.

"I'm a private investigator frequently employed by the Crown," he answered. "Surely you knew that already."

She nodded. "Not chief of criminal investigations."

So she was capable of a neatly placed low blow. "There is no one with that particular title in Montebello. But I assure you, I am qualified to undertake the investigation. I was a homicide detective in a former life." He offered her another smile. "Savannah."

"You were fired?" she guessed.

"No, I resigned." He looked around his well-appointed office as if that was explanation enough for changing jobs. The light gray walls and expensive carpet, sturdy black furniture and maroon leather chairs beat the hell out of his corner of the precinct where he'd spent his first twelve years in law enforcement. And the job here had literally saved his life and sanity.

Lorenzo Sebastiani, chief of royal intelligence, whom Ryan knew well, often called on him to dabble a little in the political intrigue so prevalent in this area of the world. In fact, Lorenzo had recommended him to the king for this particular investigation. Lorenzo had a personal interest in it. He was also half brother to Desmond Caruso, the victim in this case. Both were sons of the king's brother, Duke Antonio Sebastiani, who had died some years ago.

Desmond's mother had been one of the palace maids. She had married an Italian businessman, Guiseppe Caruso, and had moved to the States. Ryan studied the young woman sitting in his chair, a product of that marriage.

"King Marcus assured me you would welcome my help," she said.

"I regret to say he was wrong."

The door opened. Duke Lorenzo entered without preamble. "Good morning," he said formally. Nina rose from the chair.

Ryan eyed him with suspicion. "In case you two haven't met, Nina Caruso, this is His Grace, Duke Lorenzo Sebastiani."

Lorenzo reached for her hand and bowed over it. "Little sister. I regret we must meet for the first time in such terrible circumstances. I share in your grief for the loss of our brother."

"Thank you, Your Grace," she mumbled, obviously a little taken aback and unsure what else she should say.

She made a perfect curtsy, however. Her mother must have taught her court manners, Ryan decided.

Ryan managed a nod, his version of a bow, in Lorenzo's direction.

Americans generally had problems kowtowing, and Ryan admitted he was the rule rather than the exception. Also, he knew the duke well enough to know when Lorenzo was putting on airs. Ryan had seen him in his shirtsleeves, smoking cigars and dealing cards across the table.

Not that Lorenzo even noticed Ryan's nod. He was too busy taking Nina Caruso's measure.

"I am so sorry to have missed your arrival at the palace," Lorenzo said graciously. "The king has explained your mission to me."

He then addressed Ryan. "And Pavelli just informed me of your objection. I should reiterate that our Nina's participation in the investigation is not simply a request. It is her right as a sister, I believe."

"I see," Ryan said, tasting dry defeat. "Her right? Some new custom I'm not aware of?"

"Precisely," Lorenzo affirmed. "There will be no problem accommodating her in this endeavor?" Though phrased as a question, Ryan knew very well it wasn't.

He shrugged. "Probably, but I guess I'll work around it if I have to." His continued employment might be contingent on doing that, and this job was everything to him right now.

Work was his life. It was all he had left, and damned if he planned to junk it over something like this. He'd just have to invent some busywork to keep the woman out of his way while he was doing what had to be done.

"Excellent." Lorenzo offered his hand and firmly shook Ryan's, then smiled in Nina Caruso's direction. "I shall tell the king that all systems are go. A space term for launching success, yes?" He raised an eyebrow at Ryan.

"Yes. Just before blastoff. Then everybody prays there's no malfunction," Ryan said wryly.

"As we all shall do. *Grazie.*"

Grazie for nothing, Ryan thought. He liked to think this was his investigation. The king had brought him in on it, but there wasn't much doubt it had been Lorenzo's idea to do so. And no doubt at all that Lorenzo was running the show. Ryan needed to know. "Shouldn't we put all our cards on the table now. Decide who does what?"

The duke shrugged. "I provide you whatever access you need. You and your people follow through. Keep me up to date."

"Fair enough," Ryan agreed. It would simplify matters not to have to plow through the usual red tape involving court orders and search warrants. "I'll be in touch."

Lorenzo nodded, started to leave, then turned at the door. "When things settle a bit, we should arrange for another game. It has been a while."

"Any time," Ryan said, recalling the night at Pete's not long ago when he had beat the royal socks off Prince Lucas, his chauffeur and Lorenzo. A strange, if rewarding, experience.

Ryan was usually up for a card game. And the winnings were nice, but he also gleaned information from those get-togethers that sometimes proved valuable. He smiled at the thought.

"I shall leave you both to it then," Lorenzo said and exited as swiftly as he had entered.

The determined look on Nina Caruso's face instantly sobered Ryan's smile, as did the prospect of stumbling over a family member of the victim while he concentrated on finding a murderer. Lorenzo would stay out of his way and allow him to do what he'd been hired to do, but it was clear this woman wouldn't. Not when she had royal sanction to interfere.

"So, do I need to ask again for your consent in this?" she asked.

"Nope. Not necessary," Ryan said. "It's all in the way you put the question, I guess. A duke for backup definitely helped."

This was Ryan's first homicide in nearly a year. How was he supposed to give it his undivided attention and baby-sit at the same time? Nina Caruso was going to be trouble with a capital *T,* he just knew it.

In the first place, she was highly distracting. In the second place...she was highly distracting.

"You're not going to be one of those condescending types, are you?" she asked as she rounded his desk, picked up her purse and slung the strap over her shoulder. "You should know, I loathe being patronized in any way."

"Why, no, ma'am, I wouldn't dream of it," he assured

her, sounding as superciliously indulgent as he possibly
could. And as Southern as anybody from Savannah, Georgia, ever had.

The phone rang. "Would you excuse me a moment,
please?" he asked her, looking meaningfully at the door.

Reluctantly she nodded and stepped just outside and
closed it as Ryan answered, "McDonough."

"My, but you do sound put upon, my friend." It was
Lorenzo again, obviously calling from his cell phone.

"That's only because I am," Ryan said conversationally,
then added the requisite, "Your Grace."

Lorenzo continued, speaking swiftly and much more seriously, "I had hoped to arrive before she did, but I was
delayed. There was no time to arrange another audience
with the king so that he could make you aware of the situation. He sent me to inform you that Nina Caruso is to be
closely watched and that he wishes you to do this personally. Her motive for coming here bears careful scrutiny."

"Why is that? Her brother's dead and she's come to find
out what happened. Isn't that motive enough?"

Lorenzo issued a little hum of suspicion. "So she told
the reporters at the airport when she arrived this morning."

"Reporters?" Ryan asked.

"TV-news team and the usual print hounds. She must
have notified them herself. How else would they have
known she was coming?"

Ryan shook his head. "Not necessarily. You know the
papers keep a file on all you royals and everybody associated with you. Once word got out that Desmond had been
killed, they would have started calling his family to get a
reaction. If they found out where Nina worked, anybody in
her office could have told them she was on her way over
here. Especially if the caller represented himself as a friend
who was worried about her, or used some ruse like that.
The paparazzi are experts at that kind of thing. They'd have
been lying in wait when she got off the plane."

"I hadn't thought of that. Good point. But still supposition."

"You think she had prior knowledge, maybe conspired to have Desmond killed?" Ryan asked.

"Possibly. Find out and keep an eye on her while you do. A very close eye, my friend."

"Count on it."

So Nina Caruso was a suspect. Her motive for coming might be to insinuate herself into the royal family, play on their loyalty and gain their sympathy and acceptance by showing her grief. However, it was also possible that she was the one who had arranged Desmond's murder and planned to cash in on his death. No doubt there was an inheritance of some kind.

He couldn't deny she bore watching. Ryan just wished he wasn't the one directed to do it.

Since he had no choice, he assured Lorenzo he understood and would comply. Then he went to join Ms. Caruso in the outer office.

"So, we are to be partners," Ryan said, but he did so pleasantly, as if perfectly resigned to the situation.

She yanked the outer door open and stood aside for him to exit. "I'll pull my weight," she announced, her classic features set with fierce determination. "You'll see."

"Of course you will," he answered idly. As if any cop in his right mind would actually allow a civilian and family member to take part in a murder case. And he *was* still a cop at heart.

Pavelli was waiting for them outside. "Ms. Caruso's bags are in the boot," he told Ryan. "If you like, Marcello and the car are at your disposal today.

Ryan accepted the offer, gesturing grandly toward the long black beast as if he owned it. "Your carriage awaits."

She climbed into the limo and settled back against the butter-soft leather. Pavelli got in front with the driver as

Ryan joined Nina Caruso in the back. He was glad to see that the glass partition was closed. It gave them privacy.

Ryan looked at her and imagined he saw her chin tremble. Had to be a trick of light. Nevertheless, he was prompted by it to ask, "Why are you really so intent on doing this, Ms. Caruso?"

She met his gaze with one just as intent as his. "Because Desmond was my brother."

"He was Duke Lorenzo's brother, too, and the duke trusts me to handle this."

She granted him a short nod. "That may be, but I still want to be involved."

"I can understand if you came over for the funeral, but why horn in on my duties? You don't know a thing about investigations." Then it occurred to him that she might. "Do you? Are you a cop or something?"

"No, I'm a graphic designer."

Ryan snorted, not knowing—or caring much—what that entailed. He knew it didn't have a damned thing to do with detective work.

"I have an excellent eye for detail," she assured him, chafing her arms with her palms as if she were cold. "To tell the truth, I have to *do* something. Can't you understand that? I have to do something for Desmond."

"You and your brother must have been very close," he said.

"Yes, of course." Then she added, "But he's been away a long time. Since he was twenty." The admission cost her, he thought. She didn't like confiding anything about herself, but it was his business to pry out secrets. And he was curious.

If she was anything at all like Desmond Caruso, there might be excellent reason to keep close tabs on her. By most accounts, the man had been a crass opportunist. Ryan had met him once and thought he was a jerk. But even jerks deserved justice.

"How did you find out about the murder?" he asked, carefully noting her body language for an indication that she would lie.

She sighed. "Someone from the palace phoned me. I'm sorry, I didn't get the name. The call woke me, then I was so upset."

"Yeah, well, that's understandable," Ryan granted. "When did you receive the call?"

"The morning he...his body...was discovered. The person who called me suggested that I would be welcome if I decided to come. But I would have anyway," she added.

"I see," Ryan commented. "Was this official who notified you a man?"

She looked directly at him then and frowned in consternation. "I couldn't say for certain. A husky voice, but not too deep."

Couldn't say, or wouldn't? Ryan wondered. She gave no outward signs that she was lying or withholding the truth, but that meant very little other than that she could be accomplished at it and had studied body language herself.

Nina understood why she was being so adamant about participating personally in the investigation of Desmond's death, even if Ryan McDonough didn't. She *did* think it surprising and somewhat peculiar that the king would allow and even encourage it. The best she had hoped for when she'd asked permission was, as McDonough had suggested, to be kept informed as events unfolded. And to hound someone for answers if they weren't forthcoming.

Much to her surprise, the king had sent her to the P.I.'s office with the suggestion that she assist him. That alone indicated to her that the investigator might need a push to get things done, that the king either knew him to be short-handed or lacking in initiative.

Nina glanced out the tinted windows at the city surrounding them. It was so lovely here in San Sebastian, an interesting combination of old-world architecture and innovative modern buildings that signified a successful transition into the twenty-first century.

Had Desmond loved it? Had he felt at home here? Accepted?

There had been a time in her life when she had absolutely idolized her older brother. He had been so handsome, so aloof and tragic even as a teenager. How proud she had felt whenever he took the time to notice her and smile down at her.

Looking back, she realized that he'd had much the same affection for the family dog. Still, all her friends had sighed, giggled and mooned over Desmond. He had actually championed her a few times when Dad had called her on the carpet for one transgression or another. Later however, she had noticed that Desmond routinely argued with her father on just about everything.

Had they been close? No. As much as she had wished it so, her brother had been little more than an enigmatic stranger.

If she were perfectly honest, this hurried trip and her involvement here were more in the nature of alleviating her guilt. She had sailed through life without a glitch, taking for granted the love of her parents, her success in school, her wide circle of friends and her sense of belonging. Desmond had suffered every step of the way.

He had always been at odds with the adults in his life, parents and teachers. Desmond had been a loner and had never quite fit in anywhere. He'd either tried too hard or, in some instances, not tried at all.

Nina hoped he had found his place here in Montebello, where his birth father had once lived. She wished she had been able to discuss it with the duke, who must have known him very well. She had to admit, royalty intimidated her.

Desmond was born of royalty, though he hadn't known about it until after Nina's father had died. To a very young and impressionable Nina, that discovery had fully explained Desmond's difficulties in adjusting to life as they had known it. A prince among paupers, she recalled thinking at the time.

Now she could laugh at that childish conclusion. Her family might not have been rich, but they were solid upper-middle class with a healthy bank account. Love and affection were also in ready supply. Neither she nor her brother had ever lacked for a single thing they truly needed.

Nina missed her parents. Her father had succumbed to a virulent case of pneumonia just before Desmond left. The revelation that followed his death—that Desmond wasn't really his, but was instead the illegitimate son of a Monte-bellan Duke—had further alienated her brother. The loss of both husband and son had been too much for Nina's mother. She had died only months later, finally giving in to the weak heart that had plagued her for years.

Of course she had romanticized the sad figure Desmond had become. Most of his problems were of his own making. But he was her brother, faults and all. Poor, handsome, tragic Desmond did not deserve such a sad end.

If she could just do this one last thing for him, see his killer brought to justice, Nina thought she might be able to put aside the guilt she felt for having a childhood that was so much better than his. She had always felt she owed him something to make up for what he had missed and she had enjoyed, and this was all there was left to do for him.

"When did you last hear from your brother?" Mc-Donough asked, interrupting her bittersweet thoughts.

She turned to look at him. "The last time? A few weeks ago." Desmond had contacted her for a loan, but that was none of this man's business. It had nothing whatsoever to do with the murder.

"You said you once entertained a close bond with him. That was not true lately?" he asked, the intensity of his gaze absolutely unnerving.

"Is this an interrogation, Mr. McDonough?" she demanded, feeling defensive, especially since she did not want to answer the question.

"Yes," he readily admitted. "And what happened to calling me Ryan? I thought we were supposed to become more familiar. It was your idea...Nina."

They had stopped at a traffic light and she had the overwhelming impulse to get out and slam the door shut in his face. Instead, she took a deep breath and prayed for patience. Only when she had collected herself did she answer. "My brother and I were as close as can be expected given the eight-year difference in our ages and the fact that we had not visited much since he left home." And not at all since he had come to Montebello.

He pursed his lips and nodded. Then he smiled sadly. "And there was also the fact that you had different fathers. How did that affect the two of you?"

Nina shifted in her seat, gritted her teeth and met his gaze with a glare. "If you're considering sibling rivalry as a possible motive, I do have an alibi. I was on the other side of the world at the time Des was killed."

He smiled more naturally. "And that can be verified quite easily, I'm sure."

"Absolutely. So you can eliminate me from your list of suspects, McDonough," she snapped. "If you have any suspects."

"I have several hundred thousand at the moment. But you're going to remedy that with your input on the investigation, aren't you? When would you like to begin?"

"Now."

"First I'd like an answer to my previous question. *Was* there any sibling rivalry between you and Desmond?"

"Certainly not on my part!" she exclaimed. "Are you always this abrasive?"

He shrugged those shoulders she couldn't help but admire. "Nope. Sometimes I'm even more so. It's a plus in this line of work, trust me. Looks like you have the attitude down pat, if nothing else.''

Then he cocked his head to one side and raked his bottom lip with his straight, white teeth. She thought she saw a glint of amusement in his eyes. ''But you obviously don't trust me, do you? If you did, you would be content to lie around the palace eating grapes or whatever it is the royal *cousins* do, and let me handle this case.''

Nina refused to rise to the bait. Calmly she crossed one leg over the other and smoothed the knee-length skirt of her new gray suit. ''You know very well I'm not a royal cousin. But Desmond was. You said we could begin the investigation now. Will you give me something specific to do?''

He cleared his throat, quickly looking away from her legs. ''You should get settled first. Get over your jet lag.''

''I don't have any. And I'm already settled, as you put it. Mr. Pavelli has arranged a flat for me.'' She gave him a smug little smile and raised her brows. ''The vacant apartment next to yours is no longer *to let.*''

To his credit, he managed not to groan. His sigh of resignation provided her a brief moment of victory. Then he seemed to recover. ''I guess he thought it would be convenient for us. Would you like to go there first, or get right down to business?''

''Right down to business,'' Nina declared. ''That's why I'm here.''

He nodded once and leaned forward to push a button, obviously an intercom, because he spoke to the driver. ''The palace, please.''

''The *palace?* You're not talking the king out of this,'' Nina warned him. ''You heard Lorenzo.''

''I did. And, good little Montebellan subject that I am, I wouldn't dream of bucking the powers-that-be.''

Before Nina could comment, he continued, this time very seriously. ''We're going to the scene of the crime.''

Her eyes widened. "Oh."

His eyes were piercing as his gaze fastened on hers. "This is for real, Ms. Caruso. Not like you see on television."

"Please tell me you don't believe I'm stupid enough to think it is."

"All I'm saying is that if you're going to help me, get objective because I don't have time to baby you. A man has been killed. I need to discover who did it, and time is all-important. It's already been nearly forty-eight hours. Will the sight of blood make you faint?"

Nina sucked in a sharp breath of shock. He sounded horribly heartless.

"I know that seems cold," he admitted, his features rock hard and uncompromising. Unsympathetic. "But if you're going to accomplish anything at all, you have to divorce your emotions from what you will be doing. Do you understand?"

"Yes."

"I hope so. You cannot deal with murder if you don't. It's ugly. It will give you nightmares. Sometimes it will make you cry and wake up screaming. This is particularly true if you knew the victim."

He was trying to scare her off. She had crossed her arms over her chest and was clenching her biceps until they hurt.

Then she saw something in his eyes that told her he was speaking from experience, that he knew exactly what he was talking about. He'd said he worked homicide before. Did he have these nightmares?

"That means I must see…the body."

"I wouldn't advise that." His voice gentler now, thoughtful. "It shouldn't be necessary."

"I want to," she said, steadying her voice, making up her mind to do it. What help could she be to this investigation if she allowed her emotions and her fears to rule every decision she made? "Yes. I should."

McDonough shook his head and heaved out a deep breath. "You're that afraid I might miss some clues?"

"Have you even looked for any?" Nina asked.

"I haven't seen the body yet, if that's what you're asking. The king only put me on this late yesterday. I've been catching up on what the police have done so far."

"A second pair of eyes never hurts, does it?" she asked.

"Your eyes will hurt if you insist on this," he said, betraying a little of that emotion he had just warned her to bury. "I'm afraid yours will. It's going to be difficult, if not impossible, Nina, to forget the victim was your brother."

"I can do it," she said as convincingly as she could. "I can be objective if that's what it takes. Couldn't you, if the victim was a relation of yours?"

He gave her the strangest look, then tore his gaze from hers. Well, let him be angry, she thought. This wasn't about Ryan McDonough's pride anyway. It was about Desmond and finding out who killed him.

She probably would be able to handle seeing Des. At least, she could fake it for the short time it would take. She'd never been squeamish. And she knew very well that a person's essence left the body when that person died. It wouldn't be Desmond she was seeing. Not really.

Suppose McDonough did miss something? Would she know enough to find it? And if she did, would he admit the error? At least if she was courageous enough to see what a real investigator should, he might take her wish to help more seriously.

"I won't faint," she assured him. "I've seen bodies before."

He nodded and offered no further argument. Nina only wished she had convinced herself as easily as that.

Chapter 2

Ryan wished he could insist on taking Nina to her apartment before going to the palace as he had planned. Her arrival had thrown a monkey wrench in his schedule.

Strange as it seemed, that old adage about criminals returning to the scene of the crime did hold true occasionally in homicides. Consequently, Ryan had stationed one of his best men, Joseph Braca, at Desmond's house at night to keep watch. The back doors purposely had been left unlocked for easy access, and Ryan had hidden two motion-activated cameras in strategic locations to record the image of any intruders.

In addition to bringing Joe up to date on the preliminary forensics report, Ryan needed to make him aware of the new wrinkle in the investigation. Nina. While Ryan kept her busy later today, Joe would be running her background, checking the alibi and going over the victim's phone records to see if there had been any contact other than what she'd admitted.

Ryan could have phoned Joe instead of coming over,

probably should have, given the circumstances. Or he could have requested that Joe report to him at the office before going off duty. The truth was, Ryan employed any reason he could think of to get out from behind that desk and into the field. Also, this might satisfy Nina Caruso that he was allowing her to assist him.

A scant quarter hour later, they drove through the gates of the palace. Ryan scanned the royal compound, realizing how many hundreds of people must be residing, employed or visiting there. Any one of them might be responsible for killing Desmond Caruso. And it was up to him to discover the needle in this palatial haystack.

The landscaping prevented driving right up to the front. There was a large paved parking area for vehicles situated between the wing of the palace that contained the heritage section and the wing housing the throne room. In deference to Nina, who must be tired and was wearing high heels, Ryan decided to forgo the walk from there. The flagstones and graveled paths would be hell on her feet in those shoes.

He pushed a button and gave the driver his orders. "Bypass the regular parking area. Pull around and park as near the guesthouse as you can. Once you let us out, you can drive Mr. Pavelli back around front. I'm sure he has a report to make."

He turned to Nina. "The guesthouse where your brother lived is virtually isolated," he explained, pointing as they rounded the heritage wing of the palace. "It's there, just beyond those trees. As you can see, the gardens between the palace and the guesthouse conceal it from view. Even if someone had been looking out the windows of the throne wing, which is usually deserted late at night, they wouldn't have seen anything."

She concentrated, leaning forward and looking up, stretching within the seat belt as far as she could. "And the second floor?"

"It's called the first floor here. Ground floor, then the

first," Ryan informed her. "Those are the princesses' bed-chambers above the throne room, and there would be a better view of the guesthouse from there. *If* anyone had been up there and looking in that direction. Unfortunately, none of the princesses are in residence. I haven't had a chance to question their staff yet."

"I'll do it," she volunteered, sitting back and clasping her hands in her lap. "I'm not afraid."

Ryan chuckled. "Well, neither am I, but it probably won't prove useful. You can bet your favorite lipstick the king has already determined whether anyone on duty has any information to add to the investigation. If they did, it would have come to me through channels already."

"Channels?" she questioned. "Are you serious?"

He shrugged. "Protocol. I'll be given a list of who was on duty and work from there."

She shook her head and gave a disgusted huff. "This whole thing is going to get buried in bureaucracy. Mired down and unsolved. I just know it."

Ryan let that go as the car came to a stop, glad to change the subject. Protocol was a sore point with him, but one he had to live with. In this instance, he trusted Lorenzo would make sure he got what he needed. "Here we are."

His fellow passenger was frowning, worrying her bottom lip with her teeth and eyeing the guesthouse now like she might be dreading this. *Wait until we get to the morgue,* he thought with a reluctant pang of sympathy.

He could keep her from viewing the body if he chose to, but he wanted to see her reaction. It would tell him more about the relationship between Nina and Desmond Caruso than hours of interrogation.

Ryan couldn't envision Nina Caruso actually killing any-one. If she had anything at all to do with her half brother's death, she had probably hired it done. And if she had, that would mean Murder One, premeditated, conspiracy, not the crime of passion indicated by the evidence.

God only knew there were plenty of wackos out there greedy enough for a buck to kill anybody anywhere. Though security was fairly tight, someone with a little ingenuity might gain entrance into the palace grounds. Service people came and went, as did numerous tour groups. But Ryan was pretty sure that the victim had known the person who killed him. That narrowed the field considerably.

He assisted Nina out of the limo and kept a grip on her elbow as they marched down the pathway that led to the building.

There was no yellow-tape boundary visible out here to mar the beauty of the fairy-tale setting. Outside, all looked right with the world in happily-ever-after land.

"This is it," he announced. On the door was a discreet sign clearly printed with Entrance Forbidden in both English and Italian.

Ryan pushed the doorbell and heard the muted chime inside. The door opened almost immediately. Joe Braca, built like a refrigerator, dressed impeccably in silk suit and tie, gave them that little leaning-forward nod with head inclined that Italians used when they wanted to look subservient or greeted ladies they wanted to impress.

"Good morning," he said, his dark gaze roving over Nina as if she had answered his call to an escort service. Natural for Joe, of course.

"This is Nina Caruso, the victim's half sister. She just flew in early this morning. Nina, Joseph Braca, my right-hand man." Ryan called them both that, Joe and Franz. Truth was, they were a crackerjack duo and he was being sincere.

Joe effected his most sympathetic smile and took the hand Nina offered. "I am so sorry for the loss of your brother, Ms. Caruso," he said gently.

"Thank you, Mr. Braca," she replied, her gaze slipping past him to the foyer and a partial view of the living room.

Joe stepped back and allowed them to enter. He glanced at Nina's back, then raised an eyebrow at Ryan in unspoken question.

"You know the drill," Ryan ordered. "Get Franz going on the computer. You make the calls."

"Yes, sir," Joe agreed, fully understanding who the subject of inquiries would be. "I'll phone you tonight if anything turns up."

"You'll phone me in either case," Ryan said. "Before six o'clock."

Braca nodded. Ryan passed him and followed Nina to the arched entrance to the living room where she had stopped. She was staring at the stain, black on the patterned Persian carpet. Her eyes were wide and her face bone-white.

"Th-that's where it happened?" she asked, almost in a whisper.

"Yes. Tests confirm he was struck with a statuette that was found sitting on the credenza there." Ryan pointed. "He died instantly. One of the sharp edges made contact with the left temple area. If it had struck anywhere else, it probably would only have knocked him unconscious."

"So it wasn't planned." she guessed.

"*Probably* wasn't," Ryan said, not certain of that by any means. Maybe whoever had hit him had fully intended to beat him to death with the thing and had hit a home run on the first swing.

She started to walk into the room but Ryan caught her arm. "Not yet," he told her. "I've ordered Forensics to make a final sweep before anyone else goes in. We can walk around back. That could have been the point of entry."

"Someone broke in?" she asked as she walked back to the front door.

"No sign of it. The French doors to the patio were probably open. Either that, or Desmond knew the killer well enough to invite him or her in the front door.''

She picked up on the pronouns. "*Her?* You think it could have been a woman?''

He shrugged. "Entirely possible.'' In fact, Princess Samira Kamal of Tamir, Desmond's former lover, had said in her statement that when she'd dropped by to see him a couple of weeks ago, Desmond had been getting cozy with an unidentified woman.

Farid Nasir, the princess's bodyguard, had threatened Desmond's life publicly. Fortunately for Farid, he had an ironclad alibi, as did the princess herself.

Rumor had it those two had just revealed they were married. Ryan had already decided he needed to interview Samira again to determine just what her relationship with the victim had really entailed and how Farid figured into the equation.

They might not be guilty, but they could have useful information that they hadn't given the police.

"Let's go,'' he said, placing his hand at Nina Caruso's back to usher her out. Touching her was a mistake. She tensed beneath his palm as a current passed between them. Not a good sign at all, and Ryan was sure she felt it, too. Still, he didn't break the connection. He didn't want to think about why that was.

The three of them went out the front, Joe closing and locking the door behind them as they headed around the side of the building. Ryan guided her past the tiny, landscaped fishpond that decorated the garden directly in back of the dwelling.

There were large windows in the living room that allowed a broad view of the garden. Conversely, anyone interested would have a terrific view of those rooms from the garden if the lights were on. French doors between the windows allowed access into the room.

"It looks so…safe,'' Nina murmured, staring into the

room where the murder had taken place. She moved out of his reach and walked over, almost touching the glass-paned doors that were now shut, a yellow band taped across them.

She stooped a bit and examined the levers that served as door handles. Ryan watched, thinking idly how much he missed the land of round doorknobs. But he wouldn't go back there. Not for anything.

What was she thinking about? he wondered. Was she bemoaning the loss of a brother, or gloating over the fact that she'd gotten her money's worth from a hired killer? He exchanged a look with Joe, who pursed his lips as if he was wondering, too.

When she crouched farther down, ostensibly to examine the flower bed next to the window, Ryan stepped back just out of hearing and motioned for Joe to accompany him. Quickly, he related what new information he'd gotten from Forensics, which was little more than they had already guessed.

There was no need to reiterate what he wanted done in the way of investigating Nina. Joe was an expert at that and needed no direction.

"You want me back here tonight?" he asked Ryan.

"No, we'll have to let the regulars handle security. The cameras are all set, right?"

"Maybe we could have used a couple more, but at least we've got the doors covered," Joe assured him.

"Good. I need you on the BI." Background investigations were Joe's specialty, and God only knew there were enough of those to run.

Joe nodded, smiling slightly at the sight of Nina Caruso on her knees, bending over to part the foliage in the flower bed. "Searching for tracks," he observed. "You should hire her. She seems quite thorough."

"Bite your tongue," Ryan said, turning so that he

blocked Joe's view of Nina. That cute little behind of hers was enticing enough when she was standing up. "Why don't you go phone for a guard to get over here?" he suggested. "You need to grab a couple of hours' sleep and then get started on the other business."

As soon as Joe started around front, Ryan stepped across the flagstones nearer to Nina. "We might as well go unless you've found something we overlooked."

She glanced up at him, frowning. "Did you check for footprints around here?"

"We found the head gardener's, but he has an alibi. Would you care to question him?" Ryan reached down and helped her up.

She brushed the soil off her hands and straightened her short jacket and skirt. Her dark, silky hair had fallen forward over one eye. Ryan had the craziest urge to brush it back in place for her. He shoved his hands into his pockets instead and backed off.

"I'd like to see him now," Nina said, taking a huge breath as if to fortify herself.

"The gardener?"

She rolled her eyes, then closed them. Probably praying for patience. "No. I would like to see Desmond." Ryan watched her swallow hard and brace her shoulders in defiance of her fears. "His body."

Ryan's hand, acting independently of his better judgment, took Nina by the elbow as he escorted her around the building. The driver had returned with the limo, minus Pavelli, who was probably giving the king an earful about the uncooperative American investigator.

Though Ryan knew it might help him gain information about Nina, he wished she would change her mind about going to the morgue. Hell, he wouldn't even go there if it wasn't necessary. It was, however, and he would be going anyway, whether she went or not. "I could drop you at the apartment. Are you sure you want to do this?"

She snatched her arm away from him. "Yes. I have to see him. If nothing else, I need to say goodbye."

For a long, tense moment, Ryan held her gaze, trying to judge how she would hold up. "This is not like viewing the dearly departed in a funeral home, Nina. He's on a slab. In the morgue."

"Has…has there been an autopsy?" Her voice had dropped to a whisper again as if she couldn't bear to ask the question out loud.

"No, not yet." But there would be. Probably late this afternoon. "If we're going, we'd better go now and get it over with," he suggested. "Sure you're up to it?"

She nodded, clutching her purse with white-knuckled hands. He wanted to take them in his and warm them a little because they looked so cold. Damn, she was tying him in knots. What was with him, wanting to touch her every chance he got?

He hated that she dredged up his protective instincts. Hell, she was a suspect, for crying out loud. How was he supposed to stay objective when she was batting those big brown eyes, pursing her lips and making him want to do a caveman act? This was not like him, not at all.

Damn Lorenzo and his bright ideas anyway. Why hadn't he sicced her on the police? They probably weren't doing diddly down at the station.

In the States, a private investigator would never have been put in charge of something that so obviously fell under official police jurisdiction, but the cops here hadn't had the experience he'd had and the king and Lorenzo knew that. For the first time, Ryan regretted the royal appointment. More to the point, he resented its unwritten *other duties as assigned* clause.

"Come on, then," he said to Nina. She got into the car and he followed her. At least he got to ride in style when she was along. He was sorely tempted to break open that fancy bar and try to get her drunk before the next stop. He could use a shot himself, but he'd sworn off.

As they cruised through traffic toward the new part of San Sebastian and King Augustus Hospital, Ryan felt obliged to give her some preparation. "When we get there, you'll wait in the corridor. There's a camera, so you won't actually have to go into the lab. You'll be able to view—"

"No," she interrupted. "I need to see him. Up close."

Ryan leaned his head back against the seat and pressed his lips together to stifle a curse.

She laid a hand on top of his. It felt delicate. Cool. None too steady. "Please?"

He caved, knowing it was a mistake. "Okay." God, he was such a pushover. He was never like this! Never. What was the matter with him today?

Ryan reached into his pocket, pulled out his cell phone and punched in the number of the morgue. Ryan figured the least he could do was notify Doc to clean up things as best he could for Nina.

Dr. Angelo answered the direct line himself.

"McDonough here," Ryan said and skipped right over the usual pleasantries in the interest of time. "Look, Doc, I'm on my way over there now with the sister of Desmond Caruso. We won't be using the viewer. Our ETA's around twenty minutes. Can you manage?"

As he'd expected, Angelo tried to dissuade him, using the same arguments Ryan had used with Nina. Ryan cut him short in the middle of a sentence. "She insists. Set it up, will you?"

Nina had focused all her attention out the car window as if she were trying not to listen to the conversation.

Ryan couldn't help himself. He reached down and grasped the hand she had fisted on the seat between them. To his surprise, she didn't jerk it away, but opened her hand and clutched his fingers like a lifeline. She didn't look at him or acknowledge his gesture of comfort in any way whatsoever. But she was damn near cracking his knuckles.

"It'll be okay," he told her, inane as it sounded.

She didn't answer, and neither of them said another word for the rest of the ride over to the hospital, but she kept that death grip on his hand.

Damn. He knew what this felt like to her and wouldn't wish it on his worst enemy. Well, at least it wasn't a husband she was going to have to look at. It wasn't her child.

The sudden image and echo of a laughing little girl, blond hair flying in the breeze as she ran, skittered through his mind. Ryan gritted his teeth and forced his mind away from the past. Six long years had given him lots of practice, and he should have been more successful at avoidance by this time.

When the car stopped in front of the hospital, Ryan exited with a calmness he did not feel. He knew his face showed nothing that would betray the roiling in his gut.

He focused on the nearby man-made lake, the precision of the landscaping surrounding King Augustus Hospital, the pink marble of its unusual structure. All the beauty that disguised an approaching nightmare.

Automatically he opened the car door for Nina Caruso and gave her his hand again, this time to assist her out. He let her go as soon as she was steady.

But he needed the connection, even if she didn't, and placed his hand under her elbow. Yeah. Gentleman to the core, official as the day was long, a steady rock to lean on. *A consummate liar and a fraud.* He was shaking inside like he had d.t.'s. He was dreading the morgue, possibly more than she was.

He had been there before in the course of his duties. The reaction was nothing new. He had dealt with it and would again, but he knew it would always be the same. The memories would flood right through that dam he had laboriously constructed. And then he'd have to rebuild it.

Maybe if he concentrated on her reaction, he wouldn't be dwelling on his own so intensely. With that in mind, he was maybe a bit too solicitous on the way through the hospital and in the elevator that led to the lower level.

"Just try to focus on the fact that what you're going to see is not really your brother," he advised, still holding on to her arm. "It's just a lifeless shell he once used. Disassociate if you can."

She frowned at him, her dark eyes curious. "Are you all right?"

Ryan took a deep breath and tried a smile that felt unsuccessful, more like a grimace. "Yeah, sure. You?"

"I'm okay," she replied, still frowning as they stepped out of the elevator.

The smell hit him, and they weren't even close to the lab. She looked as if she'd noticed it, too. "Chemicals," he explained. A lie. It was the smell of death. "Breathe through your mouth."

Her lips opened as she complied. Full, tremulous lips that begged him to draw closer, to warm them. To warm his own.

Yeah, he thought, go ahead and think about that, fight the other thoughts. No, he reminded himself, her lips were definitely off-limits. Better lock on to something else.

But what? The odor of the place seemed to seep into him, to permeate his sinuses, to leave its taste on his tongue. Nothing was audible but their determined breathing, the echoes of his footsteps and the click of her high heels on the tiles.

Someone had placed pictures along the corridor, perhaps to distract visitors from what was to come, but the paintings were made up of shapes he didn't recognize, done in vapid tints that reminded him of badly colored Easter eggs.

Nina removed her elbow from his grasp and took his hand as if she, too, were looking for a port in a storm. He laced his fingers through hers.

They halted in front of a door marked Laboratory, next to which was a window set into the wall. The window had kept distance between the viewer and the body before modern technology, with its camera equipment, had made it unnecessary. The blinds were drawn on the inside.

He gave Nina's hand a bracing little squeeze and then released it as he tapped on the door with one knuckle.

Doc opened it and stood back to allow them entrance. Ryan forced himself to enter before Nina, as if he could police up the area and make it less terrible if Doc had not. Of course there was nothing he could do about it at that point, but he'd have acted the same upon entering any room with a woman where there was a chance of anything threatening. The urge to run interference for a female had been ingrained from childhood, and he'd never been able to shake it. *Thank you, Mama.*

Doc had removed the body from the drawer, had placed it on a table and had covered it with a pale green sheet. There was nothing else in view—no instruments or other cadavers—to cause her any horror, but Ryan supposed the remains of her brother would be enough to do that.

Even though they weren't touching now, he could feel her tension. Or maybe it was his. Ryan couldn't tell. She appeared calm enough, though the lights in the lab faded her complexion to white.

Doc stood waiting to be introduced. Ryan jerked his attention to that chore and kept it brief. "Nina Caruso, Dr. Angelo."

They nodded to one another and Doc spoke in that deep, resonant voice that reminded Ryan of Boris Karloff. "My condolences, Ms. Caruso." He looked a bit like Boris, come to think of it.

"Thank you," she said in automatic response. "May I see him now?"

She wanted to do her duty and get the hell out of there, Ryan thought, but no more than he did. He fought the flashes of memory and pain associated with another time, another morgue, two pull-out, refrigerated drawers containing...

He shook his head, cleared his throat and tried to clear his mind of his own feelings so he could observe hers. After all, that's the reason he'd let her come, he reminded himself.

She looked up at him, silently asking him to accompany her to the table. Ryan slid an arm around her, his hand at her waist, and guided her to the examination table.

Doc turned back the sheet so that only the head and shoulders were visible. Thank God he'd done everything he could. There was no blood. Even the gash on the temple, deep as it was, didn't look particularly lethal now that it had been cleaned up.

Contrary to Ryan's warning to Nina, the body didn't look radically different from what she might have viewed if it had been prepared for a funeral and lying in a casket, except for the absence of a suit and tie and a bit of flesh putty to fill in the wound. Ryan had not been involved in the case or seen the body at the crime scene before it had been removed and brought here. But even there it wouldn't have been nearly as gruesome as some he'd seen.

Nina stepped closer and touched the forehead, brushing a lock of dark hair from the brow. "He's...so cold." Two tears made tracks down her cheeks and dripped off her chin. For a long moment, she stood looking down at the remains and mouthed the word *goodbye*.

So much for disassociation. Ryan turned away. He realized he should have done what she was doing six years ago. He should have touched. He should have wept. He should have said his goodbyes and let go. Instead, he'd felt a welling of rage so great he hadn't been able to contain it.

Hell, he couldn't even remember what he'd said then, what he'd done, but he knew it hadn't been anywhere near as dignified as this. The things he did recall he was still working to forget.

His partner, Sam, had gotten him out of that morgue somehow, and when reason had returned—a brief spate of it, anyway—Ryan had been able to do what had to be done. Only when his obligations had been met had he fallen apart. Then had begun that lost year, twelve months of nothingness.

Dragging his mind back to the present, now almost thankful for where he was and for any excuse to dismiss the past, Ryan carefully examined the victim's wound and checked the rest of the body for bruising and lividity. He noted the hands. No trauma there, which meant no fistfight. Hardly a surprise. No needle marks that he could ascertain. "Any evidence of illegal substance?" he asked the doctor.

"None evident. Wait for the lab results. That will be in the autopsy report."

"I guess that's it," Ryan said, backing away from the table as the doctor covered the body. A memory flashed. Another covering up, the finality of it triggering something savage in him.

"I'm ready to go," Nina said.

"Thanks, Doc," he muttered to Angelo as he guided her out. "I'll call you later."

He would have to come here again, Ryan thought with resignation. After the autopsy, he'd have to come back. It never got any easier.

She appeared to be completely recovered, Ryan thought when they exited the elevator on the ground floor. Dry-eyed and composed now, she seemed to be in deep thought. Not at all the emotional wreck she might have been after seeing a beloved brother's dead body.

Ryan filed away the impression that the bond of affection between Desmond and Nina Caruso must not have been all that tight if her grief was this superficial.

Chapter 3

When they emerged from the hospital, Ryan sucked in a deep breath of fresh air. Better. He squinted against the bright sunlight, welcoming it.

The limo cruised up to the curb and Ryan automatically reached past Nina to open her door. She slid inside.

When he got in, she turned to him and said the last thing he would have expected. "He wasn't struck from behind."

"No," Ryan agreed as he fastened his seat belt and motioned for her to do the same.

"Then whoever did it was facing him, holding the statuette?"

"Yes, given the placement of the wound."

"Could I see the weapon?" she asked.

He sighed. "Nina, you're taking this *Murder She Wrote* business a little too seriously, you know that?"

"Maybe," she admitted, "but I think you should humor me. I do have permission to assist you."

Well, hell. Ryan couldn't tell her the real reason the king had sent her directly to him.

"Okay. Tomorrow. We'll go over the evidence then. Today I think you've done enough, don't you?"

She looked pointedly at her watch. "It's barely one o'clock."

"We'll grab a bite of lunch and drop you at the apartment so you can rest."

"But—"

"No buts," he warned. "This is not the only case I'm working on, Nina. There's plenty I have to do this afternoon that has nothing to do with this. I can't drag you all over the island while I take care of business."

"But tomorrow you'll be back on this case, right?"

"Yes, tomorrow morning."

"And I can go with you?"

He nodded emphatically. "Now, what would you like to eat?"

In a self-conscious gesture, she tucked her hair behind her ears, crossed her arms beneath her breasts and looked out the opposite window. "Oatmeal," she mumbled.

"Excuse me?"

Defiantly, she turned her head and pinned him with a glare. "I said *oatmeal*. With wheat toast and butter and cinnamon. And hot tea. Earl Grey with lemon."

"You're joking, right? I don't know anywhere in San Sebastian that serves oatmeal."

She raised one dark brow in challenge. "Well, you did ask."

Ryan shook his head. He'd known she would be trouble from the minute he'd laid eyes on her. "Your wish is my command. Apparently that's turning out to be my phrase for the day."

He leaned forward, pushed the intercom button and ordered the driver to stop at the nearest grocery.

"You'll have to cook it yourself unless you want me to send you back to the palace," he told her emphatically. "I don't do oatmeal."

*   *   *

Almost an hour and three grocery stores later, Nina Caruso, her oatmeal, Earl Grey tea, and various other containers of comfort food were safely deposited in the apartment adjacent to his.

She could eat her wallpaper paste and take a nap. He had to figure out how he was going to solve this murder while she was poking her lovely little nose into every aspect of it. All in all, he'd rather stick pins in his eyes, but he had his orders.

Her presence and demands had crowded out the possibility of his lapsing into a couple of hours of depression after the visit to the morgue the way he usually did. For that distraction, he ought to thank her.

It bothered him that she hadn't seemed all that upset to see her brother's body. Oh, she'd acted nervous and cried a little, but that could have been for show. Ryan just wished he hadn't had his own renewal of grief to deal with at the time. He could have been a hell of a lot more accurate in judging whether hers really existed.

He arrived back at his office and went over the other cases he had pending, made a few necessary phone calls and worked on putting Nina Caruso out of his mind until Joe called just before six. "Turn on the news," Joe advised.

Ortano's news clip stated that Nina had never been to the island before. She had come now to see that the investigation of her brother's murder was carried out expeditiously and to offer what assistance she could. Her words to Ortano verified that.

Other than stating the family connection and capitalizing a bit on the emotional aspect of the event, the reporter had little to add of any consequence. The clip was surprisingly low-key. The video was fantastic. Ryan switched off the set and returned to the phone call.

Joe assured Ryan that calls between Nina and her brother—all except the last of which had originated with her—had been few and far between and of brief duration. The last had been two weeks ago, placed from Desmond's guesthouse to La Jolla, California, where Nina lived. She had neither made nor received any calls since she'd arrived in Montebello.

As for her possessing a motive to have Desmond killed, Joe had not discovered one. Fear, Ryan dismissed. Revenge or jealousy were possibilities. Greed was a contender, too, but Joe assured him that Nina Caruso had a substantial trust fund and a very healthy investment portfolio.

There was an insurance policy her father had taken out on Desmond when he was a child. The premiums on it were paid through a trust which, now that the original capital was no longer needed, would also become Nina's. But was that enough to prompt her to arrange a murder when she was already fairly well off?

Ryan's gut told him no. At least, he hoped that was his gut and not another part of his anatomy.

When he called her around seven o'clock to make dinner arrangements, he received no answer. Jet lag must have finally caught up with her, he supposed. Just as well, Ryan thought, totally denying the spark of disappointment he felt that he wouldn't see her again until morning.

Maybe he should stop in and check on her. She could have experienced a delayed reaction to all that had happened, he told himself. She might be all alone and crying herself sick right now. Suddenly he found himself hurrying to get there and see if that was so.

Nina wasted little time planning the rest of her day after Ryan McDonough left her alone. It was like pulling teeth to get him to let her do anything with regard to Desmond's murder, and she needed to get on with it. She had a few weeks' vacation built up, but her job at home wouldn't wait forever.

She mapped out what she would do as she prepared her

lunch and ate it. Rest was necessary. Ryan had been right about that, so she would take an hour or so in preparation for tonight. Later, she would call a cab, return to the palace and see what she could learn about the last days of Desmond's life. After that, she meant to go over the scene of the crime with a fine-tooth comb.

Forensics should be finished with their official duties there by now. They'd had all day yesterday and today. Nina seriously doubted she would find anything significant that professionals had overlooked, but she needed to get back into that guesthouse all the same.

If nothing else, seeing how Desmond had lived, getting a feeling for his lifestyle here and walking the rooms he had inhabited might give her some clue as to the man he had become since they had last seen each other.

If Ryan McDonough objected when he found out she'd been there, too bad. At least he'd know she wasn't going to be satisfied with little pats on the head in lieu of his accepting her help. She might not be a qualified investigator, but at least her dedicated involvement might speed things up a little.

When she'd finished eating and cleared the dishes, Nina went into the bedroom, kicked off her shoes, lay down on the puffy slate-blue comforter and closed her eyes.

She liked the accommodations arranged for her well enough. Efficiency over elegance, more practical than pretty. It suited her. Nina liked to think of herself in just those terms. She wondered whether Ryan McDonough's place next-door suited him. She fell asleep trying to decide what sort of decor would.

She awoke at seven-thirty, disgruntled when she realized she'd slept most of the day. Hurriedly she showered, then chose a lightweight navy jacket and skirt with a matching silk shell. She found her lowest-heeled pumps—dressy, but still great for walking.

What she was wearing looked businesslike, she thought, like something an investigator should wear. It wouldn't quite do for dinner at the palace, of course, but she wouldn't presume to impose on the royal family anyway. If she could manage to avoid them, they wouldn't even realize she was there. This evening, she'd stick to speaking with employees who might have served Desmond in some capacity. Surely there would be footmen or maids around somewhere to give her some names and locations of people who had served at the guesthouse. She would simply explain what she needed and tell them she was working with Ryan.

And then she would see inside his home. She nodded with self-satisfaction, recalling how stealthily she had checked the French doors at the back of the place and noticed that someone had left them unlocked. Didn't leaving the crime scene vulnerable that way indicate McDonough was not taking his job seriously enough?

She couldn't figure the man out. She'd only known him for a day and during that short span, he'd exuded charm and exhibited annoyance, very nearly simultaneously. He'd declared his dedication to the job and talked a good game, but had done remarkably little in the way of investigating, as far as she could tell.

He had offered her compassion when they'd gone to see Desmond's body, but had broken out in a sweat himself. He hadn't even asked the doctor many pertinent questions.

She picked up a hint of humor occasionally, yet he certainly could be brusque.

What a mass of contradictions the man was. She wasn't at all sure she wanted to know him any better than she already did. He made her nervous, and she wasn't certain why.

But leaving the back entrance to the victim's guesthouse open was definitely careless on the part of the investigator in charge of the murder case. If he gave her any grief when he found out what she had done tonight, she'd be quick to point that out to him.

The best defense was a good offense, and that was a fact.

Nina called a cab. When the doorbell chimed a few minutes later, she grabbed her purse and headed for the door, remarking to herself how prompt the taxi service was here.

She probably should have rented a car on her arrival, but she hadn't had time to go online and see if there were any peculiar driving rules in Montebello. Or if an international license would be required to drive here. Besides, she absolutely hated driving unfamiliar vehicles. With her luck, she'd have to accept one without an automatic transmission and with the steering wheel on the wrong side. Montebello wasn't that large. Wherever she couldn't walk, she'd take a cab.

When she opened the door, her heart sank. "McDonough!"

He smiled, his eyes focused on her shoulder bag. "Going somewhere?"

"Uh, out to eat." Nina couldn't meet his eyes. He seemed to divine her every thought, and she was no good at lying. Would he guess what she was planning?

"I'll join you," he said.

Ryan had no clue where she'd been planning to go. If he'd been using his brain at the time, he would have pretended not to notice she was holding that purse and how she was dressed when she answered the door. He would have asked how she was doing, wished her good-night, then waited out of sight and followed her. But she could be telling the truth about going out to eat, in which case, he was only doing the hospitable thing, escorting her to a nice restaurant and buying her evening meal.

He knew he was bending too far backward, giving her too much benefit of the doubt because he didn't want her to be involved in this murder. And to be honest, he really didn't believe she was. Given how attracted he was to her, however, Ryan wasn't sure he could trust his instincts right now.

"We'll go somewhere close by," he said, determined to give her the chance later to do whatever she intended. And he would follow. It was his job, after all. "It would be best if we make an early evening of it so you can rest."

"Yes, that would be good," she agreed, still not looking directly at him. Guilt was written all over her.

Either she was up to no good or his presence made her uncomfortable. She sure as hell had that effect on him.

"I'm expecting a cab," she told him.

He smiled cordially. "We'll wait for it then." His own car was less than thirty feet away, but she didn't know what he drove and he wanted to keep it that way, at least for tonight.

It was no chore to keep up a running patter about the local sights she should see while she was in Montebello. She didn't seem to be paying much attention anyway, preoccupied as she was.

"Ah, here we go," he announced as the white Audi pulled up to the entrance to the building. He took her arm and led her out to the vehicle where the driver was already opening the door for them. "Hey, Luigi. How's the wife?" he asked the man.

"She is good, sir. We have another son since last I saw you."

"Congratulations, *mano!* That makes five, right?" Ryan asked as he got in.

"Four, sir. Our second was a daughter," the driver said, beaming.

Ryan noted Nina's consternation. He smiled again. "Our world is small here. Tourists and visiting businesspeople are the only strangers."

She made no comment on that, but he could see that it

upset her. Another mistake on his part, giving her that information. Now she would be leery of hiring another cab for fear he'd find out where she was going. If she planned on going anywhere she didn't want him to know about, of course.

Ryan felt a little better about his lack of objectivity now. He was back on the job as he should be. Everyone was a suspect, even the woman who had temporarily thrown him for a loop.

"You like Thai cuisine?" he asked hopefully. Ryan hadn't been crazy about the time he'd spent bumming around in that country, but the food had been good. He had regained a few of the pounds he'd lost and begun his recovery there.

"No, nothing oriental," she said, looking rather glum.

"Please tell me you eat something besides hot cereal or we're out of luck."

To her credit, she managed a grin. "I love Italian food."

"Well, you're in luck." He nodded and instructed Luigi, "Take us to Pirandello's."

"They have a new chef there," he informed Ryan. "You must try his tortellini."

"Will do." He turned again to Nina. "I hope you have a good appetite. Picky eaters annoy me."

She pursed her lips for a second. "Well, I surely wouldn't want to annoy you."

Ryan laughed full out, thinking about how annoyed he'd been for most of the day because of her. Right now he was feeling pretty damned confident again, since he was on top of the whole situation.

So she was beautiful, he thought as he looked at her without even trying to conceal his interest. So she rang his chimes a little. Okay, a lot. He had faced the worst nightmare included in this job with that trip to the morgue today and had managed to handle it much better than usual.

Maybe his heart had hardened enough now that nothing could affect him to the point where he couldn't function.

Even if he discovered Nina Caruso had paid someone to cap Desmond, Ryan could do what had to be done. He'd feel disappointed, sure, but he would be able to carry through and process her as he would anyone else.

Feelings did pass, he knew now, if you shoved them aside enough times and replaced them with a purpose. Giving in to them could wreck your life in nothing flat. He'd found that out the hard way.

"What is it? What's the matter?" she asked. Demanded.

Ryan forced a smile. "Nothing. Just hungry." And he was. "I skipped lunch," he said.

And he would skip feeding this hunger for her, too, he thought as he tried not to devour her with his eyes. "Sometimes I get busy and forget," he admitted.

But he wouldn't forget what he was supposed to do with respect to Nina Caruso, he promised himself. Or what he was *not* supposed to do.

Nina had hardly been able to do justice to the meal. McDonough's arrival had thrown her plans off-kilter. Now she wouldn't arrive at the palace in time to interview anyone about Desmond. But she could still go to the guesthouse, if the guards would let her onto the grounds. There had been no problem that morning when she had identified herself, so she didn't anticipate any tonight.

As soon as McDonough said good-night and left, she hurried to the phone and called a different cab company. Thankfully, there were three to choose from. Hopefully, this driver wouldn't be one of the detective's friends.

Perhaps she had lucked out, Nina thought, as she entered the taxi a quarter hour later. This guy was obviously Middle Eastern and both his English and Italian were nearly nonexistent. He did understand where she wanted to go, however, and took her straight to the palace.

Nina paid the cabbie at the gates and then identified herself to the smartly uniformed guard who stood there holding a wicked-looking machine gun. He examined the pass she'd been given that morning when she had first arrived, compared it to her passport, gave both back to her. He required her to open her purse, which he gave a cursory examination.

"Shall I phone for a cart to transport you to the palace?" he asked politely. "It is some distance."

She smiled up at him. "No, thank you. It is such a beautiful night, I prefer to stroll. That is allowed, isn't it?"

"If you wish. May I ask the purpose of your visit this evening, the better to give you direction?"

Nina knew he was not asking out of politeness, but that he was required to know. "My half brother was the king's nephew. The one who was recently killed. A couple of the maids who knew him invited me by to talk."

"Ah yes, such a tragedy that was. Please approach through the main entrance. I will ring up and have someone meet you at the door. Have a pleasant visit, signorina."

"Thank you very much," she said, smiling, amazed that he was actually going to let her roam around unaccompanied.

She took the well-lighted path to the left of the fountain and flower beds that graced the center of the enormous courtyard, though it led to the opposite side of the palace from the guesthouse where Desmond had lived. Periodically, she glanced over her shoulder until she saw that the guard had turned to mind his station at the gate. Then she quickly cut across to the other side.

Once surrounded by the verdant gardens, Nina felt even more vulnerable, rather than safe as she'd expected. So many times she had read about people experiencing the feeling of being followed and she felt that now. It must be guilt that prompted it, she realized, since she was not supposed to be here doing what she was doing.

So large were the palace grounds, it took her a good half hour, squeezing around hedges and ducking low-hanging limbs of trees to reach the back entrance to the guesthouse. She stopped to listen often to see whether anyone was behind her, but never saw or heard any indication that there was.

She had been on the lookout for guards patrolling, but had only noticed two marching slowly around the outer wings of the palace itself. They looked as if they were there for show more than anything else since they stared straight ahead, didn't alter the precision of their steps and never even scanned the grounds. Those offering real protection would probably be outside the walls to prevent the entry of anyone unauthorized. Nina shivered to think how easily she had gotten in. Had Desmond's killer gained entry this way? Surely the police had interviewed the guards on duty to find that out. She'd remind Ryan to get the names and do just that.

The lights were off in the guesthouse, and no one stood guard out back. There might be someone in front, she figured, so she would have to be careful, at least until she had completed her search. At that point, she wouldn't really care if she were caught. She would enjoy informing McDonough that he should have secured the place if he didn't want people inside it.

Boldly, Nina walked up to the back doors and opened them. One of the hinges squeaked in protest. Just inside the doorway, she slipped off her pumps and picked them up.

Through the large back windows, moonlight combined with the muted electric lanterns placed about the garden provided enough illumination to see her way around the dining and living room areas. Nina had a penlight in her purse, but didn't want to use it unless she had to.

The place seemed sterile as a newly built home, containing no feeling that anyone had ever lived here.

The floor felt a bit gritty beneath her feet. Nina crouched

down and touched it, discovering another reason why the room lacked any warmth or lived-in qualities. Someone had rolled up the plush Persian rugs and removed them since she had been there.

Perhaps McDonough had ordered it done to go over the rugs for further traces of evidence. She hadn't thought he would be that thorough. Maybe she would have to reassess her opinion of him if that were the case.

She approached the area where the bloodstain had been, where Desmond had lain after the attack. She could see where his lifeblood had seeped through the rug and stained the light marble tiles. Unwilling to stand on the exact spot, Nina kept as close to the wall as possible.

"Ouch!" she yipped as she stepped on what felt like a tack. Quickly, she backed up to the hearth, dropped her shoes and sat down to pull the sharp object out of her instep.

When she extracted it, she found it was not the tack she'd expected. Fishing out her penlight, she held it close to the object and examined it.

An earring! A clue? She had found a clue!

Of course, it might have been here for ages. Or it could belong to one of Desmond's friends, not the person who killed him. Still, it was something Mr. Royal Investigator had missed. Nina felt a glimmer of satisfaction in that. Now he would have to admit she could be of help to him.

She tucked the earring into the zippered compartment inside her purse, switched off the penlight, slung the purse over her shoulder and continued her search. Maybe she could find something else.

The house was larger than it seemed from the outside. The second bedroom she checked was the largest and probably the one Desmond had used. There were no clues to be found as far as Nina could determine. The drawers and wardrobe had been emptied. A fine dust coated everything. Fingerprinting dust, she supposed.

Nina had just reached the open door to the bathroom when she heard the noise. The hinge from the French doors off the dining room creaked.

It must be the guard from out front doing a routine check, she thought. She listened for a few seconds, then ducked into the bathroom and quietly closed the door. She stepped into the bathtub and crouched low behind the door of thick frosted glass to hide.

Oh, lord, where were her shoes? By the door? On the hearth?

Her heart hammered so loudly, she was afraid whoever had come in would hear it and find her immediately. Surely it was the guard from the front door doing a regular check. She hated to think who else it could be or why she was so frantic not to be discovered after all.

In spite of that reluctance to guess who was in the house with her, Nina did recall that no lights had come on just prior to or just after she'd heard that creak of the door. Wouldn't a guard need light to check the place out? No reason for him not to light up the place. *Oh, God.*

She remained exactly where she was as time passed, scarcely daring to breathe or shift her position against the end of the tub enclosure.

The air inside the bathroom felt exceedingly warm and she wished she could shrug out of her suit jacket. But she didn't dare move. Her silk blouse clung to her skin and her hose felt like they would melt on her legs. Perspiration dotted her face and made her scalp tingle. She was breathing through her mouth, practically panting. Nerves.

Now was no time to develop panic attacks, she cautioned herself. *Be calm. Wait till they leave. Grab your shoes and get the heck out of here.*

Furtive rustling sounds from the bedroom had her scrunching down even farther in the bathtub, holding her breath until there was a roaring in her ears. When she did draw in a deep breath, she recognized the acrid odor. Her nostrils began to burn and her eyes stung. Smoke!

The place was on fire!

In full-blown panic now, she scrambled to her feet and out of the tub. She grabbed the door handle, then stopped herself and flattened her palm against the door. *Hot!* She didn't dare open it. The fire roared and crackled audibly on the other side.

Hurriedly climbing up on the commode, Nina raked the curtains aside and shoved open the tiny window. No way could she fit through it, she thought, but she had to try.

Shoving her head, one shoulder and arm through the opening, she screamed for all she was worth. When she grew hoarse, she stopped and began wriggling, gaining only an inch now and then in her struggle to break free. Frustrated and panicked, she screamed again.

This time a siren screamed back. She glanced to her left. Glass and flames had burst outward through the front window of the living room.

People were running toward the guesthouse through the gardens, two men dashing toward her. McDonough shouted, but she couldn't distinguish his words.

"Help!" she cried. "Over here! I'm stuck!"

Together, Ryan and the other man dragged over a wrought-iron bench, climbed up and began hammering at the top part of the window that had her trapped, breaking the panes and mullions until the entire thing gave way. They roughly shifted her sideways so that her hips fit through the opening and finally yanked her free. The three of them tumbled into the bushes below, landing in a heap.

She'd no sooner hit the ground than McDonough had her in his arms and was running away from the building. Oddly, she thought of the purse and the earring inside it. Grasping at the shoulder bag, she clutched it to her and sighed with relief. It was still on her shoulder. She hadn't lost her clue.

If it was a clue.

Chapter 4

Ryan dumped her unceremoniously into the back seat of a waiting car. "Are you hurt?" he growled, grasping her hands and bringing them to his face. He took a deep breath in each of her palms, then released her. A strange thing to do, she thought, looking down at them, flexing her fingers.

"Um, no, I don't think," she replied, sounding rough, either from the smoke or the screams. Her hips were banged up and her throat felt raw. She glanced down and saw a cut on her lower leg from the broken glass. It stung a bit, but she was out of that firetrap and that was all that mattered to her at the moment.

"Good God, you're bleeding," he muttered, running his hand beneath her calf. Without warning, he slid both his hands up under her skirt and tugged down her ripped panty hose. She had no thought to object, as she watched him discard them and straighten her clothes.

"Medic! Over here!" he called, his voice deep and carrying on the night air above the racket around them. Then he spoke softly to her. "Listen to me, Nina. Did you see anyone inside the house?"

"No," she rasped. "Whoever set the fire was there, but I didn't see them."

"You didn't start it," he said. It wasn't a question.

"Of course not!"

A man in white came loping over. "Her leg," McDonough said, holding it to examine it himself now that it was bare. "Superficial cut, but it needs cleaning." He allowed the medic to look. "Let's get her over there."

He helped her out of the car and picked her up again, carrying her to the small white emergency vehicle that had pulled up several car lengths away in the middle of a flower bed. He set her inside the double doors in back. "Get in there and stay in there, you hear me? I'll be back in a minute."

Nina nodded and crawled up on the cot. She was exhausted. And scared. But no one would dare try to hurt her in front of so many people. Would they?

In the confusion, anyone could approach. The EMT started to climb in. If he closed those doors, she would be alone with a stranger. God, anyone could steal a white coat!

She scrambled out before he could stop her and began running. "McDonough! Ryan!" she yelled. Her voice wouldn't cooperate, emerging at little more than a ragged whisper. *Oh, God, oh, God, where had he gone?* "Ryan!"

Strong arms closed around her from behind and she began to struggle, determined to get away.

"Nina! Calm down. It's me. You're okay now," he said, his tone sounding angry, yet with the only power available to relieve her mind. He turned her around, grasping her shoulders. "Look at me."

Nina flung her arms around his neck and held on. "Don't leave," she gasped.

He lifted her again, holding her close, his jacket rough against her cheek, his face pressing hard against her hair.

"I've got you. I'm here, Nina. Settle down now. We'll go back to the ambulance and I promise I'll stay with you. Okay? You'll be fine. Safe."

She nodded, sniffling, as she burrowed as close to him as she could get. There was no one else in this entire country she could trust at the moment. "Thank God you were here!" Then a thought occurred. "Why were you here? How did you get here so quickly?"

"Followed you, you little nitwit. I just gave you too much slack in the leash."

"Leash?" she demanded, suddenly incensed. "What am I, a puppy?"

"Don't start with me, all right? I was minutes behind you, but you faked me out. From what you told the guard, I thought you'd gone into the palace to ask questions. By the time I found out you weren't there, the fire alarm sounded. Now hush. We'll discuss that later. Count on it."

"Okay," she murmured, grasping him tighter as another stranger approached.

"Take it easy," he said soothingly. "It's Dr. Chiara. He's the palace physician."

Ryan placed her back inside the ambulance and left her there with the doors open while he spoke with the doctor. Nina gave up trying to hear what they were saying. The noise outside obliterated everything else. She did keep her eye on him, however, to make certain he stayed near.

The doctor checked her out, administered oxygen and gave her an injection.

"I should send you to the hospital overnight," he told her.

"No!" she argued. "I just want to go back to my apartment."

Dr. Chiara addressed Ryan. "She should be fine, but watch her. If she shows any sign of respiratory distress, get her over to Augustus on the double." He patted her arm.

"I will, Nick. Thanks," Ryan said.

After the doctor had bandaged the cut on her leg, Ryan carried her back to the car he had taken her to after the rescue. This time he put her in front and went around to the driver's side.

"I wish you'd agree to go to the hospital," he grumbled.

"Not a chance."

"Stubborn."

Though he was obviously angry with her, he still hadn't upbraided her the way she'd expected, nor had he threatened her with any reprisals. But she knew he wasn't through with her. Not by a long shot.

As soon as he fastened his seat belt and checked hers, he sat there, silently pinning her with a gaze so intense, she felt interrogated already. Tired. Wrung out. Incredibly sleepy. "What in the world was in that shot?"

"Antibiotic," he snapped, then abruptly launched into another tirade. "You had no business being in that guesthouse. You nearly got yourself killed."

"I wanted to see for myself," she muttered, "because… because Desmond lived and died there. I promise you I didn't strike any matches."

He said nothing, and Nina felt obliged to fill the silence.

"I swear I didn't," she insisted, her words slurring. "I only wanted to be in there by myself, see if I could feel what he felt, what he was like. Only…only there was nothing there of him." Tears leaked down her cheeks and she swiped at them angrily. "And then…"

"Did you see anything?" McDonough asked finally.

"No, nothing. I was in the bedroom. Heard the back door creak. I hid in the bathroom, in the shower. Next thing I knew, the place was on fire."

"Whoever started it used an accelerant. Had to, in order for it to spread that quickly," he told her. "The arsonist went out through the back. As soon as the guard out front saw flames through the window, he reported it."

"You sniffed my hands," she accused. "You thought I

set it.'' Nina wished she could summon the energy to get really angry about that. But she was so tired.

"And now I know you didn't.'' He sighed. "You need to get to bed.''

Panic begin to rise again. "You won't leave?''

His mouth quirked, more in resignation than reassurance, she thought. "No. I won't be leaving.''

"Thanks,'' she said, breathing the word as she leaned her head back against the headrest and closed her eyes. She felt like a hundred and ten pounds of molten lead.

Nina was vaguely aware of the car stopping near the flashing lights of the fire truck and Ryan speaking to someone out the car window, but she couldn't seem to rouse herself enough to listen to the conversation.

Tomorrow he would tell her everything he had found out. Tomorrow, when she showed him the earring, he would have to agree that she'd discovered something his team had overlooked, even if it was insignificant. Then he would take her attempts to help seriously. He would have to.

The car rolled forward, soon picked up speed, and the noises associated with fighting the fire faded into the distance. She yawned widely, drawing in much needed oxygen to try and stay awake, but her eyelids refused to open.

"Not antibiotic,'' Nina guessed.

"Nope.''

"'Gainst the law,'' she said, yawning again, wishing she sounded more irate.

"Sue me in the morning.'' Had he chuckled? Was he laughing at her?

"Found a clue,'' Nina murmured, hardly able to form the words.

"What?'' he demanded. No humor now, she noted. "What did you find?''

She sensed his full attention on her now. Payback time. Nina allowed her head to loll to one side on the headrest and faked a soft snore. She knew the second or third snore would probably be for real and tried not to smile.

The smell of fresh coffee ought to bring her around, Ryan thought as he waved the steaming cup of it close to her nose.

She gave a little grunt of pleasure in her throat and turned her head on the pillow, following the scent. Her eyes opened slowly, lids still at half-mast as she licked her lips.

Ryan could no more suppress his rush of lust than he could have held back the tide in the harbor. The feeling took him by surprise at the oddest times. She should be haggard and pale after the night she'd endured. Instead she looked as if she'd given some lucky man a wild night of hot sex. No, not that exactly, he decided. Too innocent for that. Too unaware of her sensuality.

He continued to tempt her with the coffee, moving it closer, then drawing it away to watch her seek it out. Then he realized what he was doing and stopped the motion immediately.

He took a fortifying breath and looked away as he spoke. "C'mon, Nina, wake up. How am I supposed to get any work done if you sleep all day?"

She slowly pushed herself up until she was leaning on one elbow. His peripheral vision caught that and also noted the covers slipping down around her waist.

He'd undressed her in the dark last night, leaving her bra and panties on so she wouldn't freak out when she woke up. Still, he'd had a rough time getting to sleep on her sofa after that. His imagination had been working overtime, fueled by the remembered sensation of her velvety skin against his hands.

The touching had been unavoidable, of course. Inadvertent and innocent. Totally innocent. Reliving it later and adding fantasies was not, he admitted. Neither were his thoughts at the moment, seeing her deliciously rumpled, tousled and sleepy-eyed.

"Timeizzit?" she grumbled, reaching for the coffee like it was an antidote to poison she'd just ingested.

"Nearly seven o'clock. Up and at 'em. I've been up for two hours." And awake a lot longer than that, damn her luscious hide.

She grunted and gulped another slug of caffeine, eyeing him evilly over the edge of the cup. "Not fair. *You* weren't drugged."

Ryan shrugged. "*I* wasn't a basket case."

"Neither was I," she argued, shoving the cup back at him as she swung her legs over the side of the bed and sat up. "Get out of here so I can change."

As she looked down at the scrap of lacy pink bra and whisper thin silk bikini bottoms she was wearing, he watched the light dawn.

"Wait a minute! Who took my clothes off?"

Ryan backed out of the bedroom, stopping in the doorway. "Who do you think?"

"Pervert," she growled. She snatched the covers up to her chest, leaving an excellent view of those long, long legs, lovely despite the six-inch bandage marring one of them. When he managed to drag his gaze up to her face, he saw her shooting daggers and gritting her teeth. "I think I'm reporting you to the police! That's what I think!"

"Okay, enhance my reputation if that's what you want to do. In the meantime, I'm on my way to rehash some of the evidence and see what else needs doing. I just wanted you awake and aware before I left. Be sure you keep the doors locked while I'm gone."

She jumped up, dropping the sheet, abandoning her attempt at modesty. "Wait! I'm coming with you."

He'd known that. He'd already decided it would probably be better if he didn't leave her here alone anyway. The fire might have been meant to destroy the crime scene, but

Nina had almost died in it. Whoever set that fire must have seen her enter the guesthouse and realized she was still there. Setting it in the bedroom adjacent to the bathroom where she was hiding could have been meant to prevent her escape.

It was his responsibility to see that nothing like that happened again, and the best way to do it was to get her out of Montebello as soon as possible.

Ryan downed the rest of her coffee as he watched her dash for the bathroom. The back view was as nice as the front. "Ten minutes!" he called out as she slammed the door.

He prepared to wait thirty. She was ready in fifteen, marching into the living room, looking like she'd spent a full hour in front of the mirror.

Not bad, he reflected, remembering how long it used to take... No, he wasn't going there this morning. But for some reason, the flash of memory hadn't stabbed him in the heart the way it once had. He realized he'd been smiling when he thought back to the time when he'd been a husband, listening to the hair dryer, hearing Kath humming off-key while she put on her face and he tapped his foot waiting.

He shook it off, promising himself he would examine his reaction later when he was alone. Test the waters with one of the happier recollections and see how it went. Not here and now with the feisty Ms. Caruso raring to play Watson to his Sherlock.

"What did you do with my purse?" she demanded.

Ryan pointed to the chair by the door. "You know that's the first thing a good cop looks for when a woman's reported missing?"

She glanced up from examining the contents of her shoulder bag, zipping this pocket and unzipping that one. "Hmm?"

"Handbag. If the purse is still there and she's gone, it's

a sure bet there's been foul play. Women won't take off voluntarily without their *stuff*."

"Don't be sexist. You go anywhere without your wallet?"

"Point taken. You about ready to hit the road?"

She smiled smugly, holding up one fist. "You about ready to add to your collection of evidence?"

"The clue you mentioned," he guessed, returning her smile. "What have you got? That kept me awake last night." Among other things. It had also prompted him to search her purse and clothing.

"I meant it to. Are you going to guess which hand, or just take this and have a look?"

Ryan accepted what she offered. "An earring. Not yours, I take it." It was for a pierced ear and hers were pierced. He had assumed it belonged to her when he'd found it.

"Nope, not mine. I stepped on it last night in the guesthouse."

He managed not to gape. The thing was small and could possibly have been missed in the sweep. "Where exactly?"

"A couple of feet from the bloodstain. I think it might have been caught in the pile of the rug or tangled in the fringe. Your people did vacuum, you said, but you know how vacuums are. Mine barely picks up dustbunnies. Rolling up the carpet could have dislodged it." She focused on the bauble in his palm. "You think it could it be important?"

"Could be," he granted, squinting at the thing. It was half the size of a dime, suspended by a few tiny links of chain from a round silver ball welded to the post. "If we can get any prints from it, they'll probably be yours."

"I thought it was a tack in my foot or I'd have been more careful handling it. Sorry."

"Not your fault. We'll check it out anyway." He went to the kitchen, found a roll of plastic wrap and swaddled the earring. "I just wish we knew how long it had been there."

"I can tell you how you might find out," she cooed, rocking back and forth, pulling a face that begged him to ask her.

"I'll bite. How?"

She waltzed forward, took it from him and examined it through the transparent wrap. "I recognized it the minute I saw it."

"You know whose it is?" This was too good to be true.

"No, but I know where it came from. At least I think I might. On the plane coming over the airline furnished a catalog with duty-free merchandise. You know, the stuff you can only buy at the duty-free shops and while you're in the air? This particular earring was offered. I almost bought a pair, but the price was outrageous."

Ryan smiled at her enthusiasm. He felt pretty charged up himself. "We can find out when the catalog was issued, when the earrings were added, and how many have been sold and on which flights. Might get lucky with a credit-card purchase in a name that's familiar."

"Precisely. *Well?*"

"Well what?" he asked, slipping the earring into his jacket pocket.

"Aren't you going to say anything?" she questioned impatiently. "Like *thanks, well done* or something equally grateful?"

"Something equally grateful. I'll buy you breakfast."

Her face fell. "That's it?"

Ryan took her arm and led her to the door. "After I feed you, I thought I would show you the evidence room and the lab."

"You're going to let me help now, aren't you?" she asked hopefully. "I mean, really help you, not just putz around like a fifth wheel?"

"Sure I will," he said as he set the alarm and locked the

door on the way out. *Like hell,* he thought. If she believed accidentally stepping on a clue made her Miss Marple, let her think it. Someone had nearly killed her last night and he wasn't about to let her risk her life again. And no doubt she would, the little loose cannon. Who knew what she'd be up to the next time he turned his back?

He needed to talk to King Marcus this morning and convince him to order the woman back to the States on the next plane out.

What he needed now was a safe place to leave her, somewhere she'd stay put while he accomplished that.

"Can you handle reading the reports?" he asked. "Some are lengthy and fairly graphic. Pictures."

She looked suspicious. "Well, since I've seen the real thing, I think I can manage without freaking out. But what will you be doing while I'm doing that?"

He glanced over at her before backing out of the parking lot and lied straight-faced. "Checking on the earring. What else? You want to catch up on the case or ride out to the airport? I figure there's no point in duplicating our efforts, right?"

She only hesitated a moment, looking doubtful, then agreed.

Ryan almost heaved a sigh of relief. Once he spoke to the king and had her exiled, she was going to be mad as hell. He doubted she'd ever forgive him for it.

But what did he care? He'd never see her again after she left. At the realization, depression hit him like a train. It had hit before on a fairly regular basis and he was used to it now, but this time it was a little different. This time, there was a smattering of hope mixed up in all that gloom.

Maybe Nina would return to Montebello when all this was over. If she would just come back to ream him out about this, or visit her brother's grave, or just see the sights she'd missed, he might have a chance to convince her he'd been doing her a favor.

Stupid idea. None of those reasons would bring her back here. He was about to end it all before he even started anything with Nina Caruso. Safer that way, anyhow, he thought. He had no business letting her get a hold on him the way he'd been doing. It had been ages since he'd had anything going with a woman that lasted longer than it took to put his clothes back on. That was the way his life went now, and he would keep it that way.

When they reached police headquarters, he took her up to the fourth floor and introduced her to Franz Koenig, his forensics specialist and erstwhile computer geek.

Koenig was geeky, bless his heart, complete with post-adolescent pimples and the requisite penholder sticking out of his pocket. He'd only recently replaced his taped-together horn-rims with round granny glasses, and then only after Joe had dragged him down to the optometrist.

Franz was one of those guys who could get it all together, and then forget where he put it. The fact that he *could* get it all together so methodically was what had landed him the job. Ryan could take it from there, and actually preferred it that way. When it came to piling up seemingly insignificant bits of evidence, nobody did it better than Franz. Sorting them out was Ryan's forte.

"Franz here is our detail man," he told Nina. "He catalogs and lines up the pieces of the puzzle, and I mean *all* of them." Ryan clapped him on the shoulder. "Ms. Caruso found us a possible clue last night." He pulled the wrapped earring out of his pocket and handed it to Franz. "Give me some quick photos of this and then get what you can off of it."

Franz held the thing between his thumb and forefinger and began looking around for the camera. He found it, then tugged on gloves to position the object for photographing.

"Ms. Caruso's going to keep you company while I run an errand, Franz. I'm giving her the initial reports to read.

You see if you can answer any questions she has about them. I'll be back in a couple of hours to pick her up.''

Franz shrugged. ''Okay.''

Ryan scribbled a phone number on a phone pad and handed it to Franz. ''If you need me, call my cell phone. Here's an alternate number just in case.'' He knew he'd be required to turn off the cellular during his audience with the king.

''Okay,'' Franz mumbled again, took the paper and laid it down beside his microscope.

Ryan went to the portable file cabinet he had set up in the area where Franz was working. He unlocked it, withdrew a folder and brought it back to Nina.

She eagerly took the file, looked around for a space to work and made herself comfortable at the desk nearest the door. Good. She'd be out of the way and occupied while Ryan took care of business at the palace.

He waited around for the Polaroid shots of the earring to give to Joe, who would check it out with the airlines. Nina seemed thoroughly engrossed in reading and content to stay, but he shot a look of warning over her head to Franz, who nodded back. Ryan just wished Franz didn't look quite so spacey. Most of the time it didn't matter.

Nina, eyes locked on a page in the file, tossed him a negligent wave as he walked past her to leave.

Ryan experienced a strange sense of unease. He stopped at the table and looked down at her. ''You have enough to do here?''

She nodded, then placed her finger on the page to hold her place as she looked up at him. ''You guys have been busy after all, I see. There's much more here than I expected.''

He shrugged off the backhanded compliment. ''If you need anything while I'm gone, just ask Franz.'' He gestured toward Koenig, who was so engrossed in his work he wouldn't notice if the walls fell down around him. "Interrupt him."

"All right," she replied and went back to reading the file, dismissing Ryan as surely as if she'd slammed the door behind him.

Chapter 5

Ryan wasn't too surprised that he had to wait awhile when he arrived at the king's offices. Not that it was a bad place to cool his heels, if he'd had time to waste.

The lap of luxury hardly began to describe the palace. The furnishings were Italianate, of carved dark mahogany. The rich fabrics mirrored in the polished marble floors. Everything in the palace was as lush and exotic as the setting for the buildings themselves.

The doors finally opened and Prince Lucas emerged. He spied Ryan immediately and inclined his head. "McDonough."

"Your Highness," Ryan replied, shaking the prince's hand when it was offered. "It's good to have you back. It goes without saying, everybody's been worried about you and relieved to have you home again."

The royal expression looked sad, distracted, even if the lips were turned up at the corners. "Yes, well, it was an eventful year to say the least."

"No doubt. Bet you've had enough of the States for a while."

A haunted look replaced his official for-the-public smile and Prince Lucas gave a short shake of his head.

"Are you okay?" Ryan asked, peering a little more closely at him.

Immediately Lucas straightened, once again regal. Didn't matter if he was dressed today in slacks and a pullover sweater, nobody would ever mistake him for anything less than what he was, Ryan thought. And he guessed it was not all that politic to question the future king's health, much less his state of mind.

"I'm fine, thank you. And you? Lorenzo tells me you're heading up the investigation into Desmond's death. How is it going? I hear the crime scene was burned to a crisp last night. I suppose that won't help."

"Not much," Ryan agreed with a shrug.

"Well, good luck with it." He stood aside and nodded at the door he'd just exited. "The king's ready to see you, I expect, so I won't keep you." He turned and walked away without another word.

Ryan watched him start down the now-deserted corridor, noting his bowed head and the hands stuck in his pockets, the lack of spring in his step. Really glum when he thought no one was watching.

Did the upcoming coronation weigh that heavily on him? Ryan wondered. After all he had heard about the exploits of Lucas Sebastiani, he couldn't imagine that the mere job of running a little country would get him down. Must be something big.

Well, he had stuff of his own weighing pretty heavy on his mind without worrying about the prince's problems.

The king's secretary appeared at the door and beckoned.

When he was finally shown into the royal office, Ryan even broke his own tradition and bowed. Hell, he'd drop to his knees and beg if that's what it took to get Nina out of Montebello. He waited for the king to recognize him.

The monarch looked very distinguished in his gray silk suit, conservative tie and pale blue shirt. He might have been any chief executive who confidently exerted absolute control over every aspect of his corporation.

King Marcus was good at his job, better than most kings because he possessed the real power to rule and did so in a fair and equitable way. He was well loved and respected by his subjects and also by expatriates like Ryan who now called Montebello home.

"Good morning, my friend," Marcus said after a long moment spent studying him. "Are you here concerning last evening's fireworks?"

"In a way," Ryan admitted, then decided he should come right out with it rather than dancing around the issue. Surely his time in here would be limited. "Sir, I believe Nina Caruso's life is in danger. The person who ignited that fire did so in the bedroom adjacent to the bathroom where she was hiding. She would have died if we had not been able to break the window frame. Even then we could not have gotten her out if she were not so slender. You should send her home before something worse happens."

The king sat forward over his desk, his fingers clasped together, his full attention on Ryan. "Perhaps she misjudged the size of the window she would need to exit. The fire might have been set by her to deflect suspicion."

Ryan almost rolled his eyes. "Your Majesty, surely you don't think she put *herself* in such danger! We know for sure she wasn't in the country when the murder took place. And I've found no reason at all to think she had anything to do with arranging Desmond's death."

"We must consider that through her mother, she probably has contacts in Montebello, providing her with the opportunity to secure an accomplice. Perhaps the person she hired is attempting to get rid of her. That accomplice might see her as a threat now that she is here," the king pointed out. He narrowed his eyes at Ryan. "Also, I am not discounting her father's relatives in Italy. Family ties are strong in both places. Desmond might have shared the Caruso name, and ultimately the inheritance, but he did not share the blood. She might well have asked help of them."

Ryan almost scoffed. "That's a stretch, don't you think, sir? There's no indication she had any motive to have her half brother killed. What could she possibly gain by it?"

"The insurance policy purchased by her father on Desmond's life when the children were young. The trust fund he left has continued to pay those premiums. You know of this. True, it does not represent a fortune of any magnitude, but in addition, there is also the half of her father's estate that Desmond inherited, even though he was the adopted child and she, the natural one. That caused resentment, surely."

Ryan shook his head. "I wouldn't think either motive strong enough to warrant a solicitation of murder."

"It is your task to discover whether that is so," King Marcus reminded him with an inclination of the royal head. "She comes here without invitation, immediately, insisting that she be allowed full access to the details of the investigation. She was never officially notified, you know. Is that not suspicious to you?"

Yes. It was definitely suspicious. "I think the murderer called her for the express purpose of getting her to Montebello. Why, I don't know yet, but last night's close call is enough to make a rough guess. Somebody wants her dead."

"Perhaps. Perhaps not."

"She's loyal to her brother. That's why she came," Ryan explained, wondering why in the world he was arguing with the king over a woman he hardly knew. "I would demand justice if I were in her place. Wouldn't most people?"

"Perhaps. It may very well be that you are correct in believing her innocent. I but play the devil's advocate.

Keep an open mind and do the task assigned you. Arrest her if you find any evidence of conspiracy. If indeed, she is innocent, then no harm is done by your industriousness."

Not what Ryan had in mind. "You have hired me to solve your nephew's murder, Your Majesty. She's making that extremely difficult. Not overtly, of course. But she's… bothersome."

"What an interesting word," the king said, looking faintly amused. "Not one to sit idly by while you complete this mission, is she?" he asked.

"No, sir, she is not," Ryan admitted. An understatement.

"You must ask yourself why that is so. Will your protectiveness toward this woman blind you to the possibility of her guilt?"

"Absolutely not," Ryan assured him truthfully. "I will be thorough. Depend on it."

King Marcus smiled and nodded once. "If I did not believe that, another would take your place."

Ryan knew the best he could do now was reiterate his reason for the audience and get the hell out. "Sir, I do sincerely believe it would be best if you order her to return to the States until this case is cleared."

King Marcus sighed and sat back. "I am not inclined to do so until you discover for certain whether she is somehow involved or clear her completely. Extradition would prove a delicate, if not impossible matter if you later find evidence she is guilty. As you know, her precipitous arrival troubles me." He met Ryan's eyes. "And you cannot know for certain whether or not she set the fire last evening."

Ryan was already shaking his head. "No. She had no scent of any accelerant on her hands. No way she could have washed it off. All the soap had been removed from the bathroom by Forensics. The water was turned off."

"The report indicates petrol was used," the king said.

"Well then, she could not possibly have done it. She had

no time to acquire any between the time we parted company and the time I rescued her.''

"She could have siphoned it from one of the autos in the car park. A quick and simple procedure, is it not?''

"In what? No container was found. No hose,'' Ryan argued.

"But they were found. Melted globs of plastic, of course. A copy of this report has been sent to your office from the fire inspector.''

Ryan ran a hand over his face as he processed that and tried to think of anything else that might exonerate her. "She was searched as she came in. Braca questioned the guard on duty.''

"And she lied to that guard. An accomplice could have provided what she needed, or the petrol itself. It would be relatively simple for someone to enter the grounds as a tourist and remain behind after the gates are closed to the public.''

"I assume that is being remedied, sir?''

"I thought it already *had* been remedied, given the recent murder,'' the king admitted.

Someone's head would roll in security, Ryan thought as the king continued. "You are intrigued by this woman. Understandable, but you must not allow—''

"That is *not* a factor here,'' Ryan insisted with a sweep of one hand for emphasis. "You know it isn't!...sir.''

The king remained silent, his expression inscrutable.

Ryan paced for a minute, searching his mind for something irrefutable to validate Nina's innocence. "There are the surveillance cameras. As soon as we're able to—''

"Recovered within the past hour. Ruined.''

Ryan absorbed the kick of disappointment and went on. "Look, she even found what might be a clue last night before the fire took place, a piece of jewelry. Apparently it was missed in the initial sweep for evidence.''

The king nodded sagely, stretching out his long arms, his

palms flattened on top of the enormous hand-carved desk. "An earring, one that could quite conceivably belong to her. Interesting that you missed such a thing, is it not?"

"How did you know about it?" Ryan demanded. But he wasn't all that surprised. "Franz Koenig," he guessed.

It ticked him off that the king would think it necessary to recruit a spy from the team. Of course, it was entirely possible someone here had called within the last hour and asked for an update on the forensics. Lorenzo, probably. Franz would be duty-bound to give it. That scenario was much more believable than Franz as a spy, Ryan decided.

"You must not be upset that we insist upon keeping informed."

The royal *we?* A not-so-subtle reminder of who was boss here. Ryan shrugged and smiled. "Not upset, Your Majesty. It's just that I came to tell you myself and Franz stole my thunder."

The king smiled back as he reached for the solid-gold fountain pen and opened the leather folder in front of him. "Nina Caruso will remain until we have all the answers. Go and find them."

Ryan had no choice but to accept the dismissal. He ducked his head in his usual salute and turned toward the door. Damned if he'd bow and back out of the room.

"One further word with you, my friend."

The deep commanding voice halted Ryan in his tracks, his hand on the gilded door handle. He turned, looking in question at the head of state. "Yes, Your Majesty?"

"We have every confidence in your skills *and* your objectivity. Keep Nina Caruso close to you in the event your current assumptions are correct and there is indeed a threat to her. Keep her *very* close."

Ryan met the king's unwavering gaze with one just like it. "And also in the event that my assumptions are wrong."

"How better to judge?"

* * *

As Ryan made his way down the long hall leading from the royal offices to the enormous entry foyer, he mulled over all the king had said. And not said. He slowly realized that the sly old fox no more believed Nina Caruso was guilty of anything than Ryan did. This obviously was a smoke screen to hide the real reason the king wanted Nina to stay in Montebello. Hard to figure what that might be at this point.

At any rate, Ryan had no choice but to do exactly what the king advised—commanded, rather—and keep her as near as he possibly could. Her safety was paramount, as important to him now as solving the case. Maybe more so.

That didn't say much for his dedication to the job. And this job had been his whole life for years now. It was what sustained him, gave him purpose and prevented his sliding back into that pit he'd climbed out of.

No matter what the king had said, Ryan knew his professionalism and his objectivity were at stake here. Keeping his hands off of Nina took up too much of his energy and concentration. Another excellent argument for sending her away. But that wasn't going to happen now, so he would just have to deal with it.

Somehow, he had to find a way to distance himself even while keeping her within reach at all times. How the hell was he supposed to do that?

Nina hurried toward the grand staircase, her high heels clicking on the beautifully veined marble. She had made it halfway there when a large hand closed around her arm. Oddly enough, it did not surprise her all that much to find herself staring into the furious blue-gray eyes of Ryan McDonough.

After all, the possibility of running into him was the reason she was in such a hurry. If only she hadn't taken the time to interview those two guards, she might have made it upstairs to the residential wing before he finished his business in the royal office. Without a doubt he would object to what she was doing just because it was her idea and not his.

His long, strong fingers burned right through the sleeve of her beige linen suit. Every time he touched her, apprehension swept through her like fire in her veins. Not that he frightened her physically. Her own reaction to him as a man was what caused her fear. She worried what she might do if his touch gentled again as it had last night. No danger of that at the moment, she thought with a sigh. Right now he looked livid.

Though he wasn't hurting her, she knew better than to resist his grip. Maybe if she didn't act as guilty as she felt, he wouldn't frog-march her out of here like a prisoner. Nina smiled her friendliest smile. "I take it the audience with the king is over?"

"What the *hell* are you doing here?" His voice, though he kept it low, seemed to echo in the cavernous entry.

Nina knew he was about to read her the riot act for leaving the lab when he'd ordered her to stay put. She decided to brave it out rather than cower. "Asking questions. Something you—" she accused, poking him in the chest "—have obviously been neglecting to do around here!"

He grabbed her finger and removed it from the indentation her nail had made in his tie. "And how would you know what I've done or not done?"

"I asked!" she hissed. "The two people I've spoken with already were very eager to help. I'm on my way to request an interview with the princesses' staff."

"Oh, no you're not," Ryan assured her. "Even you have to observe protocol."

He started for the main entrance, still clutching her upper arm. She had no choice but to follow or be dragged. "So make an appointment!"

"I *have*. Now shut up and come on!"

''Where?'' she demanded, taking two steps to his every one in order to keep up.

''Out of here before you get yourself shot. How'd you get past the guards?''

Nina hated to tell him, but she knew he wouldn't let it go. He'd be reaming someone out about lack of security. ''Well...I showed my ID, told them I was Desmond's sister and, uh, that I had your permission.''

''Damn,'' he muttered, shaking his head. He glared at the nice young guards with the big holstered weapons and all but shoved Nina through the doors leading outside.

He glanced around. ''How did you get here? Taxi?''

She nodded, almost tripping in her attempt to match his haste as he ushered her around the arts wing to the parking lot to his car.

''How did you know I was here?''

Her smile was smug. ''Saw the number you left Franz. Public Affairs office, the same one I called after I arrived at the airport yesterday. You came here to see the king and get me kicked on a plane, didn't you?''

''Yes.''

Only when they were out of the palace grounds and he was occupied driving through the noon day traffic did Nina risk a question. ''So, what did the king have to say about it?''

He shot her a dark glance, then trained his eyes on the street again. ''Trust me, you don't want to know.''

Nina bridled. ''Don't be an ass, McDonough. Apparently it didn't work, since you're so mad.''

''When do you collect on your brother's insurance?''

She frowned at the abrupt change of subject. ''What?''

''Have you made the claim yet?''

Nina almost laughed. ''You've got to be joking! There's no insurance.''

''A policy for half a million, all paid up, plus the capital in the trust fund that paid the premiums,'' he snapped.

She was astounded. "How could… But that couldn't possibly… I know nothing about anything like that! Who—?"

"Don't play dumb, Nina. Your father insured you both and made certain the premiums were taken care of."

She sighed, pinching the bridge of her nose, trying to ward off the headache that was rapidly growing to gigantic proportions behind her eyes. "I swear I didn't know. There was nothing like that in Dad's papers after he died."

"And I suppose you knew nothing about Desmond receiving half your father's estate? Get real, Nina, you couldn't help but know." He scoffed.

"Yes, of course I knew about that."

"And resented the hell out of it, I bet," Ryan commented.

"No," she argued. "I didn't resent it at all. Desmond sold the property he inherited, which he was perfectly entitled to do. I guess he spent all the money."

That got Ryan's attention. He stopped at a red light and turned to face her. "What makes you think so?"

Nina hesitated, but guessed it didn't matter now what anyone thought of Des. Lots of people were not that great about managing their money. "He called a couple of weeks ago wanting to borrow a bit from me."

"A bit? How much?" Ryan asked, creeping ahead as the light turned and no longer pinning her with that laser glare.

Nina shrugged. "Twenty thousand. He said he would repay me with interest when he received his next quarterly allowance from the crown."

"Good God." Ryan coughed a laugh of obvious disbelief. "So you're here for repayment? King Marcus won't authorize you a nickel if your brother didn't sign a note, and even then—"

"No," Nina interrupted the tirade, "I didn't loan Desmond anything. My assets are mostly tied up in investments and CDs, so I didn't have access to that much cash at the moment. Besides, I never make loans, especially not to friends or family. I believe it eventually causes bad feelings.''

''You're right. It really is very bad business to loan money unless you're a bank. Why did he need it?''

''He didn't say. I told him I was sorry, that it wasn't possible, and asked him if he was in trouble of some kind. He said no, of course he wasn't.''

''Was he angry? How did he react to your refusal?''

Nina shrugged. ''He said never mind, then goodbye and hung up.''

''Nothing else? Did he ask how you were doing? Tell you anything about how things were going with him?''

Nina felt embarrassed to have to admit that her own brother had no interest in her life at all and hadn't been inclined to share what his was like. ''He sounded as if he was in a hurry. I guess he didn't have time for small talk.''

''Interesting indeed. Did he ever have time?''

Now she felt defensive, as if Ryan were attacking Desmond or something. ''What are you implying?''

''Nothing. Forget it.''

But she couldn't, of course, especially now that he had made a big thing of it. Desmond hadn't really cared much. Maybe not at all. So why the hell was she here? Nina blinked back tears.

Ryan reached over and took her hand without looking directly at her. ''Hey, I get carried away sometimes. It's no big deal, okay?''

''Okay.'' But it wasn't okay. Now she was questioning not only Desmond's feelings for her, but hers for him. Maybe she harbored a deeply buried resentment after all and had never admitted it, even to herself.

''Let it go, Nina,'' he suggested softly, squeezing her hand. ''Think about something else.''

At least the change in topic had taken Ryan's mind off her ignoring his orders earlier. His anger seemed to have lessened. She suspected that he rarely held on to it for long anyway, thank goodness. She wasn't up to a fight in her present frame of mind.

She was getting to know Ryan better now. He found vulnerable spots with unerring accuracy, that was for sure. He also gave good advice. Picking apart her relationship with her brother wouldn't do anyone any good now. He'd been killed, and she was here to find out what happened. It was that simple. Reasons no longer mattered.

She would concentrate on Ryan for the moment. Figuring him out might make the difference in her success or failure in this venture.

His bad temper popped like firecrackers and just as quickly disappeared, the residual smoke dispersing a bit more slowly, but even that was clearing with the breeze of diversion. All she had to do to diffuse a situation with Ryan was to sidetrack him.

"So, how about if I buy you lunch?" she asked, forcing a lilt into her voice.

"You make me crazy, you know that?" he asked.

Nina decided the question was about as rhetorical as questions ever got, so she didn't answer it. Instead, she made an observation. "You really ought to work on your adaptability, McDonough. Did you go through this trauma every time you hired an assistant?"

"You are *not* an assistant," he said, only pretending anger now and not doing it very well, either. "You're a serious liability is what you are. All I want is to do my job, and now I have to divide my time between that and keeping you out of trouble."

Nina clicked her tongue in sympathy. "King's orders, huh?"

"Yeah. King's orders." He heaved a gruff sigh. "You want this murder solved or not?"

"That's why I came here," she told him, exerting her best effort to sound patient and companionable.

"Yeah, well, I hope that's why." He risked another glance even as he wove through the traffic. "If it is, then you owe me some cooperation. You have to do exactly what I tell you and quit taking off on your own the way you did last night and today."

"I'm yours to command," she said primly, folding her hands in her lap.

He laughed and shook his head. She couldn't help noticing the creases beside his mouth that could almost be called dimples. His teeth could be a toothpaste ad and his long-lashed eyes crinkled just right at the corners. The laugh was infectious, but she resisted the urge to laugh with him since he was laughing at *her.*

"What's so funny?" she demanded, but he didn't answer. Once his laughter subsided, they rode in silence. He was still holding her hand while they both pretended not to notice.

Just when she thought she had him figured out, another side of him would emerge to confuse her. About the only thing she had locked down about Ryan McDonough was his firm determination not to act on his attraction to her. Oh, it was there, as surely as hers for him, but he resented it as much as he resented her helping him with the case.

She didn't care, Nina told herself. It was just as inconvenient for her as it was for him. The man was not her type at all. The chemistry between them was a purely physical thing that sometimes happened for no good reason at all. Pheromones or something equally ephemeral. An accident of nature in this case.

When the two people involved had nothing at all in common and no way in the world to make a personal connection work, they *should* simply ignore it. Or fight it tooth and nail, if it turned out to be this strong. That's what he was doing and helping her to do, she assured herself.

His strategy was working for the most part. She should

applaud that and thank him for attempting to be a jerk so she could keep her distance and he could keep his.

She ought to develop some kind of defense herself instead of testing their attraction at every turn, of analyzing it and rationalizing it and wishing it *could* somehow work.

God, where had that thought come from? She didn't wish it would work. Did she? No, certainly not with a man like McDonough, who admitted he had no time or inclination to involve himself in anything but his job.

One thing she definitely had to do was to stop questioning his ability to do that job. At first she really had believed he was shirking his duty with regard to Desmond's case, but now she knew better. She had seen the collection of files and realized the vast amount of work he and his men had accomplished in a very short period of time. She knew that she could leave today and rest assured that Ryan would eventually solve her brother's murder for her if it could possibly be solved. So why didn't she simply go to the airport and leave it to him?

Nina honestly couldn't answer her own question. She liked to think she owed it to Desmond to have a hand in bringing his killer to justice. But a small voice inside her head warned her that her original reason for being in Montebello had evolved into another that had an even less certain outcome.

Ryan parked half on the sidewalk, half in the street just outside Pietro's. Pete served the juiciest hamburgers on this side of the world and the greasiest fries anywhere. Nina could have her blasted oatmeal when she craved comfort food. He hit Pete's place when he needed a brief shot of home. Today was turning out to be one of those days.

God only knew what she'd try next if he left her anywhere so he could get some work done. He'd just have to haul her with him everywhere he went, he supposed.

Maybe his stopping for the junkiest food available in

Montebello had a little revenge attached to it. She definitely looked like a yogurt-and-bean-sprout kind of girl. Damned yuppie. Graphic designer? What kind of job was that? Probably did those so-called subtle ads with tons of blank space for products that were unidentifiable to the average guy.

He hadn't asked her about her job because he didn't want to know. The less he knew about her, the better. But then again, he had to find out as much as he could to determine whether he was right about her being innocent. God, he hoped he hadn't misjudged. The king would never trust him with another assignment if he screwed this up.

Ryan shoved the car into Park and got out. By the time he had gone around and reached her door, she was already standing on the narrow cobbled sidewalk.

"Where are we?" she asked, slamming her door and adjusting her shoulder bag. She raked her hair behind her ears, baring those model's cheekbones and strong, square chin.

"This way," he ordered, taking her arm. He knew he shouldn't touch her. Hell, just looking at her messed with his mind, and even through her sleeve, he felt the soft sweetness of her. The warmth. It made him remember how she felt without sleeves. Without clothes. This was not good. It was nonprofessional, and it was wrong.

When she recoiled a little, he held on, knowing it wasn't wise. Knowing he couldn't help himself and would use any excuse for continued contact. "The walking's hazardous in those shoes," he muttered. Lame reason, but better than none. He tightened his grip and endured—no, enjoyed— the resulting heat that suffused him.

"Oh," she said, looking down at the rough paving, then back up at him with a bright little smile. "Thanks."

Chapter 6

He led her two doors down to the hole-in-the-wall pub, identifiable only by a weathered wooden sign about the size of a car tag sticking out of the stones about ten feet up. Pete didn't believe in advertising much. Word of mouth brought him about as much business as he wanted to handle.

They entered the dark cavern lit only by candles on the occupied tables and a long fluorescent Bud sign over the bar.

"Wow, this is some place," she whispered, taking in all the details of the humble little pub's interior. Some might call it picturesque with the beer signs, names carved into the walls with pocket knives and tables covered with mismatched tablecloths.

Pete looked up from his task of wiping down the bar and grinned, showing a missing eyetooth and the wide, wicked scar on his neck. "Hey, Mac! What's up?"

"Not a lot, Pete. Bring us the usual and two iced teas, would you?"

"I'll have coffee," Nina piped up.

"No, trust me, you don't want to do that," Ryan advised. "Tea," he reaffirmed, looking at Pete.

"Gotcha, Mac," the man said, then called their order through the door to the kitchen which lay directly behind the bar. "Grab that corner over there," he told Ryan. "More romantic," he added, wiggling his bushy gray eyebrows suggestively. "Who's the babe?"

Ryan winced, then made the introductions. "Nina Caruso, Pete Jones, a fellow Yank."

She smiled and gave a small wave. "Hi, Pete. Nice place."

And thereby won Pete's heart, Ryan thought, unsurprised by it. Reckless as she could be at times, the woman did have class to spare.

He guided her to the table Pete had indicated and pulled out the chair for her.

Pete brought over two tall glasses of tea, floating three ice cubes each. On the tray with those sat a long-necked bottle of the off-the-wall brew Pete preferred. He dragged out a chair, sat down with them, pulled a matchbook out of his pocket and lit the candle on the table.

The candlelight threw a soft glow over Nina's features. Ryan realized he was staring at her and blinked to break the spell. "A singular honor when the proprietor joins you at table," he told her.

She grinned and nodded, racheting his respect for her up another notch and solidly cementing her new relationship with Pete. She didn't look down that aristocratic nose at the humble surroundings the way he'd thought she might.

Ryan wasn't sure he was glad about that. It would have thrown up another obstacle between them, and God knows he needed a few of those after last night.

Pete shifted his three hundred pounds around on the stout oak comb-backed chair to get comfortable, indicating he meant to stay awhile. So much for "romantic."

After another gap-toothed smile of appreciation accompanied by a closer check of Nina's visible assets, he turned to Ryan. "The sister."

Desmond Caruso's murder was headline news and Montebello a small island. No doubt most everyone knew who she was by now since the article in the paper yesterday.

"Half sister," Ryan clarified, reaching for his tea and taking a long swig. Sweet enough to pour on pancakes and only a shade above lukewarm, it tasted almost like home, as close to Savannah fare as he could get here.

"Too bad, what happened," Pete said to Nina, who merely nodded in reply.

Ryan set his tea glass down and began to turn it round and round slowly in the puddle of condensation that was forming. "Any scuttlebutt I need to know about, Pete?"

There was a massive clearing of throat and a marked hesitation.

"Nina's helping me on the case. You can talk."

"My girl Jonet says Desmond made a play for Princess Samira Kamal. Succeeded, too. You know about that?"

"Pete's stepdaughter Jonet works at the palace," Ryan explained to Nina, then answered Pete. "Yeah, we know about Princess Samira. Anyone else?"

Pete cast a wary eye at Nina. He took the time to down half his beer before answering. "He was seeing somebody else on the sly."

"Got a name or where she hangs out?" Ryan asked.

"Nope. Could be somebody just saw him with a pros," he added with a shrug.

"A *pros?*" Nina questioned, then seemed to suddenly realize Pete was using street slang for prostitute. "Oh." She blushed.

"Thanks, Pete. You get anything else, you'll call me?"

"Natch. If I run across anybody knows who she was, I'll give you a buzz." He upended the bottle and chugalugged.

Pete was upward of sixty and had come here straight from 'Nam back in the seventies. Ryan felt he had a lot in common with Pete despite totally different backgrounds and the generation gap. Both had run from dreaded reminders of the past and settled in a place that bore no resemblance to home.

Neither had talked about it much, but they'd made enough oblique admissions in the past couple of years to establish they shared a motive for transplanting here.

Pete was the only American in residence on the island that Ryan called friend. He had also proved to be a valuable source of information, since he had stepchildren and children by Sophia, his Montebellan wife, working in just about every occupation on the island. There were thirteen of them in all, not counting a slew of grandchildren. Quite a network.

Pete excused himself, bowing slightly to Nina after he got up. "Pie's on the house," he declared, making the first offer of free food Ryan had heard in the two years he'd been frequenting the place.

"You made quite an impression," Ryan told her. "Free pie."

"I like him," Nina said, watching Pete's pillowy frame squeeze through the opening to the back of the bar. Then she dropped the smile. "This woman he mentioned that Desmond was seeing. You think she killed Desmond?"

"Possibly. We'll need to talk to Jonet and see if she can give us a description or tell us who might."

"I still want to see that statuette," Nina said.

Ryan smiled. "You want to check the angle of that projection against the wound, right?"

Her mouth dropped open. Then she recovered, propping her elbow on the table and resting her chin in her palm. "That's why you're the detective, I guess."

"I already calculated and confirmed it with Doc. We agree the angle of the blow, combined with the force of it, probably indicates the perp was around five-six or -seven and not very strong.''

''Ah, a small wimpy guy or a woman. Is that what you're saying?'' She sounded insulted for some reason, but she was right on the money.

Ryan inclined his head in agreement. ''It was a lucky blow. Because of that and the choice of weapon, I really don't think the murder was premeditated.''

Nina huffed. ''Maybe not, but last night's fire certainly was.''

''Maybe whoever set it didn't know you were in there. Could have been to destroy any trace evidence.''

''Then why wait until you'd already made the sweep?'' she argued. ''They knew I was there, all right. I had the distinct impression I was being followed all the way to the guesthouse.''

''Later.'' Ryan shushed her when Pete's son, Jack, started over with their food.

Ryan attacked his burger immediately, amazed that Nina did exactly the same.

''Umm,'' she crooned, the look on her face one of ecstasy as she chewed a mouthful of the juicy fat hamburger.

A smudge of mustard dotted her lower lip, enticing him the way mustard never had before.

The frosty attitude he'd worked up against her that morning had thawed down to acceptance, then warmed up to something he didn't even want to name.

Ryan reached for the sugary tea, grasping at any kind of reassurance that his life hadn't changed all that radically. He was in trouble here. Even his ice cubes had melted.

When Ryan took her back to the lab over the police station, Nina didn't bother apologizing to Franz Koenig for her earlier escape. As for Franz, he didn't even seem aware that she had been gone.

Ryan got right down to business, asking Franz to produce

the murder weapon from the evidence vault downstairs. Nina felt edgy about seeing the thing that had killed Desmond, but also eager to check out what had occurred to her about it. Ryan remained quiet while they waited, ostensibly reading over a page of notes Franz had been writing when they arrived.

Once she had the statuette in her hands, she turned the small bronze figure this way and that, holding it by the marble base while she examined the arm of it through the plastic bag. The sculpture depicted a standing nude, one arm fused to the side of the body, the other raised with the hand buried within the hair at the nape of the neck.

"The bent elbow there inflicted the killing blow," Franz mumbled, pointing clumsily at it.

"It had been wiped, but we found traces of blood and skin particles in the crevices of the arm where the bronze is textured," the tech related in a monotone with just a hint of a German accent. "We also have isolated a half print, not yet identified."

She wondered what sort of person would have the presence of mind to wipe off the makeshift weapon after bashing Desmond with it and watching him die. Somehow she couldn't believe it had been someone so stricken with outrage they didn't know what they were doing. Whoever had done it must have recovered their senses pretty quickly after the so-called crime of passion.

"Not squeamish at all, are you?" Ryan commented, inclining his head toward the object she was holding.

Nina realized he'd been watching her, his eyes narrowed, as she'd handled the instrument of her brother's death. It did seem strange, even worried her, that she felt so little.

"I'm being objective, as you suggested," she replied. She could hardly blame him for wondering about her lack of emotion when she wondered about it herself.

Maybe it was because she really hadn't known Desmond well. Not the man he'd become after he left home. Maybe she had used up all her grief over losing him when he had left the family without a backward look.

Her little-sister grief had turned to anger eventually, then finally to acceptance. The victim of this crime was a virtual stranger to her. While she truly regretted Desmond's death, Nina knew she would feel almost as distressed about anyone who died so needlessly.

She was doing this for the memory of that brother she had worshiped so long ago, for her mother's son and especially for a boy who had been so angry he'd allowed no one to get close to him.

She hefted the slender little sculpture to feel its considerable weight. It was only about sixteen inches high, but could no doubt make a truly serious dent if wielded with some force. Desmond's wound had not looked terribly deep, just lethally placed.

"Hold it like this." Ryan took her hand and positioned it. "That puts your thumb where we found a partial print. Stand here like this," he told her, moving her in front of Franz. "He's about the same height as Desmond. Draw the thing back naturally and swing in slow motion."

"*Very* slow motion, please," Franz said, exhibiting the first sign of full awareness she had noticed in him. She'd pegged him as a space cadet, wrapped up in his work to the exclusion of everything else. She was glad to know he at least had a sense of self-preservation.

She raised the object and swung. When the plastic-covered arm of the statuette touched the technician's temple, she immediately saw that the angle was wrong to inflict the same kind of blow Desmond had suffered.

"See that? Your mark would be too vertical," Ryan said, following the angle of the protrusion on the statue with one long finger. "The person who struck him must have been taller than you. Say, around five-seven or -eight, we think."

"Nearer Desmond's height," she confirmed and he nodded his agreement.

Nina gladly released the thing when Ryan closed his fingers around hers and took the object with his other hand.

"It was a woman," she said conclusively. "This demonstration and the earring convince me."

He shrugged. "Well, you have a fifty-fifty chance of being right."

"More like eighty-twenty," she argued, hitching herself onto a stool next to the counter by the lab table. "You said a man would probably have hit harder, too, and made a deeper wound. I agree."

"Okay," he said. "There's a good chance our perp is female. But it could still be a man with a weak swing. Hopefully we'll get something useful on the earring."

He penned a note in one of the folders and snapped it shut. "We're finished here for today. Let's go back to my place.

"I'm taking copies of the files with me to go over some of the interviews tonight," he told Franz. "I need to make lists of further questions before I reinterview. You check out the rest of those things that were bagged out of the bathrooms. I want the results in the morning."

They left Franz bent over a microscope, either engrossed in his work or sulking. Nina couldn't tell. The man was none too happy with their long interruption of his afternoon, or Ryan's berating him for his premature report on the earring to the king's office.

Despite Franz's pouting and Ryan's gruff manner, Nina realized she was beginning to feel a part of the team. Ryan was now being fairly generous with information and in allowing her access to everything he and his men had discovered.

"Thanks for not shutting me out," she said as he deposited the box of folders in the back of his SUV.

"No problem," he muttered, slamming the hatch and walking her to the passenger side. He opened the door, waited for her to fasten her seat belt, then closed it.

He was lying. He had a problem with it, all right. Though he had apparently relented, he didn't look very happy about it. He hated to relinquish one ounce of control, she decided.

She had really misjudged him at first, when she'd assumed he didn't care one way or the other about apprehending Desmond's killer. Everything he did seemed directed toward that end. She could see by the volume of files alone that he had put forth a bigger effort than she could have expected from any police department this quickly.

After a silent drive through the city, Nina followed him into his apartment without waiting for an invitation. She stood by as he set the box of files on the dining table.

"I'll help you go through them," she offered. "A fresh eye might help, don't you think?"

"Right," he snapped. Then, almost as an afterthought, he tossed her a half smile to soften the reply.

That wasn't exactly a plea for assistance, but she wouldn't quibble. At least he wasn't chasing her out of the place with the broom.

She looked around. His apartment had the same floor plan as hers, only reversed. There was a living room/dining room combination, separated from the small kitchen by a waist-level bar with stools.

It looked very similar to any midpriced apartment in the States, only the rooms were more spacious, the unscreened windows larger, offering a view of the distant ocean. And there were no closets, making her wonder whether Montebellans were taxed by the number of rooms as they were in some European countries.

His furnishings looked expensive, but not outrageously so. The color scheme consisted of beige and browns, more masculine than her rose and green. This decor seemed incredibly boring for a man such as Ryan.

She noticed no personal items at all. No photos, plants, no original art, no brass or bright colors to spice up the

monotony. Maybe he was going for restful here. It was
enough to put anybody to sleep immediately, she thought
with a yawn.

"Sleepy?" he asked, almost hopefully.

"No, wide awake."

"Hungry?" he asked, this time reluctantly, as he
shucked his jacket, hung it on a dining room chair and
headed around the breakfast bar to the kitchen.

"Not much. Lunch was substantial."

"It will have to be soup and sandwiches, then. I'm not
much of a cook."

"Can I help?"

"No, I'll get it." He rummaged through the few cans
she could see on a shelf in one of the upper cabinets, his
back to her. "Tomato or chowder?"

"Tomato. I hate clams."

His actions stretched his shirt smoothly across his broad
shoulders, emphasizing their width. Nina hitched one hip
onto a stool and propped her elbow on the counter, resting
her chin in her hand.

No question, the man was very easy to look at. Incredible
buns, she thought, idly tracing her smile with one finger.

Every move he made was a study in graceful economy.
Amazing how much he accomplished and how quickly he
did it without seeming to hurry.

"When I do the interviews, I guess you'll want to sit
in," he said.

"You bet." She continued to watch as he bent over,
retrieving sandwich things from the small, European-size
refrigerator. "Do you realize that almost every conversation
we've ever had has centered on the case?" she asked.

He straightened and turned around, frowning. "So?"

Nina shrugged. "So, I thought maybe we could take a
break from it. Talk about something else for a change. Sort
of rest and regroup."

Ryan yanked open a drawer and fished out the silverware. "I don't break until the case is closed." He met her eyes directly. "To me, that means solved."

She flared her hands in surrender. "Okay, fine. It was just a thought. How *is* your solve rate, McDonough?"

"Pretty damn good. I mean to keep it that way."

"A fanatic, huh?" she guessed. "Pitbull tenacity?"

"Somethin' like that," he admitted, methodically slicing a thick loaf of crusty bread.

Nina reached across and grabbed one of the knives, the mayo and the plate of bread. "I'll do that. You do the soup."

He placed a slice of bread on the plate just as she took it and their fingers touched. For a second, neither of them moved. With a short embarrassed laugh, Nina pulled the plate toward her and Ryan turned away.

She began spreading the condiment, slowly to make the task last since it was all she had to do. "You know, you had me fooled in the beginning. The way you move. The way you talk. I admit I worried you might have an idle streak."

He gave a self-deprecating grunt, plopped the tomato soup into a pan and ran a canful of water to add to it. He stirred while she watched the subtle play of shoulder muscles beneath his shirt.

Nina continued. "But you don't have. I guess you're the proverbial duck. Serene and smooth on the surface, and paddling like hell underneath."

He glanced at her over his shoulder. "That's how you see me? A *duck?*"

She grinned back at him, loving his Southern drawl, now knowing how deceptive it was. The guy was no duck. If he only knew how she saw him. What would he do?

"How do you see me?" she asked.

He drew his mouth to one side and frowned in thought. Then he held up one finger. "Cat," he said with a firm nod and a reluctant smile. "Yeah. Sly. Independent. Unpredictable and untamable."

"Lots of 'uns,'" she remarked, not totally displeased with his comparison. He couldn't seem to hold on to that determined resentment of his for long. Nina decided doing that just went against his nature.

"And you're a little bit wild and scary when riled," he added.

She also purred when she was stroked, but he hadn't found that out yet. Probably never would. But she figured it was smart to drag him out of that mood of his if she ever planned to get on his good side.

"See there?" she said. "I've tricked you into a break after all."

He had put down the spoon he'd used to stir and was now propped against the kitchen counter, arms crossed over his chest. "You always get your way, don't you? Smiling like the kitty that ate the canary."

His intense gaze lingered on her mouth, then roamed every inch of her visible above the bar. Nina had the distinct impression that he was filling in the rest from memory, since he had undressed her after the fire.

His voice was a near growl when he spoke again. "Yeah. Definitely a cat."

Nina pursed her lips and raised her brows, not certain whether she should read more into this sudden rapt attention than simple teasing.

Then she looked past him. "You might want to paddle around to that soup, Ducky. It's about to boil over."

They laughed together as he rescued their dinner and began dishing it up. She loved his laugh, the spontaneity of it. He always sounded a little surprised by it, as if he'd never expected it to happen again.

"Tell me, Chef Duck, what brought you here to Montebello?" she asked, satisfied that she was making real progress, establishing camaraderie.

Suddenly he ceased what he was doing and slowly raised his eyes to meet hers. His were as cold and desolate as midnight in the desert. Though he refused to offer even one word in answer to her question, Nina understood the break was now over. She had encroached on forbidden territory.

The familiarity he'd allowed a few moments ago no longer existed. There would be no more banter about ducks or cats or long, sensuous looks or accidental touches that generated sparks. It was as if he'd thrown up an impenetrable fire wall between them.

Nina knew her question had caused the sudden turnaround, but told herself she should be glad it had happened. While a brief fling with a man like Ryan might be an experience worth remembering, Nina was all too afraid it would be impossible to forget when the time came to do that. She never had brief flings anyway, so it was for the best if nothing happened. If he could pretend no electricity passed between them, she could, too.

The man obviously had baggage. Big-time baggage she had no business exploring. He was an admitted workaholic, a man who lived for his work. She could see it clearly now.

He would never give up. He'd keep doggedly at it until he got all his answers. Then he would dive directly into another case without a pause, she would bet.

Had he always been that way, or was it connected to his leaving his job with the police force in Savannah and coming here to live? Beautiful as it was, she doubted he'd come here for the scenery. Savannah was a beautiful place, too, or so she had heard.

Something life altering must have happened, given his reaction to her question, but she wouldn't ask him again what it was. She knew what curiosity did to cats.

Despite her decision to leave well enough alone, Nina had to admit that she enjoyed—and, at the same time, was annoyed by—the sudden, unfamiliar, and almost overwhelming thrill of anticipation that surged through her whenever they had what she liked to think of as a *moment*.

Well, that needed to stop. No more of those moments. She would focus only on helping discover who'd killed Desmond. That was why she was here, she reminded herself.

Someone ought to teach Ryan how to pause and celebrate the small successes the way she had learned to do, but Nina didn't figure that someone would be her.

Chapter 7

Ryan didn't trust himself to sit too close to Nina, so he had put the dining-room table between them. He could still smell her perfume. It teased him across the distance, barely perceptible but certainly there. She wore a subtle scent he didn't recognize. But then, why should he? He hadn't paid much attention to things like that even when he'd been married. Another oversight to castigate himself for, he thought as he shuffled the papers within the file and then tried to look engrossed in them.

They'd been at this for a while now, and she continued to wreck his concentration with every breath he took.

"About this Princess Samira Kamal who was involved with Desmond," Nina said suddenly, looking up from her reading of the statements taken in Tamir. "What's she like?"

Ryan took his time answering as he recalled the one time he had met the princess. "Sweet, trusting. Very open. Maybe a little naive. She's led a sheltered life."

Nina scoffed. "Not sheltered enough, apparently. She managed to have an affair with my brother."

"Yeah, so he said." The fact that he had said it in front of so many people in a public restaurant sure didn't elevate Caruso in Ryan's estimation.

Ryan looked over at the typed copy of Samira's statement. "I didn't do that interview with her. I was brought into the case later. From what's in there, she thought she was in love with Desmond and believed he loved her. When she went to the guesthouse one night and saw him through the window getting cozy with someone else, she realized her mistake and decided it was over."

"She would have been furious, I bet. She could have done it," Nina said, a frown marring her perfect forehead. "Maybe Samira and this Farid guy are in it together, providing each other with an alibi." She tapped her fingers on the report. "I mean, she's a princess and he is her bodyguard."

"Actually, he's her husband," Ryan informed her. "They're married."

She looked dumbfounded, first at him, then down at the report. Ryan knew the information was not included in what she'd just read because the couple had not yet informed her family when their statements were taken.

"I hear they sort of eloped. Difference in their stations and all that, I imagine. Word's out now, though."

"There you are! Jealousy!" Nina exclaimed. "What if *he* killed Desmond?"

Ryan propped his elbows on the table. "Farid was the best bet at first. He threatened Desmond publicly. But, no, Farid and Samira were both in Tamir at the time of death. We've established that without a doubt."

Nina pursed her lips and sighed, still looking doubtful.

Ryan wished to hell she wouldn't do that with her mouth. He forced himself to look away, to stare at the ho-hum picture some unimaginative decorator had hung on his wall.

But the abstract flower petals slowly took on suggestive forms. He blinked them away.

She continued, totally unaware of his efforts to refocus. "Couldn't they have falsified flight records or something? Surely her family would—"

"Not possible. The police flew over and took these statements soon after the body was discovered. Samira's innocent and so is Farid. But I do plan to speak with her again in more detail about the woman she saw with Desmond in the guesthouse. Remember, Pete mentioned a woman, too? Could be the same one."

Excitement lit Nina's dark eyes as she leaned forward, her hands gesturing as if to grab his full attention and hold it. "We have to find her, Ryan. Surely someone else saw them together. *She* must have done it!"

"See? There you go jumping to conclusions again," Ryan warned her. "This is precisely why it's not a good idea to have an investigator involved in a case where there's a personal interest."

"Sorry." She sat back, immediately assuming a more businesslike expression. "I'm perfectly willing to consider all the possibilities. I was only throwing out ideas. Isn't that how you narrow it down to the nitty-gritty?"

"Nitty-gritty?" he questioned, chuckling at the phrase she used. "Nobody says *nitty-gritty*. It's archaic."

"Shut up," she muttered. "So, when are we going to Tamir?"

"We're not. I called to make the appointment to speak with Princess Samira and Farid, but they preferred to come here for the interview on the way back from a brief honeymoon."

She looked disappointed. "All right." And she looked tired, he noticed.

"Would you like a glass of wine?" Ryan asked. "You've been at this too long."

Big mistake on his part. She raised her arms, locked her

fingers and stretched. Her small breasts pressed against the soft silk of her blouse. "Wine sounds great."

Ryan shoved back from the table, tearing his gaze off of her before he suffered a full-blown erection. Damn, the girl was driving him nuts. He got up, quickly turning into the kitchen area where he spent longer than necessary looking for a corkscrew. "White or red?" he asked

"Whatever you're having will be fine."

"Say which. I'm not having any."

"Why not? Planning to drug me again?" she asked, but it sounded more like she was teasing him than accusing.

"Not tonight," he said, going along with it.

"I noticed you didn't have a beer with Pete."

Nosy woman. "White or red?" he demanded.

"White."

He didn't owe her any explanations of his drinking habits. But in reality he knew she was only making conversation, not prying. "I don't drink," he stated as he drew the cork on the Liebfraumilch. He kept a couple of bottles of wine in the fridge, this and a chianti. Franz and Joe often dropped by with information and would stick around for a pizza or Chinese.

He poured her a glass and ran water in a tumbler for himself. "Here you go," he said as he rejoined her at the table and sat down.

"Thanks," she said, taking a sip.

Ryan followed the motion of her throat as she swallowed, noted the drops clinging to her upper lip, watched in a daze as her small pink tongue gathered them in. God, he was going to lose it.

"So, why don't you drink?" she asked. "Problem with it?"

Prying now for sure, Ryan thought. He shook off his daze and drank half his glass of tepid water without stopping. He set it down and took a deep breath. "Something like that."

Her eyes were soft, sympathetic. "Then I admire you for not doing it. My first boss was a recovering alcoholic, so I know—"

"No, you *don't* know," he argued, carefully keeping his voice moderate. "I lived in a bottle for an entire year. Once I realized what I was doing and crawled out, it was no hardship to give it up. I don't crave it."

"Good sign," she said, seeming perfectly at ease discussing the thing that had nearly destroyed him. However, he noticed she had put down her glass and wasn't touching it.

Ryan smiled at her, recognizing her frankness and misplaced compassion. "Go ahead and drink up, Nina. Even if I do have the disease, I don't think it's contagious."

To her credit, she laughed and took another swallow. "I like you, Ryan McDonough."

And he liked her, too, in spite of himself. And, God, how he wanted her. This wasn't the same thing he felt when the urge struck him periodically to take the edge off sexual hunger. That, he'd learned to deal with pragmatically, insuring no strings were attached and both parties were comfortable with it. No, this was something else, something more intense. More involved.

He didn't like to think about it, but if he didn't, he might actually *do* something about it.

While Ryan worked silently on his stack of files, Nina fitted another piece of the McDonough puzzle into place. There was still too much of it missing to see the whole picture, but she had most of the edges filled in. She wasn't exactly sure why she felt compelled to complete it, but she did.

Bad things had happened to this man. He'd quit a job, left his country, drowned himself in drink for a whole year and now submersed himself in work. To all appearances, he had no other life. What on earth would cause a man to uproot himself and embrace a death wish? Scandal? Divorce? Somehow, she couldn't envision Ryan running from either of those.

There were no pictures of family here or in his office. When she'd excused herself to use his bathroom, she'd peeked inside the two bedrooms. Except for one unmade bed and a couple of wrinkled towels in the tub, the place looked unlived in, sterile as a hotel suite. He even had a small collection of soaps wrapped in paper with various hotel logos.

There was no music or movie collection visible, no VCR or stereo. The television wasn't even located where it could conveniently be watched. She suspected he only came here long enough to sleep and shower.

"Why are you shaking your head?" he asked, his own head still bent over the files as he looked up at her from beneath his lashes.

"Just thinking," she said, finishing off her wine. It was her second glass and her reading comprehension wasn't all it should have been. "I should go next door, try to get some sleep, I guess."

His look of profound relief dug at her vanity. He hadn't wanted her here. She had invited herself in and stayed. Then he said the very last thing she would have expected. "Sleep here."

"I beg your pardon?"

Now he hesitated. He hadn't meant to say that, she realized. Then he seemed to make up his mind about something, like he'd decided to bite the bullet. "I don't want you alone in that apartment, okay?"

And she didn't want to be alone in it, not after the fire last night and knowing whoever had set it had known she was there. "All right."

He released his breath in a rush, then covered the act with a humorless laugh and nodded once. "All right."

Nina hopped up. "Just let me help you straighten—"

"Leave it," he ordered. "We'll get back to it in the morning."

She shrugged, looking everywhere but at him, and sidled toward the front door. "I'll go get my things."

He followed and stopped her, catching her arm before she reached the entrance. "Wait."

"Why?"

Nina could sense his reluctance to spell it out. Then he did. "Look, it's late. You can't go by yourself. And even if I go with you, that means leaving you at your door while I check the place out. I don't want to scare you, Nina, but—"

"I know," she assured him. "I'm not all that eager to push my luck, either. Thanks for suggesting I stay."

His fingers squeezed her arm. "It wasn't a suggestion. If you'd refused, I planned to insist. I was just trying to decide how to phrase it so you wouldn't go ballistic."

"Why do you think I would do that?" she said, her voice little more than a whisper. She could have kicked herself. Now he'd think she was coming on to him. And she wasn't.

Now he looked really uncomfortable. "Since I undressed you last night, I was afraid you might think I was, you know, interested."

She wasn't sure where he was going with this, but didn't say a word to encourage him.

"In something besides your safety, that is." He hurried on to explain. "I'm not, so you don't have to worry."

Well, that certainly answered her question before she thought about asking it. Nina forced a smile. It felt cold on her face. "I'm not worried."

"Good. That's a relief." He released her arm and gave it a pat. Not looking relieved at all, he stepped away from her and turned. "I'll just go and get you something to sleep in," he said over his shoulder. "Towels are on the shelf beneath the sink."

"Soap's still in the wrapper," she muttered under her

breath. "Shampoo in little bottles. Pay with automatic checkout. Next guest, please." The man could make his bed, walk out of this apartment, and no one would be able to tell anyone had ever lived here.

Yes, something had happened to him, all right. Instinctively, she knew better than to ask him what it was, but something compelled her to find out.

She followed him down the hallway and met him coming out of his bedroom. "Here," he said, handing her a new white T-shirt and a pair of knit running shorts. "These are the smallest things I own."

Not exactly, she thought to herself as she looked into his eyes. The smallest thing he owned was a trust in permanence of any kind. She didn't need to be a shrink to figure that out.

Nina dredged up a smile and thanked him for the clothes, cursing her desire to know what made him tick. She had another mystery to solve that should be occupying her mind full-time. So why was she wasting time mulling over what made Ryan McDonough the man he was?

Ryan lay on his back waiting for his travel clock to buzz. Hands clasped behind his head, the sheet kicked off his legs, he stared steadily at the ceiling fan. Round and round it went, just like his thoughts. For the first time in years, he was unable to drag them back to the case at hand.

Nina Caruso was messing with his mind, screwing up his logic, threatening his job. If he couldn't stand back and look at her with a cop's eye instead of buying every word she said and watching those sensuous lips while she formed each one, he needed to get out of this business altogether.

And then what would you do? That wicked sarcastic inner voice demanded. *Tend bar? Build boats with your daddy? Hole up somewhere and drink yourself to death?*

He'd done all of those things, plus more he wasn't too proud of and some he couldn't even remember.

This woman could destroy him completely, he realized. And he was well on his way to letting her do it. *Get her out of your system,* the voice urged.

Right. Just waltz on into the next room and have sex with her. It wouldn't be all that difficult. She was attracted to him. And once she found out why he'd hit on her, she would want to get as far away from him as King Marcus would allow.

And I'd be out of a job, Ryan thought to himself. No way the king would keep him on this if he went that far to get rid of her.

Maybe he wouldn't tell her why. Maybe she wouldn't guess. People had brief affairs all the time without really talking about the reasons, didn't they? He'd never had an affair as such. Only a few minor flings for fun in college. From there he'd gone straight into a marriage that left him with no desire to play around, and then...

He skipped over that and picked up several years later, when he'd resumed a social life. If he could legitimately call it that. He had purposefully settled for meaningless one-night stands, and a bare minimum of those.

God, how bleak that seemed. Here he was, living on what was unarguably the most beautiful island in the Mediterranean, surrounded by conditions that forced beauty onto the senses, and he was no more relaxed and in no better frame of mind than he'd been when he first got here. A little more in control, maybe. But now, even that was arguable.

This woman had violated his reserve, knocked down some barrier he hadn't even admitted was still up. Ryan fought the surprise and anger he felt now that Nina Caruso was inadvertently holding up the mirror that reflected his life. He was not liking what he saw.

At least the anger cooled his other idea. No way could he approach her now with sex in mind.

"Ryan?" she called in a half whisper from his doorway. For a second he thought it was a dream, one of those where you thought you were awake. "What?" he asked, not moving.

"I heard something," she rasped, slipping inside his doorway and flattening herself against his wall. "I think someone's in my apartment next door. The walls are..." She gestured helplessly. "You know...adjacent."

Quickly he rolled from the bed and pulled on his pants. He checked his weapon and with his free hand, pressed her even closer to the wall, ordering her silently to remain where she was.

His bare feet made no sound on the carpet as he hurried down the hallway and through his living room. Carefully, he unfastened his well-oiled locks, relocked the door behind him, and crept down the outside walkway to her door. It stood open about six inches.

He kicked it completely open, then slammed himself against the outer wall. No one rushed out. No shots were fired. Crouching low, he slipped inside. Slowly, he made his way across the room, checking every possible hiding place, weapon ready.

He practiced the classic police entry that he'd performed innumerable times in the line of duty. He'd known the place was empty the minute he entered. There was a different feeling, almost a smell of expectation, a tension in the air, when a perp was still present. However, he knew comrades who had died relying on that instinct.

He flipped on the lights. The living room appeared undisturbed, so he headed for the bedrooms to check them out with the lights on. In the one where Nina had slept the night after the fire, Ryan saw a huge wet splash marring the peach-colored wall adjacent to his apartment. Shards of the water glass he recalled setting on her nightstand the night before littered the floor beneath the splash.

Burglary? No, he decided. Throwing that glass against the wall signified anger. Whoever had broken in here must have expected to find Nina asleep in this bed. He rushed back to his apartment, unlocked the door and slipped inside.

She was right where he'd left her. "Who was it?" she asked in a small voice.

He decided not to touch her. "Whoever it was was gone when I got there. Somebody broke in, all right. Looked like they were mad as hell to find you missing. Broke a glass against the wall. That's probably what you heard."

Her eyes were round as saucers. She shook her head. "All my money, traveler's checks and passport are in my purse, which I have here. There was nothing there for them to steal. Maybe that made them mad?"

Ryan nodded. "Could be that's what they were after."

"But you don't really think that, do you?"

"No." He tucked the gun in his belt at the small of his back.

Suddenly as that her arms locked around his neck. A single sob broke free and then she was quiet, trembling, either barely breathing or holding her breath.

"Ah, baby, it's okay," he heard himself say. "Everything will be fine." His hands clutched her at her waist and her neck, then slid farther around her so that he wrapped her snugly his arms.

He couldn't have spoken if somebody had held a gun to his head. Emotion choked him. His eyes were clenched and tears burned behind his lids. How long had it been since he'd held someone the way he now held Nina? Someone who looked to him only for comfort after a nightmare? Someone who really mattered?

He almost pushed her away, but found he couldn't make himself do it. She needed him more right now than he needed space to figure out what was happening between them. Later he could fall back and rebuild his defenses. For now he would just hold her.

*   *   *

Ursula Chambers stood in the shadows, clutching the handle of the large blade she'd slipped into the pocket of her summer-weight trench coat. Desperate times called for desperate measures. Anxiously she watched the door of the apartment she'd just left.

She shouldn't have slammed that glass against the wall. The second it had struck, she'd realized her mistake in letting her temper get the best of her. She'd been so sure the woman would be in there sleeping. But, no, she must have been in bed with that private dick next door. Tramp.

Desmond's sister. Why had Desmond never mentioned he had a sister? He had surely told her about the plan. No doubt they'd been as thick as thieves all their lives, considering how quickly she'd flown over here, making noise about seeking justice for her beloved brother. What a crock. On television yet! She was sending out a signal to Ursula with that announcement, trying to force a contact and get in on this venture. Wanting in on the action. Fat chance of that after Ursula had done all the work. Des's little sister wasn't getting a dime.

She'd been there at the guesthouse, probably looking for Ursula's address. The fire had almost taken care of the whole problem. At least it had gotten rid of any evidence Ursula might have left in the place, which had been the original plan. That lost earring had bothered her. She knew it must have fallen off inside the guesthouse. She might have left stray hairs and things that the cops could get DNA from like they did on TV. She hoped they hadn't had time to do that before she had destroyed the place. There'd been nothing on the news about any discoveries.

Damn her quick temper, she hadn't meant to kill Desmond. He'd been her ticket to a fortune. But she would work around that when the time came, Ursula thought, biting back the urge to cry. She didn't need him. Why had he made her so angry?

She sniffed, shrugged it off and decided to think positive.

Going into the palace grounds with that last tour group and staying behind and hiding in the gardens had worked like a charm. Getting out with the crowd of emergency workers tonight had, too. They'd never know Ursula Chambers had been there. She had the instincts of a female James Bond. Considering that, she felt a little better about the failure to get rid of the Caruso woman, both in that fire and with the knife. There would be other chances.

The question was, how long would Desmond's sister keep the secret? Or would she soon give up trying to horn in on presenting the royals with the prince's baby? If so, she might blab about the plot hoping for a reward.

Something had to be done within the next few days or Gretchen would arrive with the kid. When Ursula handed over the baby to the royals there would be nothing to keep Nina Caruso from blowing the whistle on the whole deal. Unless she kept quiet and resorted to blackmail. That could be the whole idea.

Either way would spell disaster. Nina Caruso had to go.

Ursula watched as the lights went off in the woman's apartment and came on again in the one next to it. Too late to do anything tonight. She turned and walked hurriedly to her rental car parked two blocks away, trying to think what she would do next to eliminate the threat.

One of the rescue workers tonight had mentioned the detective who pulled Nina out that window was an American, Ryan McDonough. If that woman had hired a private eye to look out for her—or worse yet, to locate Desmond's accomplice—Ursula might need to hire somebody to counteract that. She knew just the guy. Not too smart, but greedy as hell.

Maybe she could talk him into doing two for the price of one if she threw in some benefits. She did, after all, have exactly what it took to convince a man to do anything. Desmond had told her that once when they were…well, she shouldn't think about that anymore, how close they had been, what plans they had made. What was done, was done, and she had to get things back on track.

Ryan notified the police as well as the king's administrative assistant, but went back to Nina's apartment and collected the glass fragments himself, bagged them and called Joe to come and pick them up to be examined for prints. In no way did he indicate to the cops that he thought the break-in was related to the fire. There was a chance that it wasn't, and if it was, he didn't want it broadcast on the evening news. The report would list it as a simple breaking and entering with nothing reported missing.

He knew the return call from the palace would be coming. In preparation for that, he had brought Nina a dress, shoes and her makeup from her apartment. She'd acted absurdly grateful to him for what she called his "thoughtfulness," especially when his taking her to the palace was his next step in getting rid of her.

Hell, he hated that she was acting so unlike herself this morning. He missed the in-your-face attitude. All this sweetness and cooperation must mean she was scared out of her mind.

He donned a suit and was knotting his tie when his phone chirped.

"McDonough," he answered.

"His Majesty requests your presence in his office at half past ten, sir. Miss Caruso is to accompany you."

"Of course," Ryan said and pocketed his cell phone. Now maybe King Marcus would listen to reason and send her home. Surely to God he would.

"I'm nervous," Nina admitted when they were settled in his car and on their way to the palace. She kept fiddling with the seat belt while her gaze darted out first one car window, then another.

"I don't wonder," Ryan commented, keeping an eye on the rearview mirror as he drove.

''I *am* staying, you know,'' she stated with more than a hint of yesterday's defiance.

Ryan didn't argue. As far as he was concerned, the king could take the heat for it when she found out she had no choice.

They rode in silence for a while, both fully aware that danger could be following. Or could be beside them in the next lane, for all he knew.

Ryan felt like kicking himself for not requesting that the palace send one of the limos to pick them up. Those were supposed to be bulletproof.

Didn't that prove his head wasn't where it was supposed to be? And whose fault was that? He cast a glance at Nina, wanting to hold it against her.

Unfortunately, what he really wanted to hold against her wasn't the fact that she wrecked his concentration.

Just once, before she flew to safety and out of his life forever, Ryan wished he could have her. That's all it would take. Once. Then maybe he'd be able to put her out of his mind and get back to business. That was all he wanted.

Maybe tonight, if she didn't have to fly out this afternoon.

Nina knew she had to get herself together before their audience with the king. If she looked as scared as she felt, he would probably make her go home.

She had thought very seriously about agreeing to go, even suggesting it herself, when she realized someone had broken into her apartment.

Ryan was so tenacious, she certainly didn't have to worry about his finding Desmond's killer without her prodding. However, her reason for wanting to stay had broadened, if not changed completely. Going home was not an option. She could not leave with all these questions in her mind about Ryan.

Why did he—a man so obviously wrong for her—captivate her senses so totally the way he did? It wasn't love or anything like that, she was sure. But whatever it was, the sheer power of it amazed her. She had to identify what it was and put it to rest before she left here.

When she decided to love, she would definitely choose someone like her father, who had put his family first before everything else in his life. Maybe he had spoiled her. Even so, she wanted a love like the one he and her mother had enjoyed, one that included devotion as well as passion. Theirs was such a great example of what a marriage should be. No way would she settle for less.

Even an affair with Ryan wouldn't be wise. She knew the pitfalls of getting involved with a workaholic again. Her one serious relationship had been with a guy like that and it had made her miserable for almost a year.

Whenever she thought of Terry now, she pictured him with a cell phone permanently attached to his ear and a string of excuses for leaving her coming out of his mouth.

She'd thought she loved him. He'd thought she was a short recess between appointments. She wasn't a clinging vine or an attention hog, but a woman deserved to be noticed once in a while as more than a convenience.

Ryan would probably be even worse than Terry once she wasn't right in the middle of a case he was working.

He was probably an alcoholic, too. Who knew when he'd go off the deep end? Add that to his carrying a gun and living a dangerous lifestyle and he was about the last person in the world she ought to be interested in.

But she was.

Nina had never desired this keenly, to the point where she was willing to put up with almost any conditions. If she hadn't seen that same desire for her in his eyes, she would be running for her life. It was there, however, and he was fighting it. She had to know why.

Nina knew that if she didn't find out how deep it went, she would never be able to forget him. The unresolved feelings she had for Ryan would haunt her and color every relationship in her future.

She needed to stay long enough to see where this was going because if she left now, Nina knew she would never see him again.

"I am not leaving," she said again as they pulled into the parking lot between the wings of the palace.

Ryan smiled and shrugged, carefully not looking at her. They left the car and walked around to the entrance. He seemed determined to keep as much space between them as he could. Nina missed his hand on her arm or on the small of her back. Though his touch disconcerted her, she craved it.

Nina smiled and said good morning to the guards, one of whom she had questioned.

Even as she spoke, Ryan moved closer and placed his hand at her waist as if to hurry her along. Was that his purpose, or was he laying a subtle claim? And which did she want it to be? Nina sighed, increasing her pace even though she dreaded what the king might say.

Chapter 8

Nina only gave the opulence of the palace interiors her passing notice. Her mind was occupied in forming arguments for remaining in Montebello that King Marcus might accept.

A stooped yet gruff-looking man of about eighty greeted them outside the king's office. "His Majesty will see you immediately," he said, then opened the intricately carved door and announced them.

King Marcus stood as they entered. Ryan bowed formally and Nina dropped into a deep curtsy, waiting to be addressed.

The king cleared his throat and with a small flick of one hand, indicated they should rise. "Thank you for coming."

"Our pleasure, Your Majesty," Ryan replied. As if they'd been left a choice.

The king gestured toward the satin striped chairs that stood in front of his desk. "Be seated."

Nina perched on the edge of her chair, her hands tightly clasped in her lap. Though this was her second meeting with King Marcus, she couldn't help feeling awe. He was the only king she'd ever met in person, and the only one she was ever likely to meet. Desmond's uncle.

The man didn't need his royal robes to look regal. The only crown he wore was a full head of silvery hair. He was about the same height as Ryan and almost as broad-shouldered and lean.

She searched for any resemblance to her half brother, but found none other than a very slight cleft in the chin. The king's was barely noticeable whereas Desmond's had been prominent.

The king looked directly at her. "What happened last night must have given you a fright, Miss Caruso," he said. "Are you quite recovered?"

Nina ducked her head in a swift nod. "Yes, sir. I'm all right."

He nodded, then he directed his gaze to Ryan. "The plane will be available to return Miss Caruso to California this afternoon. Until then, you remain charged with her safety."

Nina rose and began shaking her head even as the king spoke. "No, please, Your Majesty. I need to stay here."

She looked to Ryan as if he would support her when she knew very well he wouldn't. And none of the reasons she had gone over in her head justified her staying in Montebello. At least none she could relate to the king. And especially not in front of Ryan. "Please?" she added.

The king motioned for her to take her seat. When she had done so, he watched her for a full minute, his dark gaze intense, before he spoke. "Do you know of an enemy who might wish to see the Caruso family destroyed?"

The very idea made her shudder. It had never occurred to her that it could be someone she actually knew. "No, sir, of course not! Desmond left us when he was twenty to come and live here. He hasn't been around to make any

enemies. And I haven't any that I know about. Certainly
none who would travel this far to get rid of me."

She frowned and thought for a minute. "Everyone loved
my father. He was a good man. I can't believe what you're
suggesting is feasible."

"Very well," the king said. "Then we must assume that
we are dealing with someone native to Montebello."

Ryan spoke up. "No, Your Majesty. It's dangerous to
assume anything until we have more information."

The king considered. "Granted. Do you have any theories you wish to relate?"

Nina waited, breath stilled, while Ryan seemed to process his thoughts.

When he began, he spoke firmly and without hesitation.
"Yes. I believe someone killed Desmond Caruso in the
heat of anger, without prior intent. When this person realized Desmond was dead, an attempt was made to destroy
any evidence. The weapon was wiped along with anything
else the killer might have touched in the guesthouse. But
there remained a chance trace evidence might be found,
hairs, fibers and so forth. Therefore the fire was meant to
take care of it."

He paused, then continued, "The fact that the fire was
set after the initial sweep by the police tells me that the
perpetrator either believed evidence had not yet been collected or had lacked an earlier opportunity to set the fire."

"What about my being there trapped in the bathroom?"
Nina demanded. "Whoever it was meant to kill me, too!
Why?"

Ryan smiled. "That's a good question, isn't it? You were
on TV and saying why you came to Montebello. Maybe
you were in the right place at the right time," he said. Then
added, "From the killer's point of view, that is. The attempt
on your life was a crime of opportunity."

"And last night's break-in?" she asked.

Ryan frowned. "Right now, all I can do is guess. If we

rule out revenge, then the killer either fears you will find the truth, that you already know something that could be incriminating, or hates you simply because you are related to Desmond. And we had better consider greed. Who would benefit if you died?''

Nina closed her eyes and leaned forward, her face in her hands. "I don't know. I don't have any relatives left except two first cousins in Milan. I've never even met them."

"Locate these cousins," the king ordered Ryan. To her, he said, "Until we judge whether the threat to you is confined to this island, you will be safer here than alone in California."

He stood, signaling the audience was over. Ryan rose immediately and reached for her hand as if she needed help getting up. Her legs did feel weak and her mind reeled with this new possibility.

The king pressed a button on his desk and the king's secretary who had shown them in, appeared immediately. "You must move from the apartments," the king said. "Albert will summon one of the cars to take you directly to the Royal Montebello Hotel. He will also secure a suite for you on the floor in reserve for our guests. Security will be sufficient there and the hotel will be convenient to the police station and the palace. Your personal things will be collected and delivered to you both this afternoon. Someone from Lorenzo's offices will bring whatever you need in the way of equipment."

He inclined his head in dismissal. "Take care."

"Thank you, Your Majesty," Ryan said, bowing again, still holding on to her.

Nina curtsied, feeling clumsy and more shaken than when she'd entered the king's office. She murmured her own thanks and they quickly left the spacious chamber.

As they retraced their steps along the long marble corridor that led to the entrance, Ryan looked ready to explode.

She realized he had been counting heavily on the king sending her away.

What if he had done so? And what if the killer had followed her all the way home and Ryan hadn't been there to protect her? She placed her hand over his where it gripped her arm.

He threw her an impatient glance, his jaw clenched. But when she looked closer, she saw he looked bleak rather than angry.

"Why are you so anxious to be rid of me?" she whispered.

He said nothing for so long, she thought he wouldn't even answer. When he did speak, his voice was low-pitched and gruff and he had stopped looking at her. His hand tightened on her arm. "Because I want you to stay. I want it too damn much. And now there's no choice. Are you satisfied?"

"Not really," she said under her breath.

Ryan tried to ignore Nina's reaction to the Royal Montebello Hotel. He resented the necessity of working out of here. They stood waiting for the elevator that would take them up to the sixth floor.

"Would you look at this place!" she insisted, her back to the elevator doors, her eyes wide with wonder as she took in the marble-and-gilt interior of the lobby. "I mean, you expect a palace to be outfitted in splendor, so I wasn't surprised there, but this…." She gestured toward the massive reception desk flanked by gigantic floral arrangements, the heavy silk draperies gracing the floor-length windows, and walls bearing enormous paintings in wide, ornate gold frames.

"I think it's tacky," he muttered, much preferring simplicity. All this was too, too. "I just hope we don't get stuck with the bill."

Nina laughed. "I'm sure the king wouldn't have sent us

here if he planned to make us pay. The manager told the desk clerk who registered us that we were guests of His Majesty.''

''Yeah, I heard,'' Ryan admitted as the elevator doors opened and they entered. ''I doubt they'll leave us alone long enough to get anything productive done. Maids in and out, meals and all that. I hate hotels.''

''Well, I don't see how you could possibly hate this place,'' Nina declared, running her forefinger along the gilded handrail that surrounded them on three sides. Gold-veined mirrors reached from the rail to the top of the elevator, making it seem larger than it actually was. After a quick glance around, Ryan kept his eyes on the door.

Trapped in splendor, he thought angrily. With Nina. How was he supposed to keep his mind on work when he'd be imagining them enjoying all this together under other circumstances?

''Come on, spoilsport, chill,'' she said when the elevator dinged and the doors parted. ''At least you won't have to boil soup for us while we're here.''

''And *you* won't be getting any oatmeal,'' he countered, pushing past her down the hallway to locate the number of their suite.

There was nothing at all common about the common room they would share. The walls were covered in patterned silk. The two sofas and chairs were striped damask and looked geared more for show than comfort. ''At least they have a desk,'' he said, shedding his jacket and tossing it over one of the chair arms. He tugged at the knot of his tie, loosening it. ''Nothing we can do until they get here with our stuff.''

''Oh. My. God!''

''What's wrong?'' He hurried over to the door of the bedroom where Nina stood gaping.

''Look!'' she whispered as she reached out and grasped his forearm. ''It's a movie set.''

He looked. And was impressed in spite of himself. Gilt, satin and lace. White, off-white and gold. "Yeah, but is the film set in Las Vegas or Windsor Palace? Hard to tell."

She laughed.

Ryan pushed away from her and crossed to the bathroom. Unable to speak, he just pointed and shook his head. She joined him, squeezing past to enter the mirrored room. She sat down on the pink marble platform that surrounded an enormous tub with gold fittings. "Ryan?"

"What?" he asked, frowning at the way his shoes sank into the deep pile of the ivory-colored carpet.

"I think they gave us a bridal suite by mistake. Did you notice those nude paintings in the bedroom?"

"Old masters, I'm sure," he said.

"See this?" she pointed to the array of exotic bath oils. "Or do you think this is standard fare for all the guests? Surely you don't think the king—"

"—is throwing us together?" Ryan considered it. "Why would he do something like that? Surely he has enough to do without trying to play matchmaker."

"I don't know," she admitted. "It wasn't anything he said, but he looked at us...you know, with a speculative gleam or something. Didn't you notice?"

Ryan shrugged. He hadn't thought anything of it then, but now that Nina mentioned it.... "But why?"

"How well do you know him?" Nina asked. "I mean, personally, with all the formality aside?"

He laughed. "Honey, with King Marcus, you *never* put formality aside. No, I don't think any of this was his idea." Ryan thoughts quickly shifted. "But come to think of it, Lorenzo...."

"Lorenzo, the duke?"

"Bingo," he said wryly, light dawning. He shook his finger at Nina. "And he showed up right after you got to my office, remember?" Ryan paced for a minute, recalling their conversation. Then he pointed at Nina. "You wait right here. I'm going to straighten this out. Damned interfering sonofa—''

"No! Wait! What if you're wrong?"

What if he was? Ryan stopped and turned to Nina, still trying to piece together some kind of reason why he might be right. Gut hunch didn't get it. Neither did the spindly facts on which he was basing his assumption.

"Why would he want to pair us off, do you think?" Nina asked, her lips quirking up at the corners. "We're like oil and water. Surely he noticed that."

"Maybe he cooked this up before he saw us together." Ryan marched into the bedroom and sat down on the edge of the bed.

"What do you mean?"

"Okay, try this on for size. You," he said, pointing at her, "are a poor little girl all alone in the world now that Desmond is dead, right?"

"Wrong! I'm not a poor little girl!" she said with a huff. "And you think I live in a vacuum? I have friends."

He waved that away. "Yeah, but no family in the States, though. Let's say Lorenzo feels sort of responsible for you in a roundabout way. I mean, he was Desmond's brother and you were Desmond's sister. Even though you two aren't related by blood, I can see where he'd feel obliged to see you settled and taken care of. Can't you?"

She scoffed. "That's absurd. But let's put that aside for a minute. Why would he stick me with *you,* of all people?"

Ryan didn't take offense at her question. And he didn't want to tell her why Lorenzo would want to fix him up with a woman, but this whole scenario was beginning to make more and more sense to him.

He gave Nina a partial truth. "I've been a little resistant to his ploys before. Lorenzo was married earlier this year. You know how newlyweds are. Misery loves company, I guess."

"Oh? He's that miserable?" Nina asked, still looking amused by the whole thing.

"Well, maybe he's not exactly miserable." Ryan felt terrible for even implying that. "Actually, he's deliriously happy. I think."

Nina laughed, sat down on the bed beside him and poked him on the knee with one finger. "You, my friend, should appreciate the thought if not the deed. I know I do. It's great to have somebody care what happens to you, even if they do meddle."

Ryan glared at her, brushed her finger away and rapidly got up. That perfume of hers had been driving him crazy all day. Worse, now that they were so close. And here in this satin-infested bedroom, he couldn't get past the image of her lying virtually naked on that bed. He didn't need to be in the vicinity of any bed with Nina Caruso right now.

"You think we should *appreciate* it? The duke should damn well mind his own business. If he's behind these incidents—"

"You know better than that. If he cared enough to try to set us up with one another, he surely wouldn't try to scare me to death, much less put me in danger."

"Yeah," he admitted. "You're right." Ryan ran a hand through his hair, then squeezed the back of his neck, trying to ease the tension there. "But I'm calling him just the same and find out what's what."

"Why? You want him angry with you?"

Ryan snapped. "Well, I'm damned well angry with *him!* Being the king's godson and nephew gives him no right to go around tryin' to arrange people's lives like some…some godfather or something." He flung out his arms. "And you said yourself that the king is in on it! He must be. Why else have we got a suite instead of private rooms? And why is it *this* suite? Damn thing looks like an upscale whorehouse. What the hell was he thinking?"

He watched as Nina fell back on the satin covers and covered her face with her hands. She was laughing.

"What's so damned funny?"

"You," she answered with a lazy chuckle. "I've never heard you talk that fast." Playfully she peeked at him between her fingers. "C'mon, Mac. A few minutes ago you were in stitches over that silly bathroom. Where's your sense of humor now? You're letting this make you crazy. What's the problem anyway? Afraid I'll take advantage of you?"

"Be careful how you put a question like that, Nina. I might just insist on it."

Actually he was more afraid of what he might do to *her,* and he didn't think she'd respond well to a one-night stand. Or a one-week stand. Or however long it took to wrap up this case. She'd get involved, just like Lorenzo probably intended. Then Ryan would have to hurt her feelings. He didn't want hurt feelings. He didn't want feelings at all.

But he did want sex.

He backed up and sat down again, careful to keep a good foot of space between them. "Okay, smarty-pants, what do you suggest?"

"Pretend we haven't noticed," she suggested. "Or we could keep them in suspense."

"Or play along," he said before he could stop himself. He leaned closer. God, she was like a magnet. He forced himself to back up a little and tear his gaze away from her lips. "Forget I said that."

"No," she said, her voice a near whisper. "I think it might be…a good idea." Her hand touched his where it was propped on the edge of the bed. Slender fingers traced the tops of his knuckles and trailed to his wrists.

"You'd better watch what you're doing there, sweet pea," he growled as he raked her body with a warning inspection.

She smiled and raised one delicate eyebrow. "Do I really scare you, Mr. Big, Bad Private Investigator?"

Ryan drew in a deep breath and released it slowly. "Yeah, you really do. Does that make you feel good?"

"It could," she whispered, those long dark eyelashes at half-mast and her lips parting in invitation.

He couldn't believe he would cave this easily, but it seemed the most natural thing in the world to lean over this smiling, sensuous woman and give up his sanity for a kiss.

Her mouth was soft, welcoming, giving, so he took, demanded and ravished. She had no right, he thought, no right to be this sweet. So incredibly sweet, and succulent as ripe peaches still warm from the sun.

She purred a warning in her throat that sang through his blood like a challenge.

Next thing he knew, he had covered her completely, pressing his chest against her to feel her breasts, fitting his arousal to her mound, moving in a shameless parody of what they really wanted. Then he felt her hands pushing against his shoulders.

Breaking the kiss, he slid to one side and buried his face in the slick satin of the bedcovers. "Okay, all right. Give me a minute." He sucked in a deep breath to keep from panting, cursing in his mind the heady scent of ripe luscious peaches that would not leave him.

Exerting every effort, he pushed up on one elbow and looked down at her. "Sorry," he said. "But you did—"

"Ask for it," she finished. "I know. But I was sliding off this damned comforter. We would have landed on the floor. If we're going to do it, let's not waste all this luxury."

She reached out with one hand and dragged the edge of the slippery covers away from the mounds of ridiculous ruffled pillows and the quilted-satin headboard.

Ryan had to smile. "You sure?"

''No. You're not, either, but that's not going to stop us, is it?''

He drew one finger across her velvety cheek and touched her lips. ''I hate like hell to admit this, but I'm not prepared. No protection.''

She closed her eyes and banged the back of her head against the soft mattress, a study in frustration. Ryan loved it.

''I could call room service,'' he offered.

She gave a nearly silent scream, deep in her throat.

He laughed, drawing his finger down her exposed throat to the V of her blouse. ''Let's see just how far ol' 'Renzo means for us to go.'' He leaned over to the nightstand and pulled open the drawer. ''Lo and behold. In Technicolor, too.''

Nina propped up on her elbows and peered at his find. ''Goodness, he's an optimistic devil, our friend the duke.''

Ryan pushed her back on the bed, making room for himself as he kicked off his shoes. ''And you, dear heart, are a bad, bad girl.''

''A temporary condition, I assure you,'' she said, shuddering when he buried his lips in the curve of her neck. ''I can be quite good.''

''Well, don't start now,'' he warned playfully, but when she tensed a little, he backed off and looked down at her, trying to gauge whether she was uncomfortable with this. ''Second thoughts?''

She looked a little sheepish. And adorable. ''No, it's not that exactly. But we should have some kind of understanding. Don't you think?''

''Spell it out,'' he said, beginning to cool off considerably.

''No strings?'' she said hopefully, toying with his chest hair.

Ryan exhaled with relief. But he also experienced a twinge of regret that things had to be this way. And that she actually *wanted* them to be this way. He placed his hand over hers. "Had strings before?" he asked.

"Could we not trade war stories?"

He smiled and raised her fingers to his lips. "Let's not trade anything but our bubble gum, okay?"

She nodded, her eyes closed, her lips so enticing he had to taste them again. This time he delved deeper, letting his mind fog with pleasure, shoving the past into the dark recesses of his mind. No war stories. No memories. Just this sweet obliteration of everything but the hot urgency sweeping through him.

Her wordless sounds of encouragement drove him faster than he meant to go. He had to touch, to claim the soft firmness of her breasts, slide his fingers under that silk to discover what lay beneath.

Lost in mindless need, he tugged at buttons, hooks, zippers and fabric until she writhed beneath him as she was meant to be. He felt her hands on him, frantically pushing his shirt off his shoulders. He shrugged out of it, lifting himself off her to yank at his belt. Already her fingers were at his waist, shoving down his pants and briefs. He kicked them off and pressed himself full-length against her, reveling in the feel of skin to skin, heat to heat.

Warn her to be still. Slow this down. Some rational part of his mind tried to interfere, but he ignored it. Instead he buried her mouth with his as he hurriedly ripped open a condom, sheathed himself and drove into her with a primal groan he couldn't suppress.

For a second the pleasure numbed him so he thought it was over. Then she pulsed around him, bringing him to life so quick and hard he gasped. He fought for control, the one thing crucial to a man who was any kind of lover. Dimly he realized he might never be where he was again and wanted to stay there as long as humanly possible.

Holding her motionless with his body, he willed himself to focus on her face, to brush the softness of her cheek, her eyebrow, her ear with his lips, to deny the almost overpowering demand to withdraw and thrust again until they found release.

"Tease!" she hissed through gritted teeth and managed to shift her hips.

"No," he growled, more in denial of her demand than her accusation, but he knew he had lost this battle even before it began. "Damn you."

Still he tried to delay, to make it last until she reached the mark. Sweat ran down his forehead into his eyes. Breath burned in his throat. Need to end this beat like an incessant drum in his lower body.

His concentration grew so labored, she took him by surprise. The rapid, tight contractions of her body triggered a reaction he'd never before experienced with anyone.

Ryan surrendered every effort at control and plunged heart first into a pleasure so mindless it took on a life of its own. Again and again he stroked in and out, shifting angles, seeking more of her to claim. To know.

Her cry erupted as she tensed around him again and he poured into her with everything he was and wished to be. His senses, so absorbed in the sound, sight and scent of her, sharpened to nearly painful clarity.

Like brands, he felt each of her fingers that grasped his lower back, the short crescents of her nails a glorious pinch of reality.

Every nuance of her voice invaded his mind and carved out a place to live. Their combined essence drifted around them, incense for the gods. Stetson, sweet peaches and sex.

He drew in a deep breath, yielded to whatever had possessed him and just held her close, not knowing, not even caring what would happen next.

Chapter 9

Nina feigned sleep. No way was she about to ruin this interlude with Ryan by talking. At least not now, when she was floating in a state of euphoria. No telling what she might say.

She didn't have to be a genius to figure out that he would regret it now that the heat was spent. She regretted it probably more than he did. No, any words they might say to one another right now would probably escalate into the granddaddy of all fights.

Exhaling a long sigh of contentment, she allowed her body to remain a boneless heap of satiation and tried to make her mind lapse into nothingness.

Her busy brain wouldn't cooperate. The fact that he was lying half on top of her with one of those biceps resting comfortably beneath her breast and the rest of him damp against her side didn't help matters.

The overpowering urgency with which they'd come together almost scared her, though she certainly hadn't minded at the time. Would she ever in her lifetime find anyone to approximate what he had made her feel?

Ryan threw himself into lovemaking the way he did everything else. One thing for sure, she'd had his full and undivided attention for the duration. She was no short recess for Ryan. She was more like an extended lunchtime when he was starving. No woman could resist loving that.

Well, she had allowed this to happen for one reason only—to find out whether her feelings for him were all lust and no substance. At the moment, her regard for him felt pretty substantial in all quarters. She could love this man. *Would* love him if she didn't watch out, maybe did a little already. She still wasn't clear how he felt about her, except that he seemed to resent whatever those feelings were.

While she was lying here in this condition, it would be easy to tell herself, and him, that they could not let anything like this happen again while she was here. It would be a mistake to take things any further. He was not the kind of man she wanted to love and, for some reason of his own, she obviously was not the woman he considered Ms. Right.

They would both be better off to cool it, to consider this a convenient sexual encounter and let it go at that. But she simply didn't want to talk about it right this minute when she felt so heavenly.

He eased farther from her, as if trying to get up without waking her. To facilitate that, she rolled away from him and snuggled down into the puffy feather pillows.

Fine. She wanted him to go. If he stayed on the bed, who knew what would happen? She knew. That long, muscled body of his all hot against her was bad. Bad for her peace of mind. Bad for her dwindling determination. And oh, so bad for her attempt at remaining physically satisfied.

A few seconds later, she felt him drape something over her. Though his footsteps were inaudible on the deep, plush carpet, she knew he had left the bedroom. There was a quiet snick of the door handle as he closed it behind him.

Nina indulged herself in a long, heartfelt sigh of regret. A tear escaped and she raked it away with the back of her hand. Damn him. The least he could have done was be a selfish lover. Instead, he had been perfect. Incredibly generous, giving, masterful and tender even while he demanded and took everything she had to give. Now how the devil was she supposed to forget something like that?

In the sitting room, Ryan pulled on his slacks and padded barefoot into the other bedroom. This one was laid out the exact opposite of the one where Nina was sleeping, he noted absently as he headed for the bathroom. And it contained fewer frills.

He turned on the tap, splashed water on his face and glared into the mirror. "Fine mess you've gotten us into now," he growled to his reflection, running his wet fingers through his hair. He leaned over and ran cold water over his head.

Just as he toweled off, he heard the discreet chimes of the bell. Yeah, this was exactly what he needed right now. Company. No shirt, no shoes and bleary-eyed from mind-numbing, heart-stopping sex. *Do come in, whoever you are.*

He strode through the bedroom and sitting room to answer the door. Through the peephole, he saw it was only one of the bellhops with a luggage cart. He unlatched the door and gestured the guy inside. "Just leave the bags here. I'll take them to the rooms." Ryan pulled out a couple of bills and tipped him.

Alone again, he went over to one of the formal-looking sofas and flopped down, waiting for the grief and remorse to wash over him and obliterate all the pleasure. Waited for them to tense him up and give him that queasy feeling he always had after indulging his hunger with a woman.

Angst. Discontent. Guilt. Where were they this time? Oddly enough, none of them materialized. Even when he sat there expecting them, ready to embrace them like old acquaintances that kept turning up like clockwork, they never came.

He still felt good. Weary as hell, but incredibly peaceful and right. *Unbelievable.* For a long time he just sat, empty of everything but stillness and gratitude. He almost felt like laughing at his unexpected metamorphosis.

Had his father gone through this? Did that explain why the man had married again while Ryan's mother had hardly been dead a year?

The thought had just popped into Ryan's mind, surprising him. He'd never considered that before. Why now? Maybe Nina reminded him a little of his feisty stepmother. Aggressive and yet vulnerable. Refined and yet sexy. Independent. Beautiful. Yeah, there definitely were comparisons there, even though they neither looked nor sounded anything alike and Trish was at least fifteen years older.

Had ol' Dad fallen in lust and been unable to help himself? Or had he simply grabbed the first woman who didn't make him feel like he was betraying the love of his life?

Ryan's gaze strayed to the phone, just within his reach. No, he couldn't call. He had hardly spoken to his father in almost seven years. A brief stilted call at Christmas just for form's sake, that was all. *Honor thy father.* Lasted all of three minutes, at most.

Their estrangement worked, though. His father didn't need any reminders of the grief he had left behind, and Ryan didn't want to rehash his resentment. Funny thing was, that resentment seemed petty all of a sudden, useless. So what if his dad was happy with someone else? What did it matter?

The question wouldn't get out of his mind. Had Dad gone through this? How had he justified happiness with another woman? And that woman's children? Ryan suddenly felt very alone. His feelings binged around like the steel sphere in a pinball machine.

Nina had done that to him. His life had settled into a

routine of work and sleep and more work. It had given him a reason for being, a schedule for survival.

He picked up the phone and dialed, holding his breath, hoping no one would answer and that would be that.

"'Lo?"

Ryan cleared his throat and took a deep breath. "Dad?"

"Ryan? Ryan, is that you?" His father's voice lit up like someone plugged in the Christmas lights. It always did, Ryan realized, kicking himself for all the years he hadn't noticed.

"Yeah, Dad, it's me. How you doin'?"

"What's the matter? Is something wrong, son?"

Of course he would ask that. It wasn't Christmas. It wasn't time for the duty call. "No, Dad, nothing's wrong. I...I just wanted to say hi."

"Well, hi, yourself! Boy, this is a treat, y'know? Trish and I were just talking about you yesterday, wondering what the weather's like over there in your paradise this time of year. Said to her I bet you were tan as all get-out, soaking up all that sun. You used to be a regular beachcomber."

"Yeah, it's great here, Dad. Weather's good. I hit the beach now and then." He paused, bolstering his decision to make nice. "How are Trish and the kids?" Ryan thought his stepmother's children must be teens by now. He'd never seen them and didn't want to. He only hoped they had replaced some of what he had ruthlessly snatched away from his father.

"They're all fine!" his father crowed. "Asleep right now, of course."

Ryan smacked his forehead and laughed. "Oh, God, I forgot the time difference. Sorry if I woke you."

"No, no, don't be sorry. Jeez, it's good to hear from you, son. You sure nothing's wrong?"

Ryan hesitated. "Can you talk, Dad? Is she...is she listening?"

"Nope, Trish's sound asleep. I was watching the late

show, dozing a little. Touch of insomnia.'' The enthusiasm had cooled a little, replaced by wariness.

No point in putting this off, Ryan thought. This was an overseas call and it was the middle of the night there. ''Dad, when you and Trish got together, did you... How did you deal with... Did you forget about Mom?''

There was a long silence without even the usual static. Then his father's voice held a note of comfort Ryan remembered so well. ''I could never forget her, son. Not ever. No one, especially not Trish, would ever expect me to. Your mother was one of the finest women who ever lived, Ryan. But Trish is another one of those. If you would just give her a chance—''

''I will, Dad,'' Ryan promised quickly, wishing he'd never phoned. Wishing he could terminate this call immediately without hurting his father any more than he already had.

''Son, is this about Trish and me, or have you met somebody? I've prayed you would, but—''

''I'll call you again soon, okay?''

''Ryan, Kathy wouldn't want you to suffer the way you have on her account. I know that sounds trite, but—''

''I have to go, Dad.'' Ryan rubbed his hand over his chest. It ached like his lungs were seizing up.

''Sure, sure, I know you do. Look, I'm not meddling, honest, but—''

''Right now I can't say any more.'' But he had to. He couldn't stop himself from saying it. ''I love you, Dad. And...I'm sorry. Tell Trish for me. I mean it. Really.''

He hung up before things got any more maudlin. Fiercely, he bit his lips together and blinked hard. Something had shifted inside him, leaving a vacuum. He didn't know what he would fill it with.

The door chimed again and he hurried to open it, ready for any distraction at all. He didn't even check to see who it was.

Lorenzo. "Greetings," he said, raking Ryan's bare chest and feet with an interested gaze. "Is the air-conditioning faulty?"

Ryan realized how he must look. He had pulled on his pants and zipped up, but the fastener was open and they rode below his waist. Without thinking first how it would appear, he shot a quick glance toward the closed door of the bedroom where Nina slept. "I was just about to take a bath."

Lorenzo smiled, following Ryan's glance with one of his own, looking very much like a wolf eyeing a herd of sheep. "Sweaty work, moving into a new place, eh?"

"What do you want?"

"Nothing at all. I stopped by to see one of the representatives from Thailand and decided to check on you while I was here. How is the investigation coming along?"

"I'm sure you already know as much as I do about it. Maybe more. Why don't *you* tell *me?*"

"Progress on that earring, I think," Lorenzo said easily, stepping past Ryan and making himself at home. "Definitely purchased within the last six weeks, because they were not available before then. Joseph has narrowed it down. You'll want to get the full report from him, of course."

"Of course," Ryan said, turning his back on Lorenzo for a minute, trying to avoid attention as he hitched up his trousers a couple of inches and fastened them. "Remind me to give Joe a raise for keeping the world so well informed."

"Good idea. How is our little Nina adjusting to the new surroundings?"

Ryan turned back around, his arms crossed over his chest. "She's resting. Last night was not conducive to sleep."

"I will assume you're speaking of the break-in." Lorenzo kept smiling, looking very satisfied with himself.

"This was your plan from the first, wasn't it?" Ryan asked him. "Throwing us together."

His grace had the grace to look shocked. "Me? The job is making you suspicious of everyone, my friend. Would I ever presume?"

"Yes, you have *presumed* before and it was all for nothing, if you recall. But never mind that now. Let's get back to the case."

"Sorry, but I have to go." Lorenzo strolled back out of the room and turned around in the corridor, a thoughtful look on his face. "Could I give you a bit of advice?"

"No, thank you," Ryan said firmly.

"All the same," Lorenzo said, shrugging one shoulder, his smile even wider, white teeth gleaming. "If I were you, I would have someone daub a bit of antiseptic on those fresh scratches and not wear a French-cut to a public beach for a while if they extend to where I suspect they do."

Ryan fumed, but his voice remained calm. "Thanks. I will take that under advisement."

"You're quite welcome," Lorenzo said and strolled off to the elevator.

Ryan slammed the door. He hated being maneuvered. Even when it took him where he wanted to go.

Nina finally ventured out of the bedroom. She had heard voices, but hadn't wanted to show herself in the state she was in. When the door slammed, and everything grew quiet, she figured Ryan was alone again.

She was without makeup now and her clothes were hopelessly wrinkled. With any luck, she would be able to change before anyone other than Ryan saw her this way. "Oh, good, I see they've brought our bags."

Before she even reached them, Ryan had her two suitcases and was headed past her into the bedroom where they'd made love. "You can stay in here," he said. "I'll take the other one."

She pursed her lips and nodded, accepting that he had beat her to the punch, insisting they not share a room. So they had come to the same conclusion separately. Relief and regret hit her with a double punch.

When he returned from placing her bags in her room, she asked him, "So, do we talk about it?"

He studied her for a full minute, his face unreadable. "Do we need to?"

"I guess not."

"A mistake, huh?"

She shook her head and looked away, chafing her bare arms as if she were cold. To tell the truth, she was. "No mistake yet, but it could become one. For one of us, anyway."

He smiled, but it was without humor. "Which one, do you think?"

"Me," she said honestly. "I need more than you can offer."

"You're right. I don't have much."

She felt so offended, she wanted to slap him, but she doubted he would tolerate it. "I was *not* referring to money," she snapped.

"Neither was I." He sounded sad.

They stood there looking into each other's eyes until the phone rang. Ryan made no move to answer it, so Nina walked over and picked it up. "Hello?"

"Is Ryan McDonough with you, Ms. Caruso?" asked a breathless deep voice with a faint Italian accent. "Is he there?"

"Yes, he's here. Who is this?"

"Joseph Braca. Is he all right?"

"Of course, Mr. Braca. Why?"

Nina heard him exhale sharply and take another deep breath. "His father just called. He said he was afraid for his life."

"His father's ill?"

''No,'' Braca said, worry obvious in his tone. ''Mr. McDonough is afraid for *Ryan's* life. It seems Ryan just phoned him and sounded—''

Ryan pried the receiver from her hand. ''What's the problem, Joe?''

Nina watched, concerned, as Ryan listened, alternately rolling his eyes and pacing. Then he gave a mirthless laugh. ''He misunderstood, that's all. Look, don't worry. I'll call and reassure him. Yes. Right now.'' He hung up, shaking his head and muttering a curse.

''Well?'' Nina demanded shaking her hands at him palms up. ''No way are you going to get out of explaining this.''

''It's nothing.''

''The hell it is! Your dad's so frantic, he's calling your employee to save your hide. What does he know? Is someone after *you?*''

Ryan groaned and sat down on the sofa, his head in his hands. ''Could we just drop this for now? I have a phone call to make before my old man has a heart attack, okay? Could I have some privacy for this, please?''

''Just to let your father know you aren't dead yet? I think not. I want to hear this.''

He narrowed his eyes and glared at her. She stood her ground. ''If that's your most intimidating look, Mac, you might as well give it up. Make the call.''

She watched him dial.

''Hello, Dad?'' he said almost immediately, still giving her the evil eye. ''Hey, I'm fine. Really. No, no, I never had anything like *that* in mind, I promise. Look, it was just a simple apology, all right? That's all it was. I got to thinking and I decided it was time to…settle things.''

Nina could hear the agitated buzz of another voice on the phone from where she stood, but couldn't distinguish the words. Ryan had sounded gentle, yet frustrated. And he still looked furious with her.

"Yeah, Dad, I thought maybe I had, but now I'm not so sure." He shifted the receiver to his other ear and released a huff of frustration. "Could I get back to you on that? End of the week, if not before. Bye. Yeah, Dad, me, too." The last words were free of impatience and sounded sincere.

Nina smiled her approval as he replaced the receiver. "What on earth did you say to him earlier to make him think you were suicidal?"

Ryan scoffed. "I apologized for something. Seems that was enough. Must have shocked the hell out of him."

"Good grief! What on earth did you *do* to him?"

He looked up at her, his eyes tired and a little bloodshot. "Nina, this is none of your business. Back off."

This time she did. He was right. She did not need to get involved in any of his family problems, even if he would let her. Maybe his father was just a little off his bean or something. It didn't matter to her. She wouldn't let it.

She backed slowly toward the bedroom, gesturing her embarrassment. "Why don't I just go, um, take a shower?"

"Why don't you just go take a shower?" he repeated.

"We've said all we have to say about the other, right?" she asked, just to have things perfectly clear between them. "Separate rooms. No more…?" She let her voice trail off as she shook her head.

"No more," he agreed.

On the fifth day of their stay in the Royal, Ryan knew something had to give soon. He and Nina had examined every report and interview in minute detail, then formed theories they either discarded or put on their lists.

Their only outing had been on their third day here, to the palace for a short memorial service for Desmond in the chapel.

Lorenzo revealed that Desmond had once said to him that he favored cremation and had no use for any kind of religious service. Nina had agreed she would wait to have a Mass said when she laid him to rest beside their mother in California.

Lorenzo promised that Desmond's ashes would be available at the funeral home and that she could take them with her when she left Montebello.

The duke conducted the eulogy himself. The only tears were Nina's, but everyone who attended gave her comfort.

Ryan thought a very public funeral might have been better, given the chance that the killer might show up. But the royals were thrust into an awkward situation, since Desmond had been illegitimate. It was strictly a family affair. He knew he'd been allowed only because of his association with Nina, to provide support for her.

Two armed guards escorted Nina and him, and they were ordered to ride in one of the bulletproof limousines, so Ryan suspected the size and location of the memorial service also had to do with the problem of security for Nina.

Being isolated with her and unable to function as he usually did on the job when he did get out of the hotel made Ryan virtually useless. Still, he worked every available hour. Somehow he had to solve this case.

The forced togetherness with Nina was driving him crazy. Every time she walked through the room, his body went on alert. He had to force himself to concentrate on what they were supposed to be doing, not on what he wanted to do.

She had made her decision and he had to abide by it. Hadn't he given her the perfect chance to invite him to share a room, to say he didn't have to stay in the other one? Of course, he could have just asked her if she wanted to, but he'd thought at the time that he should give her an easy way out.

No, to be perfectly honest with himself, he had almost hoped she would opt for stopping what they had started.

He wasn't sure he could deal with the intensity of what he felt for her. Just as well, since she obviously didn't share it.

In spite of his disappointment over that, he did feel better about himself than he had in years. The future no longer stretched out before him like some endless thing he had no right to enjoy. He was waking up each morning curious about what the day would bring. Curious about something other than which turn the work might take.

Would Nina relent and actually say something personal today? he would wonder. Would she throw her arms around his neck and beg him to get rid of some of this damned tension? Not hardly, but it was a great thought to wake up to.

Today he knew where the work was going, initially anyway. Princess Samira and Farid were arriving in San Sabastian. He would interview them this afternoon at two, right here in the suite.

Nina pushed away the remnants of her lunch and got up from the small eighteenth-century table that, along with two matching chairs, served as their dining area in the sitting room.

Breakfast and the midday meal were always a trial to get through. Dinners were not much better, but at least the scenery was different. They ate the evening meal downstairs in the dining room along with the other guests.

"You don't eat enough," he said, finishing his coffee and thunking down the mug. He'd had to order that mug special. Those eggshell china things held about two swallows.

He was deathly tired of all the froufrou and wanted to get back to his place and his plain old stuff.

"You eat enough for both of us," she replied, heading for her room again. She spent entirely too much time in there, but he wouldn't complain about it. At least he could think straight when she was out of sight.

She seemed troubled about something, quieter than usual

and a little pale. "Nina, are you okay? Did the service upset you that much?"

"No, no, I'm fine," she answered over her shoulder.

"Just bored, huh?"

With a sigh, she turned around. "I've seen every movie ever made, I think. Reruns of every sitcom on cable. So many cooking shows, I feel like a master chef. I'm sick of reading, too. If this is not over soon, I think I might drown myself in that horribly ostentatious bathtub."

Ryan laughed. "Yeah, I know what you mean." He walked over to one of the sofas and turned, gesturing for her to take the other one. "Want to work a little?"

"On what? We've covered everything time and again."

He wiggled his eyebrows and grinned. "A break on the earring. Things are looking up. Joe called while you were getting dressed."

"I didn't hear the phone." Excitement gleamed in her eyes. She hurried over and sat down, leaning forward, her hands clasped on her knees. "What? Give!"

He sat back, resting his arms along the top of the sofa, and crossed one ankle over his knee. "Hand cream."

She frowned. "Explain."

"Franz located a film of hand cream on the earring. Whoever wore it also wielded the statuette, which also bore traces. You found a bona fide clue."

"All *right!* Now we've got her!" She couldn't seem to sit still.

"Well, at least we're fairly sure it's a *her.* Impossible to tell which brand of hand cream, since so many contain the same basic ingredients. The traces weren't enough to identify it exactly."

"Even so, it's enough to tie the two objects together as being handled by the same person, right?"

"Absolutely," he agreed, thoroughly enjoying the way her cheeks pinkened with enthusiasm. "Now if we can get a description from Princess Samira on the woman Desmond was seen with in the guesthouse days before he was killed, we might have ourselves a genuine suspect.''

He watched her expression fade from enthusiastic to thoughtful. ''I guess we'll be wrapping this up soon, then, won't we?''

Ryan wasn't quite as convinced of that as she was. ''Let's not start counting chickens. Might jinx us.''

Her smile returned full force. ''Superstitious, McDonough?''

''Maybe. Celtic background and all that. It's fairly latent, though. I walk under ladders and pet black cats.''

She gave a rushed little chuckle. ''To stay on the safe side, let's not break any mirrors.''

A sudden vision flashed in his mind. Mirrors shattered, windows broken, glass shards everywhere. So much glass. Devastation. He almost strangled, trying to breathe.

''Ryan, what is it? What's the matter?''

He felt her hands on him. One patting his face, forcefully. The other grasping his shoulder, shaking. ''Sorry,'' he gasped, willing himself back to the present.

She knelt next to him, her fingers now clutching his arms. ''Tell me what's wrong.''

''Nothing,'' he said, swallowing hard, then sucking in a deep breath and letting it out slowly. ''Flashback, I guess.''

''To what?'' she asked softly.

He couldn't look at her. And he sure as hell wasn't going to tell her. ''Bad case. A long time ago.'' He pushed her aside and got up. ''Excuse me.''

Carefully keeping his stride unhurried so she wouldn't know he was running like hell, he left her kneeling beside the sofa.

He closed the door to the bedroom, went into the bathroom, locked that one behind him and leaned back against it. He closed his eyes, tried to force his mind to grasp at anything that didn't matter.

This would subside, Ryan told himself. Sure enough, the image in his mind quickly faded as it usually did, but the horror of it took longer. It would never leave him completely, even now that he was finally willing to let it go.

Chapter 10

•

Nina banged on the bathroom door with both fists. "Ryan? Ryan, open the door! Are you sick?"

To hell with his privacy. The man had looked as though someone'd hit him square in the stomach with a wrecking ball. "I'm calling someone to break this thing down if you don't—"

The door opened and she stumbled inside. He caught her in his arms just as her nose bumped his chest. Pushing away as soon as she got her balance, she searched his face, reached up to touch it. "Ryan…"

He snatched her hand down, placed it at her side and let go immediately. "Did you know you are the single most irritating woman I have ever met in my life?" he said through gritted teeth.

She nodded, slid her arms around his waist and hugged him, laying her face against his soft knit shirt and holding him as tightly as she could. "You scared me," she whispered.

"Let go, Nina," he ordered, but he didn't remove her

arms. His were hanging loose at his sides and he was very still.

Slowly, she withdrew and backed up a step. "Sorry."

"Okay." He was deliberately avoiding her eyes. "Look, just forget about it. Do me a favor and don't push."

For a moment, she studied him. His breathing was controlled, but shallow. He looked pale despite his tan, but he seemed to be regaining his composure.

"After what your father said, all sorts of things went through my mind," she said honestly, then worried that maybe she shouldn't have been quite that candid.

He brushed past her and into his bedroom, turning his back on her as he opened the double doors of the massive wardrobe. "Nina, I am *not* going to discuss this. I have the interview in about half an hour and I need to change."

"Red tie, the one with the gray stripes," she suggested, knowing the former subject was closed and that he badly needed to get his mind off of whatever it was.

He snatched the tie off the rack that held a dozen more and tossed it onto the bed. His movements less than graceful, he yanked out his charcoal suit and threw it after the tie. It landed in a heap. Nina walked over and straightened it while he searched for a shirt.

Turning with a light yellow oxford cloth hooked on one finger, he glared at her. "I can dress myself, thank you very much."

She shook her head. "But not in that shirt, please. The powder blue, I think."

His eyes widened and his mouth firmed. He was close to hyperventilating. "Will you please get the hell out of my room!"

At least he wasn't pale any longer. "I'm going."

She took her time, but she left. It was hard to leave him there. Would he lapse back into whatever had caused that flashback? What had triggered it anyway? One minute he was fine, even smiling, then the next...

They had been talking, or rather, she had. Was is something she'd said? Nina tried to think back, but the incident had made her forget exactly what they were discussing when it happened.

She had to face the fact that she might never find out. When all this was over, probably very soon now, a plane would carry her back to her old life and he would go back to his. Working long hours, obsessed with his job, suffering these spells brought on by some gruesome incident in his past. And she would never know about it.

Who would bang on his door then and make him angry enough to forget? Who would hold him when he so badly needed to be held he didn't dare admit it?

Oh God, she was in love with him. Neck-deep in love. Probably way over her head in love. It was too late to avoid it. And the man had more baggage than an international airport in the middle tourist season. She could really pick 'em.

He came out of the bedroom straightening his tie. She noticed he had on the blue shirt. It made her smile. ''That blue looks good with your eyes,'' she said, just because it did.

''Thanks,'' he muttered, then cleared his throat. ''I know you're not going to like this, but I'll have to ask you to wait in the bedroom when they get here.''

She gave a cough of disbelief, then protested. ''Why?''

''Princess Samira will probably be more open to questions if Desmond's sister's not sitting here listening to every word she says about him. That's why.''

''But—''

''No buts.'' He smoothed down his tie and straightened his jacket. ''I'm running this investigation and I get to make the rules. Your brother and this woman were lovers, I think. And they did not part friends. Meeting you would be awkward for her. So scat.''

He did have a point, she supposed. Though she had

wanted to meet the princess and her bodyguard husband. It would have been something more to tell her grandchildren. If she ever had any, which did not look very promising at the moment. Obediently, she started for her room.

"Good luck," she said, almost wishing he wouldn't find out anything. She needed more time to work all this out in her mind before she had to leave.

Sadly, solving Desmond's murder had sunk another notch on her list of priorities. After all, it wasn't as though the person who killed him was a mass murderer or anything. She hoped.

Ryan agreed the most likely scenario was that Des had made some woman furious and she had crowned him. If the statue had hit an inch or so off the mark, Desmond might even have retaliated. Not that Nina had ever witnessed his being violent, but she remembered that he had been in trouble for fighting during his troubled youth. Poor Des, who had never fit in and now never would.

She should recommit herself to her initial reason for coming and try to ignore her own dilemma for the time being. If worse came to worst, she could prolong her stay after things were settled and see how things with Ryan would work out. It would be foolish anyway to pursue it now with emotions running so high. Maybe she only thought she was in love.

It might even be some sort of syndrome where she fell for the guy in charge. Patients often experienced that with doctors, didn't they? Students with teachers? Hostages with their captors? The last thought made her wince. Right now, that felt closer to the true situation than the other examples.

She heard the door chimes and glanced at her watch. The princess and her husband were here already. *Early.* If only she had left the door open a crack, she could have peeked. But she could still listen! Grabbing the water glass from her night table, Nina kicked off her shoes and went over to the door.

Carefully, she positioned the glass against the wooden panel and placed her ear just so. Hey, it always worked in the movies, she thought, wondering if it actually would in real life.

A smile crept across her face and she shivered with success. The princess was speaking now, replying to Ryan's greeting. Though her words were soft, they were mostly audible. What a charming accent she had.

Ryan must have seated the couple already. They were obviously closer to her bedroom door than when they'd first entered. Just let that rascal Ryan try to edit this little chat. Now she could hear every word.

Ryan realized how uncomfortable this must be for Princess Samira, talking about a former lover in the presence of her new husband. He wished he could have arranged to talk to them separately, but knew better than to push his luck. It was a wonder these two had agreed to speak with him at all.

If they had refused, it would have taken more than an act of congress to make it happen. Relations between Montebello and Tamir had been shaky at best for centuries. Though they were greatly improved now, an incident might set them off again.

The princess was tiny, a few inches over five feet tall. Her long black hair was caught up in a smooth chignon at the nape of her slender neck. She was dressed in a simple, white form-fitting dress that looked like pure silk. Her pearls were understated elegance, just like the rest of her.

Her husband, Farid Nasir, had a bodyguard's build. He was almost a foot taller than the princess and was obviously heavily muscled beneath that expensive hand-tailored suit of his. The man looked as if he could be deadly or benign as the mood struck him. Right now, he wasn't leaning toward the latter, but Ryan would bet his temper had a short fuse.

"Ask your questions, Mr. McDonough," Samira told him. "We shall cooperate in every way that we can."

"It was good of you to agree to come, Your Highness. On behalf of the Crown, I thank you for your assistance in the investigation. First of all, I have to establish your actual relationship to the victim, Desmond Caruso. Did you know him well?"

She shot a wary look at Farid, who remained immobile and expressionless. "We were…involved. I believed for a short while that I was in love with him."

"And that he loved you," her husband supplied in a gentle voice. Farid looked directly into Ryan's eyes and added, "But he did not."

"Fortunately, for you," Ryan said. "You had an altercation with him, did you not?"

"I did. This happened at the Glass Swan. When he insulted my wife, I backed him against a wall and threatened to kill him."

"I see. Precisely what did he say that made you angry enough to do that?" Ryan asked.

"Must I repeat it?"

"Please. It could be important," Ryan urged, offering Samira a look of apology. He had read it in the police report and knew it would be embarrassing for both of them, but sometimes a second relating of events produced something unexpected. Memory during an episode stirring up intense emotions was often quirky. And the report only contained the gist of what was said. He needed actual words.

"Tell him, Farid," the princess ordered softly. "Desmond cannot hurt me with his vile words any longer."

"Caruso mocked her," Nasir said, his voice deep and without inflection. With one hand he grasped both of Samira's and held them. "The devil said that she was cold. A frigid woman. Then something to the effect that I should be glad he broke her in for me."

"No wonder you lost your head," Ryan commented,

wondering again why the man hadn't choked Desmond on the spot. Farid would have been acquitted in any court lined up in this part of the world.

It was a good thing Nina wasn't here to listen to this.

"So that was it? You said your piece, released him, took Samira back to Tamir and never saw Desmond Caruso again?"

"That is correct," Farid admitted, but his dark eyes held regret for it. "I did not kill him."

"Yes, we have established that. The main reason I wanted to speak with you both is to ask about the woman Desmond was with days earlier. The one you saw with him through the window of the guesthouse, Your Highness."

Ryan watched her draw her hands from Farid's and clasp them formally in her lap. Her shoulders were straight now, her delicate chin raised royally, her slender ankles crossed very properly. She wore a slight frown as if trying to recall every detail of the incident he referred to. "This person had blond hair. She seemed tall, almost as tall as Desmond, or perhaps the heels of her shoes were high enough to make her so."

"What sort of build? Body type?" Ryan asked, making notes on his small lined tablet.

"Not heavy. Slender, but not precisely thin."

"Approximate age?"

"I do not know. I could not see her face." She blushed and lowered her eyes. "They were embracing. Kissing. I left then, not wishing to disturb them."

"Of course." Yeah, he'd bet, Ryan thought. She probably had wanted to burst in there and scratch out some eyes right about then. But this dainty little princess would never have done such a thing. The lady had class. She knew exactly when to cut her losses, admit her mistake and move on with grace.

Ryan admired her enormously for carrying through with this as she was doing. If only she had seen more of that woman, she might have been the key to solving this case. "Tell me, have either of you heard any other woman's name in connection with Desmond Caruso?"

"No name," Samira said. "However he had been sitting with a woman shortly before our confrontation in the restaurant."

Ryan had not heard this. It was not in the report the police had taken in Tamir the morning after the body was discovered. Farid Nasir's confrontation with Desmond was recorded, but no one had mentioned a woman. "You saw her?"

"Again, only from the back. She had blond hair to her shoulders. I believe it was the same lady. This one was not young. I saw her hand as she lifted her wineglass from their table. Her nails were well manicured. Long. Painted red. Her hands were not young."

He wrote down *not young* in large capital letters on his notepad and let her see the words. They both smiled and even Farid's lips quirked up at one corner.

"What was this ancient lady wearing?" Ryan asked.

Samira sighed and bit her lower lip, her perfect dark brows furrowed. "Black or very dark blue, perhaps. Sleeveless. I could not tell whether it was a dress or pants. Gold bracelets and rings. I did not count them."

"Excellent description," Ryan said, praising her. "You are very observant. Mr. Nasir, did you see the woman at all?"

"No," Farid admitted. "I was unaware that he was with anyone."

He paused for a minute, then declared, "I believe we have told you all that we know of this matter. We will go now."

Ryan stood and closed his little notebook. "I thank you for your time, Princess Samira, and for yours, Mr. Nasir. It was good of you to come."

"If there is nothing more, we shall return to Tamir first

thing in the morning,'' the princess said as she and her husband got up to leave.

"No more questions at present. If I think of anything else, I will come to you next time. Again, thank you for coming and for being so forthright."

"You are quite welcome," she said graciously, offering her hand.

Ryan took it and bowed over it, then shook hands with Farid Nasir. "Congratulations on your marriage. I hope you will be very happy together," he told them sincerely.

Farid took the princess's arm in a proprietary way no bodyguard would ever dare. "We shall be, of course, but would be much happier if we could put everything to do with Desmond Caruso behind us and forget he ever existed."

Ryan nodded in agreement. "We will close this case as soon as humanly possible. Count on it."

Nina came out the minute the door closed. She wore a stunned look. And she was carrying a water glass in her hand. "Do you believe Desmond actually said those things about her?" she asked in a breathless voice.

"Dammit, Nina!" Ryan threw up his hands and shook his head. "I should have known you couldn't resist. People who listen at doors usually hear things they'd rather not—"

"Do you believe he said it?" Nina demanded, ignoring his anger.

"You knew him better than I did. Do you believe it?"

She swallowed hard and looked a little sick. "I…I honestly don't know." She sank down on the sofa and looked lost. "If he did…well, it was awful, wasn't it? To say such things?"

Ryan hated to see her this upset. He wanted to rake her over the coals for listening in the first place, but he didn't have the heart after all she had heard. "Maybe Nasir exaggerated a little. It happens. Memory works funny sometimes and he must have been jealous to start with."

Slowly she shook her head. "No. No, I don't believe he would make that up." She looked up at him. "How could Desmond say something that vile, Ryan? It was horrible."

"Come on, Nina. The man was mad at her. She dumped him—though I grant you she had good reason—and he struck out, wanting to hurt her, too."

"You don't have to provide excuses to save my feelings, Ryan. The princess went there to that guesthouse and saw him with another woman. She thought he loved her. Then the next time they meet, he's flinging these public insults. No, they were worse than insults. He was deliberately trying to destroy her reputation. I feel terrible for her. She sounded so sweet."

Ryan said nothing.

"You believe it. You believe they're telling the truth."

He sighed, sat down and took one of her hands in his. "Yes. I'm sorry, Nina, but I do."

"It didn't say that in the report of the police interview with Farid."

"No. But they had to know the specifics would get out. People overheard it."

"So did the woman with Desmond," she said, a tear trickling down one cheek. She swiped at it angrily and sniffed. "What he said might have made her as furious with Desmond as I am this very minute."

He couldn't argue with that, Ryan thought. She was absolutely right.

It was too bad that Nina had to discover that her brother was not the man she'd thought he was. That anger she was feeling would dissolve into sadness soon. Ryan knew she would dwell on it.

"Since we talked to Pete, I've had Joe asking around, trying to find somebody at the restaurant who might have witnessed what went on. I'm going to talk to the staff myself. Let me call and see what he's got," Ryan said as he picked up the phone.

When Joe answered, Ryan gave him a quick rundown on the information he had gotten from the princess and her husband. Joe imparted what he had learned, which was damned little. Ryan hung up, feeling more discouraged than before.

"So, did he learn anything?" Nina asked, frowning. She looked as down as he felt.

"Nothing new. Unfortunately, the argument between Samira and Desmond grabbed all the attention and whoever was with Desmond went virtually unnoticed as a result. So far all we have is mention of an ordinary blond female. One who might no longer be a blond. If she's guilty of killing Desmond, we can probably bank on the fact that she'd adopt some kind of disguise. No one at the restaurant who did see her remembered seeing her before, Joe said. My guess—and Joe agrees—is that she's not a native or a very frequent visitor. Might be someone Desmond picked up who was here on vacation and long gone now."

"Then who's been after me?" Nina asked with a shrug.

Ryan had no answer for that one and they both knew it. He needed to find some kind of distraction to keep her mind busy.

"You want to go over to the American Embassy with me? I need to pick up some paperwork." It was something he had been putting off, but time was growing short.

In about six weeks, he would submit his application for citizenship. He'd been operating here under a work visa for almost two years. If he intended to stay, he would have to request another extension or, more practically, become a Montebellan. Giving up his American citizenship was not a thing he looked forward to, even though he never intended to return to the States.

"Does this have anything to do with the investigation?" she asked.

Ryan looked away. "No, nothing. It's personal."

"Personal?" she asked, perking up. "You actually have a personal life? There's news."

Immediately, he felt defensive. "What do you mean by that? Everybody has a personal life."

She scoffed. "Not you, Mac. Everything you do is connected to work, do you realize that? Not once in all the time I've known you, have you done anything that didn't have to do with the job!" Suddenly she looked away and colored a nice shade of rose. "Well, all right, once, but it doesn't count. That was just an anomaly."

"That's what you call it? Well, gee, I need to look up that word in *Webster's*. I've been using it wrong all these years."

She blushed even redder. "You know what I mean."

Ryan shrugged. "So I do what I get paid to do. You ought to appreciate that. How else do you expect me to catch whoever killed your brother? That's what you came over here demanding."

She paced back and forth nervously, running a hand through her hair, pausing to look out the window as she crossed her arms. "I know." For a moment she remained quiet, then sighed as she stared out at the city of San Sebastian. "I think I made a huge mistake in coming here."

"What do you mean?" he asked gently. "You want me to admit what a big help you've been? You have helped."

She shook her head, still not facing him. "It's just that you seem obsessed with it. A lot more obsessed than I am, which is little strange, don't you think? You never think about anything else."

Little did she know, but he wasn't about to admit how much she was on his mind. Then he would have to say why that was, and he honestly didn't know. "Sorry. The work is who I am."

Suddenly she turned, frowning. "See? That's exactly what I mean."

Ryan smiled. "All work and no play makes Jack a dull

boy? Well, I am a dull boy, Nina. What you see is what you get.''

"You've allowed me a glimpse now and then of a man I would really like to know better. Then you yank down this shutter between us. I believe you use it to shut everybody out, not just me. Why is that?''

Ryan hated this kind of examination. "Who the hell do you think you are, picking my life apart like a plate of bony fish? You want me in the sack again? Is that what this is about? Okay, let's go.''

She rolled her eyes and turned back to the window. "In your dreams. If you actually *have* any dreams. I'm just worried about you, end of story. You want to live like a robot, that's your business.''

He marched over and stood just behind her, spoiling for the fight she had picked. "You're damned right about that. It is my business! And I don't appreciate all this crap. I live the way I *have* to live, Nina.''

She wheeled on him. "Why?''

"Why do you care?'' he shot back.

"Because you're miserable, that's why! You don't have any friends, Ryan! You need friends! You need some kind of connection to life besides existing in that blank space you call an apartment, running interviews and collecting clues!''

"I *have* friends.''

She flapped a hand, dismissing that. "On the surface. You shake hands, you joke around, you smile, but it always comes back to the job, doesn't it? Always. You haven't talked to a single soul since I met you that you didn't need information from.''

Ryan took a deep breath, trying to stay cool. "There was my dad.''

She clicked her tongue in disgust. "Yeah, the guy who thought you might eat your gun, right?''

"What's this attack all about, Nina?" he demanded. "Why, all of a sudden, do you feel like I need saving?"

Her eyes softened with what looked like pity. "Because you do. Because I want to be your friend, a real friend, not just someone you tolerate being close to you because you have no choice."

"I don't have a choice," he snapped. "And you're just bored. Why is it women always have to start dissecting somebody when they run out of things to do?"

"Did some woman leave you dissected, Ryan?" she asked, tongue in cheek, looking up at him from beneath those dark curling lashes.

In a rush, he released the breath he'd been holding. "Yeah," he admitted, nodding. "One did."

Nina walked around him and left him standing there by the window. "Well, someone needs to put you back together one of these days." She waited, probably for him to answer, which he didn't. The silence drew out. "Guess it won't be me."

He guessed not.

Ryan stood there where she had stood, looking out, not seeing, wishing he didn't feel as fragmented as she had accused him of being. Or as wound up in the work. Or as friendless.

There was Pete, he wanted to say. But Pete was a source. And Lorenzo was more of an employer than a friend. He liked both men, but they had lives vastly different from the one he had led and was leading now. Franz and Joe would do just about anything for him, but that's what they got paid to do. He had nothing in common with either of them if he didn't count the job.

Damn, he hated thinking about things like this. He almost hated Nina for pointing them out. For being right.

"You know, I wish we could go to the beach," she said with a deep sigh. "It's so nice out there."

He turned and glared at her. "Analysis is over then?"

"Time's up. I'll send you a bill." She met his gaze with an unreadable expression.

"So do I just chill out and chalk this up to cabin fever?"

She nodded. "Wouldn't it be wonderful just to lie in the sun and try to forget about everything for a while? I'd give anything to do that."

Ryan supposed he could arrange it. There were private beaches where the public was not allowed. He could probably get Lorenzo to set it up, especially since the man seemed so damned determined to play Cupid. "I'll see what I can do," he said, shaking off the unwarranted anger.

"Never mind," she said, looking wistful. "With my luck, sharks would probably attack the minute I hit the water."

"Did you bring a bathing suit with you?"

She stretched out on the sofa, her hands behind her head and closed her eyes. "I didn't fly to Montebello to swim."

"Hey, first rule—you never go anywhere on this island without a suit. Carry one in your purse. Keep one in your car. In your desk. Everybody swims. We'll get you one from the gift shop downstairs. I'll call down and have a couple sent up for you to try on." He reached for the phone.

She sat up. "Are you kidding? I've seen those things in the window on the way to the dining room. They're nothing but strings and patches."

He smiled evilly. "You're as well equipped for that as anyone I've ever seen. Or we could skinny-dip. The guards might snigger, but—"

"Not funny." She seemed to be working on restoring her good humor. The least he could do was match her effort.

"Let me see what Lorenzo says. Maybe he'll loan us his private stretch of sand for a couple of hours."

"You think he would?" Her excitement proved what he

had suspected. She just needed to get out of here for a while.

"Sure. What are *surface* friends for if you can't borrow their beaches?" He picked up the phone and punched in the number for the duke's offices.

By the time Lorenzo had sent word by one of his assistants about a safe location, Nina had chosen a little red two-piece from among those sent up from the exclusive shop downstairs. She had refused to model it for him, and Ryan hadn't insisted. Not with a couple of beds in the vicinity and tension running high as a kite.

Instead they went to their separate rooms and put on their swimsuits so they wouldn't have to change at the beach. Over his swimsuit, Ryan slipped on a pair of faded jeans. He quickly located his deck shoes and a freshly laundered polo shirt and finished dressing.

When he returned to the sitting room, she was already there, wearing a bright, loose-fitting sundress and strappy little sandals. She held up the canvas tote she was carrying. "Towels and sunblock. Anything else we need?"

"Nope. The less we carry with us, the better."

He didn't want anyone who might be watching to guess where they might be going and follow. He adjusted the small holster clipped to his belt at the small of his back and made certain his shirttail covered it.

He had already called the palace for the car and a couple of guards. Glancing at his watch, he figured they should be waiting downstairs by this time. It was nearly four o'clock, but he and Nina could have a quick swim and still return to the hotel well before dark.

She accompanied him down to the lobby. Ryan hoped their short outing would cheer her up. He was feeling pretty low himself, considering her observations about him.

He kept a close eye on the pedestrians and traffic nearby as they exited the building quickly and darted inside the limousine. They drew no more than what seemed the usual curiosity people afforded a couple making a dash for a limo in front of the most expensive hotel on the island. Celebrities stayed there, after all. He supposed Nina might be considered one after her write-up in the news and her connection to the royals.

He wished he had argued with the king about the hotel. It might have been better to have taken her to some isolated beachside cottage across the island where no one would think to look.

However, if he had insisted on that, then he could not have continued with the investigation. Although considering how much he had accomplished in the past week, he doubted it would have made much difference.

Right now, since they were in the safe confines of the car, he was having a hard time focusing his mind on anything besides that new red bikini he knew she was wearing under her clothes.

Also, in the back of his mind just beyond that pleasant haze of lust grew the novel idea that he could have Nina as a friend. A real friend. She had already come closer to that than anyone else had since he had sealed himself off.

Ursula Chambers pulled the straw sun hat closer down on her brow as she watched the royal limousine pull away from the curb. This did not look good. Not at all. Desmond's sister was riding around in a damned limo, guarded by a guy who could afford to put her up in the Royal Montebello Hotel.

It must be a red-hot affair since the two of them rarely left the room. Ursula grimaced just thinking about the cost of staying here herself, but she needed to be close enough to take advantage of any opportunity to get rid of Nina. Obviously, the woman was just waiting until Ursula turned over Prince Lucas's baby to the royals. Then she would demand Ursula either share what reward she received, or give it all to her. No way.

Thank God Desmond hadn't known about getting rid of the baby's mother. Ursula felt a brief stab of pity for her softheaded sister, but hadn't Jessica asked for it? She'd taken the prince in, given him a job and fell right into bed with the man without even knowing who he really was, for goodness' sake. And gotten dumped for her trouble, too. Then she had admitted she was pregnant by the Joe who turned out to be a prince. If only she had cooperated with Ursula and used that fact, she wouldn't be dead now.

Ursula knew she had to get this one last complication, Nina Caruso, out of the way and then she'd be home free. Or at least ready to proceed with the next step. God, she had to be ready. Gretchen would soon be here with the baby. Once they arrived in San Sebastian, it would be too risky to delay doing what had to be done. God, she hoped the money she got for selling Jessica's ring would last.

"Shall we go in now?" Ursula's companion asked, his accent as oily as his hair. He gestured from the car's window toward the entrance to the hotel. "I shall take care of everything."

Desperation made her force a surgary smile, assuring herself that her acting talents had always been underappreciated. "Of course you will, Jean-Paul." Fake name, fake plastic, she'd bet. Just what she needed.

"You go ahead and do that, lover, while I do a bit of shopping, okay? Something special for you," she sing-songed suggestively, tracing the long red nail of her forefinger down the front of his tie. "We'll celebrate big time after you've done the little chore for me that needs doing."

Ursula was not too trusting when it came to the locals, but she had sensed from the start that this one was a man after her own heart. Or after what was left of her money. As she saw it, they were pretty much one in the same and he'd play hell getting either one. Once he had served his purpose, he probably wouldn't be missed much. Not as much as Desmond anyway, and she was getting used to that.

They entered the hotel separately. She wandered by the shop windows inside the lobby, careful not to give the impression that she was with him as he registered at the desk. When he headed for the elevator, she sauntered along toward them herself as he held the door open for her. "You will come back down to the lobby and wait for them," she instructed. "You know what to do then."

"Yes," he said with a sly smile. "I know."

Just one more thing, Ursula kept repeating inside her head. Or two more things, if she counted Jean-Paul, and she would have it rocked. She would never have to worry about money again.

Chapter 11

Nina felt woefully exposed as she slipped off her light cotton sundress in the open air and dropped it beside the tote containing the towels. There were no cabanas set up here on this lovely hidden stretch of beach. No folding lounge chairs or beach umbrellas marred the landscape. Even the steep path that accessed the cove was invisible from where she stood.

The place looked as it might have when first discovered. The expanse of sand where they stood lay just below a natural seawall formed by rocks, some reaching heights of twenty to thirty feet. Just above those ran the narrow two-lane road where the limousine was parked. The two armed guards, one their driver, were now hidden from view, ostensibly patrolling.

Ryan's rapid exhalation, almost a whistle, made her heat with a blush. Of course she had worn bikinis all her life. She had grown up in California, after all. But having his full and undivided attention while wearing one this revealing was a little disconcerting.

"Red is definitely your color," he said, not even bothering to disguise his interest in her body.

"And tan is yours," she replied, raising one eyebrow meaningfully, just to emphasize that he was wearing even less than she was.

He pulled out their towels, dropped them on the sand and fished around in the bottom of the tote. "Want me to slather on your sunblock?" he asked, brandishing the tube of it, a wicked gleam in his eye.

"No way," she replied, willing to risk any degree of sunburn rather than risk his hands on her. She didn't think she could endure that without doing something idiotic. "The sun's low now, anyway."

He shrugged and dropped the tube back into her tote, leaving the towels lying in a heap at his feet. "It's almost five and we ought to leave here by six."

His black bathing suit rode well below his waist and fit him like a second skin, leaving nothing to the imagination but whether the skin beneath it was lighter in color. And she already knew it was. Nina feasted her eyes for as long as she dared, then turned toward the surf and ran into the water.

She knew he was right behind her. Then he was beside her, swimming out past the breakers. They swam parallel to the shoreline until she tired and stopped to tread water. He moved nearer, within touching distance, his gaze alternating between her and the two guards who were now visible in the distance.

"This is crazy," he said, grinning, water lapping at his chin, his strong arms stroking outward to keep him afloat. They also propelled him closer, close enough to take her mouth in a wet, hot, salty kiss that caused them to sink just below the surface.

Nina sputtered and laughed as their heads emerged again. Her arms encircled his neck and her body lay flush against his. She could feel the scissoring of his legs keeping them afloat.

"Put your legs around my waist," he said.

She did, her breath hitching in her throat as she watched him swallow hard and smile. The intimacy of their embrace seemed even greater than if they had been out of the water doing this. Something about the motion of the current around them increased and magnified it somehow.

They lingered there, bobbing like a single cork, while he stole breathless kisses and she clung to him, content except for a burgeoning need to get even closer. She relished the slick, hard surface of his muscles against her, the heat trapped between them and the cold swirling around them.

"We should go back," she said when the powerful urge to take things further grew too intense.

"I'd like to tow you to another island, one that's deserted," he said, almost gasping, "and keep you there."

"You'd be so bored. Nothing to do." She trailed her fingers along the back of his neck, exploring, tickling.

"Oh, I'd think of something," he assured her with a suggestive leer. "Believe me, I *am* thinking of something right now."

"I know, but you'd better cool it," she advised, darting a glance toward the guards who were waiting for them near the car. "We probably have an audience."

"They'd better not be watching us. They're paid to watch in the other direction. Kiss me."

She did, but kept it brief. His lips tried to cling when she released his neck and unwound her legs from around him. She began to tread. "Did you come here to neck or swim?" she taunted and began swimming back the way they had come.

"Neck!" he called out and glided past her to swim a length ahead. With each stroke, as his face turned to the side, he glanced back, wearing a grin. Suddenly he circled her, cutting through the water like a dolphin. Swimming beneath the surface he nudged her playfully, emerging with a laugh when she squealed.

He seemed so totally at ease in the water, she thought, wondering whether he had always lived near the coast of Savannah. He must have grown up in the surf. Now, with his blond-streaked hair slicked back and his tanned muscles gleaming wet, he certainly had the look of a beachboy. And he swam like a fish.

When they reached the spot nearest where they had left their towels, they headed in. Nina felt pleasantly exhausted as she got her feet under her and plowed through the waves lapping forcefully around her.

Ryan reached out, smiling as he offered her his hand. She took it, remarking to herself how natural it felt to lace their fingers together. After so many days of carefully avoiding one another, being with him this way was like coming home after a long time.

Only now she realized that actually going home, returning to the house in California where she had lived all her life, would never bring her this feeling again. No, the old sensation of warmth and comfort and being loved had died with her parents. Her fingers tightened and she wanted to hold on forever, even though she knew that was impossible.

Ryan was not the sort of man to want any permanent ties. She had the impression that eliminating the ones he'd had was why he had come here in the first place. Reluctantly, she released his hand when they left the water.

She watched as he bent over to pluck up one of the towels. Nina started to reach for hers, but he stopped her. "Let me," he said.

Nina stood stock-still while he drew the soft towel around her and slowly, too slowly, began drying her. Only the thickness of the towel lay between his palms and her body. She shot a glance toward the guards, but couldn't see them now for the rocky outcropping that sheltered the sandy paradise.

Surrendering to the inevitable, she closed her eyes and relished the sensations. Through the stretchy Lycra patches concealing her nipples, the nubby weave of the towel roused her. He lingered there, teasing, then molded her bare waist and hips. His body drew close as his palms and the towel cupped her bottom, moving in a circular motion that drew a groan from deep in her throat.

"Wet," he whispered close to her ear. He wasn't kidding, she thought as she felt him begin to kneel in front of her. On his way down, his breath and his mouth warmed her cleavage, her midriff, then the top of her thighs.

Eyes still closed, legs trembling, she braced her hands on his shoulders, hot shoulders, sticky with saltwater and kissed by the afternoon sun.

Nina forgot about guards and everything else when his lips began branding her just to one side of the triangle of red fabric. His teeth gently grasped the string that held it in place, tugged it away from her and let go. A sharp little sting of pleasure shot through her and she cried out, a definite plea for more.

"Enough," he gasped and his touch was gone.

Breathless and shivering, Nina forced her eyes open and saw that he had backed away, holding the towel in front of him while he scrubbed at the center of his chest with one end of it.

Wordlessly, he crouched, picked up the other towel and tossed it at her. She caught and held it close, unmoving, ignoring the granules that now coated her chest, stomach and the tops of her legs.

"Get dressed," he ordered. "We need to get out of here."

Yes. Out of here and back to their suite, she thought numbly. Back to seclusion. Good idea.

She shook off the fog of desire that held her immobile, turned away from him and snapped the towel sharply to get rid of the sand.

It took only a minute or so to mop off the remaining seawater and slip her dress over her head. Frustrated, she raked her fingers through her hair, pulling it behind her ears.

"All right, I'm ready," she said, watching with interest and a little vindication while he struggled to zip his jeans over his arousal.

"Serves you right," she grumbled.

To her surprise, he agreed. "Yeah. Sorry."

She stuffed the damp towel into her tote and trudged back toward the path that would lead them up to the road. He followed, passing her just before they reached the top as she had known he would.

She bowed to his need to protect and defend. That was, after all, who Ryan was. He was never a beachboy except on break. Never a lover except on break. And his infrequent breaks were brief and timed to the minute, she suspected.

She couldn't even accuse him of not warning her. *The job is who I am,* he had said. And even if he could manage interludes such as this afternoon, Nina knew she would never be satisfied living with a man like Ryan. Not while knowing that his first and foremost thoughts at all times centered on his work. It just wasn't enough.

Ryan kept his hands to himself and his attention firmly focused out the window until they had almost reached the hotel. No way could he return to that room without violating their agreement not to have sex. She wouldn't object. He wouldn't hesitate. And then what?

He had let himself get entirely too attached to this woman. Had even considered they might have something going that could last awhile. Even tried to broach the subject with his father on the phone.

What the hell had he been thinking? After she had told him flat out she had considered it a mistake the first time. That it wouldn't be wise. She'd all but said she wanted more than an affair. Anything else was certainly out of the question. She had a life. Why the devil would she want to think about sharing his? It sure wasn't anything to aspire to, now was it?

Work, work and more work. The infrequent game of poker with people he hardly knew. A bleak-looking apartment that said more about him than he wanted to admit. Yeah, she had noticed all that, all right, and pointed it out with no mercy. Add the occasional dip in the ocean while he committed a desperate act to somehow connect with another human being. No, not just any human being, but the only one he had wanted any connection with in six long years.

Boy, he had almost lost it today. Came that close to breaking out of the mold that had held him together since tragedy ripped him apart.

Still, he didn't feel the guilt. What he felt was more curious now than scared about what would happen to him if he changed. Did that mean anything significant? Like maybe he had healed a little while he wasn't looking?

One thing he did know, there was a lot more thinking he had to do about that before he committed any more acts of lunacy like he had today.

When the limo pulled up in front of the hotel, he got out with her and rushed her inside. The elevator ride was silent. He unlocked the door to their suite and stood aside for her to enter. When she had, he stayed where he was. "You'll be all right by yourself for a while, won't you?"

"You're going somewhere?" She turned and frowned up at him.

"Uh, yeah." He handed her the tote bag with their damp towels. "I'm going to the office for a while." He hadn't left her alone here before. "You will stay put, right?"

"Yes. What do you want to do about dinner?" she asked, but she already looked resigned to eating alone. He could also see that she understood why he was leaving.

"I'll stop by the desk and have them send something up for you," he told her.

"Okay, fine," she said. "Chef's salad and mineral water."

She sounded defensive and a little bit hurt. That was the last thing he wanted. He tried a smile. "One of those strawberry things, too, huh? With whipped cream?"

She shrugged and he noticed her bare shoulders were pinkening from their exposure to the sun. He wanted to kiss them, feel the heat on his lips. God, he had to get out of here. *Now.*

"I'll be back by nine. Promise," he told her, a real concession when he wanted to stay gone all night just to be on the safe side.

He listened to make certain she locked the door, then retraced his steps to the elevator. All the while he kept thinking how he had just reinforced her opinion of him. Damn. Using work as a refuge was beginning to seem a little unhealthy, even to him.

At precisely nine o'clock, he was back, nothing accomplished and his thoughts still in a whirl about what to do. He knew very well what he wanted to do. But he also knew that Nina was vulnerable right now, had been since she got to Montebello. She was totally without family, if you didn't count those two relatives in Italy he had checked out. They hadn't left that country since they'd been born and probably didn't even care that this little cousin existed. While they were not in any way involved in the threat she faced here, neither were they people she could count on for anything. Naturally she was lonely. Ryan knew he was just handy.

She was attracted to him, he knew. And she was reading more into it than she should. So was he, for that matter.

He slipped the key card into the door and called out to her as he entered. She was sitting in a chair at the table sipping the wine he had ordered for her. Wine she would

never order for herself when he was around because she
knew he didn't drink. It had become a standing joke during
their dinners together that she always asked for water and
he would ask for the wine. Then he would switch glasses
and she would smile at him, his reward, Ryan supposed,
for an alcoholic refusing the evils of drink.

How sad was that, his allowing her to think, after only
one denial, that he was recovering? Hell, maybe he was,
but he didn't think so. But she could make him feel like a
king with one of those proud smiles of hers and he would
take them any way he could get them.

"Find out anything?" she asked.

"I spoke with the maître d' at the Swan and he gave me
the name of another one of the waiters working the night
Desmond and Farid had their confrontation. Might get an
ID on the woman Desmond was with, or at least a better
description."

"That's good," she said, but with no real excitement.

He strode over to join her and poured himself a cup of
coffee from the silver pot that always accompanied their
meals. He even used the little china cup and didn't bother
going to find his mug.

"You want half this salad?" she asked, removing the
silver cover that kept it chilled. "They always send enough
to feed an army."

"Why haven't you eaten already? You weren't waiting
for me, were you?"

She shook her head while she improvised another salad
bowl, using the cover that came on hers. Ryan reached for
the salad dressing. Then he noticed something. A pointy
piece of leaf tucked against a slice of cucumber. Bay? No,
too thick. But he recognized it. Automatically, he reached
out and grabbed Nina's wrist that held her fork. "Don't
eat. Wait just a minute."

He poked carefully through the various greens and found

more of the unusual leaf. He looked up at her. "Who brought this up? The regular guy?"

"Alonzo? No. I didn't recognize…what's wrong?" She glanced down at her bowl and back up at him. "What's the matter with the salad?"

He pointed to the leaf. "Oleander. Poison that simulates a heart attack. And it doesn't take much of it." He pushed away from the table and reached for the phone.

"Send security up to 612," he growled into the receiver. "Not one of your house dicks. I want Tatro himself and if he's not around, you find him and get him up here *now!*"

His hands were shaking when he hung up. Sweat broke out on his face and sent a chill right through him. He knew from the look on Nina's face that she didn't need a fuller explanation. Someone had tried to kill her again. And if he had returned ten minutes later, he might have been too late to save her.

"Ryan?" she said, her voice a mere whisper, her dark eyes wide with fright.

"Come here," he said. Not waiting for her to move, he closed the distance between them, pulled her close and held her. He knew that very soon, maybe only hours from now, he would have to let her go for good.

Nina answered Signor Tatro's questions, but she couldn't keep her eyes off that table holding the deathly dose of salad she had almost eaten. Ryan paced like a caged lion, his frustration palpable.

One of the house detectives who had arrived with the head of security came in to interrupt them. "Signor Tatro, I need to speak with you outside a moment," he said in Italian as he darted a look at Nina, then Ryan.

Ryan had stopped and was listening. He protested in the same language, probably to let the guy know his ploy was useless. "If it has to do with what's happened here, then you don't need to keep it private."

Tatro nodded. "Go ahead. What is it?"

The detective inclined his head toward the corridor. "The waiter who usually serves this floor is missing. He was last seen in the kitchens arranging the food on a cart to bring up here."

Nina spoke up. "We usually eat dinner in the restaurant. I thought nothing of it when I saw it wasn't Alonzo. I assumed the shifts changed in the evenings."

"How is it no one observed the switch?" Tatro demanded.

The detective wiped his forehead and sighed. "The corridor leading from the kitchens to the special sixth floor elevator was left unguarded. A key card is always needed to access it. It was thought to be safe."

Ryan interrupted, speaking English again and not addressing anyone in particular. "He must have seen us come back this afternoon. Hair wet and carrying that tote, probably realized we'd been swimming. Figured we might stay in for dinner."

He had resumed pacing, busy reconstructing what might have happened. No one interrupted. He was looking at the floor, one hand on his hip, the other gesturing. "No, wait. He could have been hanging out in the lobby, heard me order up your salad and wine. Has to be how. Then," he said, nodding to himself, "he heads for the kitchen, hoping for a chance."

"The leaves?" Nina reminded him.

"Outside. The flower beds outside." Ryan stopped, turned to the detective and ordered, "Go see if there's oleander."

"There is," the detective assured him. "I called down to check."

Ryan nodded again. "So he steps outside, plucks a handful, then goes to the kitchen to wait. If there's an opportunity, he'll take it. If not, he'll wait, do something else."

"Something that will appear a natural death or an accident," Nina added. "Like the fire."

"Exactly," Ryan said, agreeing. "No guns, knives or whatever, but he obviously knows how to kill. Oleander's not exactly a poison of choice, but it can be very effective and, as I said, simulates heart failure."

"How did you know about it?" Nina asked.

"Worked in a plant nursery one summer when I was a kid."

The phone rang just as Signor Tatro stood to leave. Ryan answered, then passed him the receiver. The man nodded, hummed a couple of answers, then barked an order in Italian. When he turned to Ryan, he lowered his voice and spoke apologetically. "The regular waiter has been found unconscious in one of the supply rooms near the elevator. The injury is not serious, they say. If you had succumbed to the poison and the coroner discovered it was not heart failure, this fellow might have been blamed. I shall go and question him now."

"Yeah, you do that," Ryan said. "Meantime, I'm getting Ms. Caruso out of here. Nina, go get dressed. We're going to the palace as soon as they can get us a car over here."

"Ryan, it's almost ten. We should wait until morning."

Tatro agreed. "Please, Signor McDonough. If you will stay, I shall post two guards at your door and more beside both elevators. On my word, no one will get past them."

Ryan was already shaking his head.

Tatro persisted. "I will go myself and oversee a meal prepared for the lady and for you."

Nina scoffed. "Thank you, *signore,* but I seemed to have lost my appetite. But I do think we should wait, Ryan."

Reluctantly, he acceded. "All right, but first thing tomorrow, we go to King Marcus with this."

"I guess we have to," she agreed reluctantly. "Who knows what this guy plans for us next?"

Not for *us,* Nina thought, for *me.* They both knew Ryan was not the target. After tonight's fright, she realized there was no place safe in Montebello, even the palace. After all, her brother had died right there on the palace grounds.

After Tatro and his men removed the dinner tray and left, Ryan locked the door and came to join her on the sofa. He sat close and took her hands in his. He said exactly what she expected him to say. "Nina, you'll have to leave."

She sighed wearily. "I know."

"The king will probably insist on it now. He'll make sure you have adequate protection wherever you go, so don't worry about that."

"I'll go home."

"No, that wouldn't be wise," he told her. "You need to go somewhere no one would expect you to go until we find out who's after you and why."

Well, that was easier said than done, she thought. "You know I don't have any relatives except those cousins in Italy and they're strangers. No friends that don't live in La Jolla. Where would you suggest I go?"

He seemed hesitant to answer, but finally did. "You could go to Savannah. I've still got connections there. Favors owing. I could make some calls, set you up with a safe place to stay, get the locals to keep an eye out for you. Hell, King Marcus even has a business located there, did you know that? Flies over there once in a while."

"But you don't," she guessed, "even though your father lives there?"

"No," he said. "I don't." A statement of fact. No explanation.

"Was he terrible to you as a boy?" she asked, giving him the benefit of the doubt. "Or to your mother maybe?"

She saw the answer in his eyes, though he said nothing for a long time. Finally, he answered simply with a small shake of his head. "No."

"So family's never been way up there on your list," she said, accepting what she had suspected all along.

This time he didn't answer. But she didn't miss the flicker of sadness, maybe even yearning, before he carefully concealed it behind that damned mask of his.

He wanted family, she realized. He wanted her. She couldn't see it now, but it had been there in his eyes before when he hadn't purposely hid it from her. The need was in his every touch, intentional or accidental. Or was it only her hope that made her imagine it? She had to find out before she left. "Come with me to Savannah, Ryan."

The silence stretched between them until she thought she would scream.

His stoic gaze slid away. "I can't."

Anger and frustration boiled up and over. She yanked her hands out of his and crossed her arms over her chest. "Oh, I forgot," she said, not caring that she sounded sarcastic and mean. Maybe anger would snap him out of this. "There's that precious job of yours, right?"

When he didn't reply, she added, "I guess it really *is* who you are."

He looked at her again, his expression as unreadable as it ever had been. Then he got up. "Go to bed, Nina. We should get up early in the morning and get this over with."

Nina left him and went to her room. There was nothing else to say. She had already thrown her pride away, revealed her feelings for him and had been soundly rejected. Tried to help him and he'd turned away.

Somehow that upset her more than the poisoned salad. There was a very good chance they would apprehend the person who did that. But for Ryan and her, there was no chance at all for anything to turn out the way it should.

Once she got on that plane back to the States, no matter which state she went to, she knew they would never meet again.

Chapter 12

Ryan breathed much easier when King Marcus acted predictably and ordered Nina to leave. She would go to Savannah on one of the private jets the royal family kept at hand. Ryan had already called in some favors last night and knew she would be safe once she reached Savannah.

After his pronouncement that Nina must leave, the king looked at Ryan. "Is it your considered opinion that these attempts are of local origin?"

"Looks that way, sir. Ms. Caruso?" He thought Nina should add her bit of information to back that up.

She nodded. "The man who delivered the meal did speak with an accent that sounded local. I know I've only been here a short while, but I did grow up with an Italian father and a Montebellan mother. This person said very little to me, but what he did say indicated to me that he was from here."

Ryan added, "One thing I do know. He could easily have killed her when he delivered the food. From Nina's description, he was certainly large enough to overpower her."

No need to list the ways that might have been done silently if the only object was to see her dead. Even now, Ryan shuddered at the thought of a garrote or a knife. Or someone's hands around Nina's neck, choking the life out of her.

"So how would you explain what he did? Your best guess."

"I think he was hired to get rid of Nina and told to make it seem accidental, Your Majesty. Death by natural cause. Either that, or he intended for the regular waiter to take the blame."

"Do you believe the incidents are related to Desmond's death?" the king asked.

"Anybody's guess, of course," Ryan answered, "but my instinct says yes. We have agreed that she should go to Savannah. No one will know to look for her there."

"Lorenzo will coordinate with our security staff there to assist with protection," the king said, then addressed Nina. "Mr. McDonough will escort you to your embassy now. Your consulate will arrange for guards to travel with you on a private flight. We believe you will feel safer with Americans at this point."

"Thank you, Your Majesty," Nina said.

She sounded dispirited and unconcerned, as if it mattered little where she went or who went with her. In spite of his relief at seeing her safely out of harm's way, Ryan couldn't deny an insistent urge to comfort her, to assure her he would always be there for her if she should need him. But, of course, he couldn't do that. He wouldn't be available. He would be here.

"We sincerely wish the best for you, my dear," King Marcus said. "And we are aggrieved that you have suffered such trials since arriving on our island. Perhaps someday when matters are settled and no danger remains, you will return."

Her smile looked shaky and faltered completely as she

answered. "I should not have come at all. I clearly see now that my interference in the investigation was uncalled for and unnecessary. Thank you for the invitation, but I won't be returning, Your Majesty."

The king stood, came around his desk and took Nina's hands in his. "Then farewell, little Nina, and be happy."

She curtsied, withdrew her hands and Ryan ushered her out. The king followed to the doorway and called him back. "One further word with you."

Ryan stepped back into the office while Nina walked down the corridor out of earshot. "Yes, sir?"

"You could accompany her. There are others capable of finishing this. Lorenzo will see to it."

Tempted as he was, Ryan knew he couldn't leave until he had closed the case. There were no *unsolveds* on his record. "I finish what I start, sir." He opened the door, then realized he hadn't been dismissed.

The king looked down the corridor to where Nina stood waiting. "That remains to be seen, does it not?"

Ryan knew he wasn't referring to the investigation. Without any further verbal comment, he nodded once.

Ursula marveled at Jean-Paul's nerve. He had argued against using the poison, saying it was too iffy. Even after the uproar his failing caused last night, he now seemed obsessed with doing the job. A matter of pride, he'd said. She, on the other hand, just wanted to get away from the man. He was sick.

He said he needed a crowd around Nina to do what he had in mind. She was leaving it up to him this time. All those phone calls to newspapers seemed weird. And the story he'd fed them about Nina, outrageous. That she had discovered a plot against the crown! She'd be covered up with press the minute she left the palace. Ursula couldn't see how that would help matters any.

Maybe he was smarter than she gave him credit for. He

was right about one thing: accidental death was damned hard to plan.

She was supposed to wait for him here in his room, then pay him before they checked out, both for completing the job and for the room. Right. Ursula adjusted her dark wig, stuffed her filmy nightie into her purse and went down the back stairs.

If Jean-Paul screwed this up, got caught and squealed, she wasn't about to be hanging around here waiting for the police to come after her. She'd never told him her real name or where she'd been staying before they met. Her tiny flat over in the artists' quarter was paid up through the end of the month. In cash. Nobody could find her there, least of all some loser like Jean-Paul.

It was a short distance to the American Embassy. The limousine stopped directly in front of the imposing granite building. A steep flight of steps led up to a portico now crowded with a gaggle of paparazzi. "Damn. Who alerted the press? I'm gonna have somebody's head for this!"

In spite of the inconvenience of wading through a badgering crowd, Ryan knew he should find a way to get Nina inside. His contact with her was to end right here. There probably was a back or side entrance, but the reporters would have that covered, too.

"I'm not taking you through that," he said. "We'll call and have guards sent to the airport."

"No, let's do it," Nina argued, reaching to open her door. "You're the one who insists on getting this over with. And for once, I agree! They're just reporters, Ryan. It might even help if they report I'm leaving."

Ryan reached for her arm and stopped her. "I said no."

She tugged away. "Don't be ridiculous. This is a public place with dozens of witnesses. Reporters with cameras, for goodness' sake! Who would be stupid enough to—"

"Okay, okay, I get your point, but I don't like this, Nina."

She sighed. "I'll tell them I'm leaving. If the story's in the papers, the killer will think that I've given up the investigation and gone home."

"We're not certain the threats to your life are connected to the investigation," Ryan reminded her.

"You know as well as I do that they are. All you have to do is watch who buys the next ticket to California. I won't be there anyway, even if they manage to slip by you. So come on," she said. "Let's do it."

Ryan pushed the intercom button and spoke to their driver and the two guards riding with them. "Paolo, you stay with the car. Arletti, Sergio, we surround her. Nobody gets close. Got that?"

They exited the vehicle. Ryan took point, leaving Arletti and Sergio to flank Nina. The swarm descended on them almost before they reached the steps and moved up just ahead and to either side of them, firing questions in English and Italian, bumping and shoving, juggling microphones and cameras.

"Ms. Caruso...Ms. Caruso! What about the threat to the king? Is it a terrorist plot?"

"Is it related to the troubles with Tamir?"

"Have you any word on your brother's murderer, Nina?"

"Is the threat to Prince Lucas? Will the coronation go as planned?"

The noise was deafening, the camera flashes blinding. Ryan fought his way through, cursing, feeling the tug of Nina's grip on the hem of his jacket.

Suddenly she let go. Ryan whirled just in time to see her tumble. Arletti was on his knees, in Ryan's way, scrabbling to prevent his own fall. Ryan's eye registered just for a split second, a man's face, a face that held no surprise, no eagerness for a story, only satisfaction. Ryan batted him aside, leaped over the guard, flew down the steps and reached Nina.

She lay sprawled about two-thirds of the way down. Knowing she would be trampled in seconds, he scooped her up and headed for the limousine, praying she had no injury he might be compounding.

"Go, go!" he ordered, motioning for Paolo to get them away from the locusts about to cover the car. He couldn't see Arletti. Sergio was running interference, blocking the advance the best he could, but he was only one man. Ryan shouted, "Floor it, Paolo! The hospital! Call ahead!" Tires screeched as the limo leaped forward.

Nina stirred then. She lay on her back on the seat where he had placed her. Ryan was on his knees beside her in the spacious floorboard. She tried to sit up.

"Be still," he ordered, placing his open hand over her middle. "Don't move!" She would be numb, almost surely in shock. He ran his hands over her lightly, checking for protruding bones and bleeding. "Do you hurt anywhere?"

Her laugh was thin, breathless, nearly hysterical. "Kidding, right?"

"Shh. I'm sorry. God, I am so sorry." He looked carefully at her face for the first time and saw the reddened skin and goose egg rising at her hairline on her forehead. "God, Nina," he rasped, resisting the need to grab her close and hold her. Fingers trembling, he gently brushed back her hair. A straight purple-red imprint cut directly through the bruise that was darkening even as he watched. "Your head hit the corner of a step."

"Several steps, I think," she gasped and reached up to touch it.

Ryan took her hand away and held on to it. "Try not to move now. Just be still." He had to get calm. Think rationally. He sucked in a deep breath, blew it out forcefully and unclenched his eyes. "Okay." He patted her hand, then checked her pulse. It raced, just as his was doing. Respiration was shallow. "You're shocky. But you'll be all right. I promise." She had to be. She *had* to be.

He shrugged out of his jacket and laid it over her. "Now then, listen to me, Nina. Can you wiggle your toes a little?" She had lost one of her shoes in the fall. He yanked off the other one and waited. "Wiggle your damned toes!" he shouted, frowning at her.

She had passed out. He cursed, foully and creatively, wishing he could get his hands around the neck of the son of a bitch who'd pushed her.

The face he had seen immediately afterward flashed through his mind. "I've got him, hon," he growled under his breath as he held Nina's hand, his finger on the pulse at her wrist. "I *know* him now."

For the time being, he put thoughts of retribution aside and kept watch over Nina. The short ride to the hospital seemed like hours. The emergency room crew took over and ordered him to the waiting room. He ignored them.

He followed her gurney up to X-ray, never letting her out of his sight. Only after they had her situated in Intensive Care and the doctor asked to speak with him, did Ryan leave her side. A nurse was with her, once again checking her vital signs.

"Does she have family here?" the doctor asked when they were outside in the hallway.

"No family. I'm her…" What was he? He had to say something. "I'm her, uh, significant other." For now, anyway.

The doctor frowned. "Lover?"

"We're not married…yet," Ryan added, hoping that would be sufficient to override doctor-patient confidentiality.

"But she is not—"

"Dammit, tell me how bad this is! She's got no one else. I'm the one who cares about her, okay? Give it to me straight."

The doctor shrugged and sighed. "She has a concussion. Though no bones were broken, she has severe bruising to most of her body. We'll have to keep her here under close observation."

"How long?" Ryan asked.

"I cannot say. The head injury rendered her unconscious and we must wait until she wakes to assess—"

"She *was* conscious," Ryan interrupted. "She spoke to me in the car. Made sense, too."

"Ah, good. That is very reassuring," the doctor said with a smile. "Then I expect she will come around soon and we can move her to a regular room. Only when she wakes again will I be able to evaluate and suggest a possible time for her release. We might need more tests and she will certainly need our care. So she must stay for now."

"Oh, I *want* her to stay. And I'm staying with her!"

The doctor placed a hand on his shoulder. "I regret that will be impossible, sir. Once she is moved to a private room, then perhaps."

"But you don't understand, doctor. Someone's trying to kill this woman and today's not the first time. That danger's just as great as any of her present injuries. No, greater. I'll have King Marcus call and verify this if you don't believe me."

That got his attention. "The king?"

"Yes. Ms. Caruso is half sister to the king's nephew, the one who was murdered."

The doctor's dark eyes widened. "Ah, yes. *Caruso.* I saw the article in the news when she arrived. I did not make the connection."

He worried his chin with the tips of his fingers for a minute, then came to a decision. "Then she must stay in this unit. It is more isolated," he added by way of explanation. "Why not have guards stationed outside the doors to screen everyone who enters?"

"I can do that," Ryan said, "but I don't want to leave her."

"No one likes to leave a loved one when they are hurt, but I assure you, she will not be alone. And you may wait beside her door if you wish."

The nurse came to the door. "Dr. Ponti, she is awake and asking for someone."

"Me," Ryan declared, worry and impatience overruling politeness, rules and anything else that got in his way. He pushed past the nurse. "Nina?"

She reached one hand out to him and he grasped it, bringing it to his lips as he leaned against the side rails of her bed. "Oh, baby, you scared the life out of me! Thank God you're okay."

"I was pushed," she said, her voice a mere whisper. However, she sounded more as if she didn't want anyone to overhear than weak from her injuries.

"I know," he told her. "Don't you worry. I saw his face. I'll get him."

"You do that," she said, squinting against the light. "And do it *now,* would you?"

The doctor had followed Ryan in and was looking at him pointedly.

Ryan kissed her hand again and placed it on the bed beside her. "I will. Let me get somebody up here to stand sentry and that bastard's toast before the day's out. You've got my word on it, Nina."

She closed her eyes. "Always get your man, don't you?"

"Always," he assured her, then winced when she turned away.

"Well, *go!*" the doctor urged. "We have work to do here and you are a hindrance at the moment." He smiled to temper the order. "She will be fine."

Ryan nodded, scribbled down his cell-phone number and tucked it into the breast pocket of the doctor's white coat. "You call me if she needs me. For *anything.*"

After a final prolonged look at Nina, he left her room to make his call to Lorenzo.

A half hour later, leaving Nina under heavier guard than the crown jewels, Ryan went downstairs. On the way, he removed his suit coat and tie and rolled up his sleeves. His whole shirt was wet with the cold sweat of adrenaline. No time to change, though. He was pretty sure he wouldn't have to go far or wait long to locate his prey.

When he stepped off the elevators in the main entrance lobby, he noticed many of the reporters had followed and were hounding the staff at the counter there for information.

He quickly ducked behind one of the decorative fluted columns that flanked the bank of elevators and watched.

His gaze flew from face to face, estimating about fifteen people. It was hard to count when they were swarming. Most of the local press, he knew at least by sight, but there were some freelancers, the ghouls from all over the globe who hounded celebs and the royals. But he didn't see the man he was looking for among them. Not yet.

Ryan waited. He knew if he were the one after Nina and had failed in this attempt, he would be right here, concealing himself in this bunch of scavengers. The perp would be here to discover her condition if nothing else. He would be hoping everyone who cared about Nina was too upset right now to be looking for him.

There! Ryan suddenly recognized him. He had donned a brown cap and horn-rimmed glasses and was carrying a notebook of some kind. Rushing him was not a good idea. As soon as the rest of the pack saw Ryan, they would be on him like a bad case of hives. No way could he take the guy down in that crowd. Better to wait until they dispersed.

He watched for a good five minutes, one arm propped against the column, still out of sight of anyone who did not approach the elevators. Ryan straightened when he saw the man edge away from the others and start to move in his direction.

Carefully Ryan kept out of sight. His target drew closer then veered toward the double doors just past the matching column on the other side of the elevators. So he was going upstairs, probably to try for another shot at Nina. Perfect.

Ryan waited until the doors opened and closed. Then he followed. When he entered the enclosed stairwell, he could hear the rapid scuff of footsteps just above, probably nearing the door to the first floor.

Ryan wished he were armed, but had known better than to carry when he was visiting either the palace or the Embassy. That's what the damned guards were supposed to be for.

He took the steps two at a time, knowing he couldn't muffle the sound of his hard-soled dress shoes. He flew, unable to hear the other man's progress for his own clatter. The door to the second floor was just closing softly on its pneumatic hinge as he reached it.

Ryan halted for a second, listened, heard nothing on the stairs. He pulled the door open and rushed through just in time to see the elevator begin to slide shut. Damn! If he didn't get on the stick, the bastard would make it all the way up to ICU.

He grabbed the elevator door just in time to stop its closing. And he smiled at the man inside. "Gotcha," he muttered.

His quarry scrambled to get out. Ryan tackled, grappling to subdue while the man fought one-handed, clawing at Ryan's face and trying to bite, of all things.

The doors closed while they scuffled and the elevator started up. Ryan reared back and clipped the guy on the chin just as a gunshot exploded, deafening within the small space.

The man beneath him collapsed, the clawing hand now dormant, the other trapped beneath the body. Ryan reached under him, securing the wrist, knowing what it held. With his free hand, he felt for the pulse at the neck.

"Help...me," the man gasped.

"Tell me who hired you and I might think about it," Ryan growled. He couldn't hear a damned thing. "And talk *loud!*"

"Please...."

"Who, dammit? Who paid you?" He fisted his hand in the guy's shirtfront and gave him a shake. "You dick around with me, sheep-dip, and I'll kill you right now."

"No name. Woman. The Am-Amer—"

"American?" Ryan demanded, shaking him again when he didn't respond.

The eyes were open, glazed now, the mouth slack.

Well, *damn.* Ryan got off the guy and rolled him over. The bullet had entered just above the waist. A .22 caliber. Would have bounced around, maybe hit the heart. Something vital, anyway. He was dead.

The doors opened and a woman screamed. Ryan sighed and tried to ignore the ringing in his ears. He had wanted the bastard dead pretty bad, but not like this. Not accidentally. And sure as hell not before he got more information out of him.

He reached up and punched the button to keep the doors open until hospital security arrived. The screaming woman had run back toward the nurses' station. Ryan could hear a commotion down the hall now that his eardrums were recovering from the report of the gunshot.

Quickly, using his handkerchief, Ryan fished for the guy's wallet and read the name and address on his license. He checked the amount of cash in the leather folder and returned it intact to the pocket where he'd found it.

"Damn, damn, damn," he muttered, looking down at the lifeless thug sprawled on the floor, gun still clutched in his hand. Ryan hadn't touched that, even to remove it. The jerk was good and dead. He wanted no questions about whether the man had back-shot himself.

Two uniforms appeared, weapons drawn. Not hospital

employees, either. These were the real McCoy. He knew both of them, though not well. "Hey, Mylonas. Take care of this for me, would you? I'm here on royal orders. Got someone under protection up in ICU. This guy was trying to get to her."

"Yes, we know about Ms. Caruso," Mylonas said with a curt nod. "We heard about the embassy incident. That's why we were here." He proceeded to pat Ryan down, checking for weapons.

His partner, whose name Ryan couldn't recall, had immediately disarmed the dead guy, bagged the .22, and was now busy checking the body for signs of life. Ryan watched the second cop shake his head at Mylonas.

"You must come with us to the station house, Mr. McDonough," Captain Mylonas said, sounding as official as he looked in his snappy green uniform. "Just a formality, to be sure."

Officer Starch-butt did relent enough to offer a half-hearted smile as he took the cuffs off his belt and snapped one on Ryan's right wrist. "Sorry. Regulations, you see."

"You're liking this way too much, but okay." Ryan knew the drill. He had hoped mentioning the *royal orders* thing would get him off the hook, at least for a couple of hours. Obviously not. "No problem," he said as the other cuff clicked shut behind his back.

No real reason not to go peacefully without a fuss. Nina was safe for a while. Maybe for good. At least the bitch who had hired that misbegotten excuse for a human would need time to find another one like him. If she could. At least he'd confirmed it was a woman he was after. An American. Maybe. Or that last garbled word might have been a reference to the target. Nina.

This perp was a small-time hood off the street. While it was true that professional hitters often used a cheap .22 caliber throwaway just like that one, Ryan imagined they generally dressed a lot better and had more than the price of lunch in their pockets. And any pro worth his salt knew how to fight. This one was broke, dressed like a wanna-be and fought like a girl.

He winced at the politically incorrect thought. He also remembered that, unless he was way off the mark, some *girl* had taken out Desmond Caruso without much trouble. Nope, only a fool underestimated a female's abilities just because she was female.

His hunch told him there was something bigger going on here than some frustrated bunny knocking the playboy upside the head in a fit of rage. If that was all there was to it, she would have hopped the next plane out of here and that would have been that.

But she obviously hadn't. She had hired ol' Slick back there in the elevator to kill Nina and make it seem accidental. That fact right there, Ryan thought, threw up the red flag.

It wasn't Nina's cousins, up to no good, greedy for any inheritance. That much Ryan had already determined. So the motive for all this had been narrowed down to two things now—hatred for all things named Caruso, or fear of discovery. The first didn't make any sense. Desmond and Nina hadn't even known the same people since they were kids. That left fear.

The means, obvious. Motive, probable enough to run with. All Ryan needed to do now was find out who had the opportunity. He would solve this one. Things finally were falling into place.

If he didn't count personal things. He loved Nina Caruso. As surely as he was doomed to live without her, he loved her. Funny, that little epiphany should occur right now. Even more ironic that it didn't surprise him. The subconscious was a wonderful, awful thing sometimes in the crazy way it worked.

Ryan barely paid attention as he was assisted into a police vehicle and hauled off to the station downstairs from the lab he'd helped set up himself. Instead his mind was now fully focused on the woman back at King Augustus Hospital in ICU.

What if he told Nina exactly how he felt and asked her to come back to Montebello when all this was over? She had assured the king she wouldn't.

There were bad memories for her here that must heavily outweigh any good ones she might have. Ryan certainly could identify with that. It was the bad memories of Savannah that kept him from ever going back there, that had sent him halfway around the world to live in circumstances as different as he could manage to find.

Soon as she was feeling better and in a mood to talk it over, he would see what she thought about it. First, he had to finish up the investigation. She'd just have to understand why he couldn't let it go.

Chapter 13

Ryan chafed at delays. Patience was not his long suit anyway and especially not now, with Nina lying in the hospital. At least she wasn't in any immediate danger, he thought.

He sat in one of the interrogation rooms, a place much like the ones he had used many times as a detective to question suspects and witnesses.

They had brought him a soft drink and provided him a bandage to stick on the place where one of the perp's fingernails had cut into his chin. He pressed his sore knuckles against the cold can of soda and moved the paper on which he'd written his statement away from the circle of sweat left by the condensation.

The dead guy wasn't prime talent. In fact, he must be the scraping off the bottom of the barrel when it came to hired killers. Ryan figured this meant two things. First, whoever was calling the shots didn't have good contacts here, or very much money. And second, Nina would be safe if she left the country. It would take both money and resources to find her. Even more to do something about it.

Most likely Desmond Caruso had been up to no good, mixed up with some unsavory element here in Montebello. God only knew what that was. But someone, some woman, obviously considered Nina a threat.

Detective Andreas entered the room wearing a smile. "We have identified the man you killed," he said, beaming.

Ryan sighed and shoved the paper toward Andreas's end of the table. "I didn't kill him."

"A matter of semantics. The two of you struggled. The man died."

"I told you, the idiot shot himself trying to get the weapon out of his pants," Ryan snapped. "You arresting me or what?"

"No, no, of course not," Andreas insisted, picking up the statement and eyeing it with a smile. "This fellow was wanted for several other offenses. We probably should thank you."

"I did not shoot him," Ryan insisted. "I was unarmed."

"Yes, we know." Andreas smiled even wider and gestured toward the door. "You may go."

For a second, Ryan thought he had misunderstood. "Go?"

"Certainly. Only I would ask you not to leave the island just yet. We might need more information from you."

"You've got all I know. The man tried to kill Nina Caruso. At least twice. It's all right there," Ryan said, pointing to the account he had just written. A recap of the truth that he had told a number of times since entering the interrogation room. He stood and headed for the door. "I'm going back to the hospital, just so you'll know."

Andreas followed him out, practically swaggering. "Certainly. We will go with you."

"Just give me a ride to my apartment so I can get my car."

"My partner and I will accompany you. I insist."

Ryan's patience was almost gone, but he made the effort to be polite. "Suit yourself."

The ride back to the hospital was silent, the two officers in the front seat watchful as the police car worked its way through the heavy traffic.

Andreas had not come with them after all. The fact that two uniforms, armed to the teeth, were along meant that someone had ordered Ryan protected. Lorenzo, probably. Andreas had called the duke's office immediately at Ryan's insistence.

The cops flanked him going into the hospital and all the way up to Intensive Care. At the desk outside the closed unit, Ryan asked to see Nina. There were no guards around. Nobody but a couple of nurses.

"She is not here," one of the nurses informed him.

"Could I have the number of her room?" Ryan asked, relieved. They had moved her to the private room already. That meant he could stay with her.

The woman hesitated, then said, "Sir, she is no longer within the hospital."

"Then where the hell is she?" he demanded.

"Gone, sir. I do not know where. The men who were waiting about here and some others who arrived took her down in the service elevator."

Ryan grabbed the phone and punched in the duke's number. This was Lorenzo's doing, he knew it. The woman who answered put him on hold and left him there. He slammed down the receiver and rushed back the way he had come. The cops followed.

He knew exactly where they had taken Nina, at least initially. "I have to get to the airport," Ryan snapped.

In all fairness, he had to admit it was a good move to get her away this soon. She needed to be out of here before some other goon went after her. This way, she'd be in the air before anyone knew she was gone, and her destination would remain a secret.

Ryan just couldn't get his mind around her leaving without some kind of goodbye. He would never see her again. That thought brought a rush of something like panic inside him.

"No, no. It's best," he muttered under his breath. He said it again to try to banish his unreasonable anger. Nina had been snatched out of his grasp, out of his life, without so much as a wave.

He drew in a deep breath, closed his eyes and fought for control. It would be stupid to arrive at the airport and deck the duke before he said hello. *Damn Lorenzo.*

That was the reason he'd been held at the station and grilled for so long. Lorenzo had ordered it.

Ryan and Nina had been joined at the hip ever since the day she'd arrived in Montebello. Wherever he had gone, she'd been right with him. Anyone looking for her would certainly look for him to find her. Yes, it had been smart for Lorenzo to get Nina to safety before whoever hired that gun found someone to replace him. Ryan couldn't argue with that.

"Turn around," he ordered the cop at the wheel. "I've changed my mind. Take me home."

The dark gaze of the driver met his in the rearview mirror. "Are you certain, sir?"

"Yeah," Ryan muttered. He would arrive too late to catch Nina anyway. The police would not have released him unless Lorenzo gave the okay, and he wouldn't have done that unless Nina was already off the ground.

"Might as well do something constructive," he said, ore or less to himself. He would get in touch with Lorenzo, find out for certain where Nina had gone, then try to get some work done. He would drive back to the police station, upstairs to the lab, see if Franz had found any new developments since this morning.

Back to square one, nothing left but the job. He hadn't really gained much ground in square two anyway. Nina was better off. Safe now. This was what he wanted, wasn't it? What he had wanted all along.

So he loved her. Big deal. Love sure didn't equal happiness. He should have learned that a long time ago. He had really, but he'd been stupid enough to forget it for a while.

Now he could get somewhere, devote his full attention to the case and not have to worry about her every damned minute of the day and night. Wouldn't even have to think about her.

He would just take a minute, thank God she wasn't lying in the morgue now, and then get on with what was left of his life. At least she hadn't left him with nightmares.

Nina lay in the rear section of the Gulfstream jet. Never in her life had she seen such incredible luxury on a plane. Everywhere there was exotic wood, rich fabrics and butter-soft leather. Appointments for a king and his royal entourage.

Ryan would probably call this tacky, too, as he had the hotel. The thought brought tears to her eyes, but she smiled in spite of them and tried to divert her mind.

The cabin was divided into three areas. She had been placed aft and left alone, ostensibly to give her quiet time for recovery. She occupied the sofa, which was large enough to qualify as a bed. The carpets were so thick she probably could have rested comfortably on the floor. There were two club chairs in front of the sofa where she lay, one holding a bag of toiletries and makeup someone had brought for her.

She had been able to shower and change in the spacious lavatory. Thankfully, someone had brought clothes for her to replace the flimsy gown she had worn when they brought her from the hospital. The clothes weren't hers. Though she dressed well, she had never dressed quite *this* well. The loose-fitting, pale yellow raw-silk pantsuit was obviously hand-tailored, as was the silk underwear. The designer shoes were an exact match for the outfit. Her size, too.

While she liked to imagine she was dressed in one of the princesses' ensembles, she realized the clothing was new, probably purchased immediately before the flight. A weekender packed with similar garments had been provided. She wondered who had shopped for her.

She had to admit she'd hoped that Ryan would appear before takeoff. But he hadn't come. Hadn't even sent a message by anyone. He must have taken her at her word when she'd ordered him to go find the man who had pushed her. With that one-track mind of his, he probably didn't even realize she was gone yet.

The three guards who accompanied her were Americans, one of them a woman. They had left her to go forward where there was another seating area with tables. She could hear muted conversation and the vague clinking of silverware.

One of the guys had a Brooklyn accent, the other man and the woman were obviously from somewhere in the South. All looked extremely capable as bodyguards, and from the bulges beneath their suit jackets, she could tell they were armed.

Nina had refused anything to eat. Hunger was the last thing on her mind. Her head still ached and worry wasn't helping. Now that she'd had a nap, a shower and had gotten over the surprise rush from the hospital to the plane, she needed to assert herself here.

No one had told her their destination yet. The duke had overseen her removal from the hospital, ignored her questions and simply told her that she need not fear. Ha. Who wouldn't be apprehensive, flying God only knew how high in this airborne palace, with no idea where it would set down?

The female agent named Martha who had assisted her in showering and dressing hadn't said anything about where they would land, either. But then, Nina hadn't asked. They had treated her like an injured child, and Nina was embarrassed to admit she had acted like one. That fall must have shaken her more than she'd thought.

What worried her most right now was what she would do once they landed. Where would she be and would she know anyone at all there? How soon could she safely resume her old life? And how would she ever forget Ryan McDonough?

She never would, of course. Not in a million years. But she would have to put their relationship—if she could call it that—in some sort of perspective in order to get on with things.

"Please don't let this plane land in Savannah," she whispered to herself. Nina didn't think she could deal with the hope that Ryan might suddenly decide to come home while she was there. That she might see him again. He'd made it clear that wouldn't happen.

Nina sniffed, grabbed a tissue from the box on the handsomely carved table beside the chair, let herself cry. Five minutes, she told herself. Five minutes was all she could afford to spare for this wave of disappointment or self-pity or whatever it was that made her heart feel cracked in two. Then she would get up, wash her face, comb her hair and join the others.

She might not like the information she got, but she definitely meant to demand it anyway.

The flight was a long one and they put down in Savannah, after all. They were staying at a hotel near the airport. Nina was glad she'd insisted on a room to herself. The guard, Martha Baxter, didn't seem offended. She simply arranged for an adjoining room.

Martha informed her that King Marcus apparently had an excellent security force at the plant he owned locally. They were coordinating with several of the people who worked for that company to serve as Nina's temporary protectors. The three embassy guards were to transfer her care to them this afternoon and fly back to Montebello in the morning. The new guys supposedly were taking her to a safe house.

Nina resented that, but was resigned to added weeks of seclusion—this time without the benefit of having Ryan around. She took a shower, changed into one of the casual outfits someone had bought for her and flipped on the television for the early morning news.

She was idly thumbing through a magazine with pictures of Savannah's tourist sites, wishing she could see some of them, when the name McDonough jumped out from one of the advertisements. *Custom-made boats. Small craft. Call William McDonough.* Ryan once mentioned his dad making boats. She smiled at the simple, straightforward ad.

If this was Ryan's dad, she wished she could call and reassure him that his son was perfectly all right and that she knew firsthand that Ryan had absolutely no intention of doing anything foolish. The man must have been a worried wreck when he'd phoned Joe Braca to see whether Ryan had been about to kill himself.

Martha had warned her not to contact anyone she knew, but Nina rationalized. She didn't actually *know* Bill McDonough. What could it hurt? Nina looked at the phone. It wouldn't do to call from her room. But she could sneak downstairs to a pay phone.

By the time she had and was dialing the number, an idea had formed. What if she disappeared and arranged for her *own* safe house? If no one knew where she was, including the king's people, she would be just as safe as she would be hidden away in a place where they'd give her no freedom at all. Heck, she could buy a straw hat and sunglasses and roam around Savannah all she liked. And after she'd seen the sights, she would be free to leave.

The ringing stopped. "Hello," a woman answered.

"Is the William McDonough at this number the father of Ryan McDonough?" Nina asked politely.

"Yes, is something wrong? Is Ryan all right?" the woman asked urgently.

"He's fine. I'm a friend of his who just flew back from Montebello. I thought I would call and give his dad a first-hand account of how well Ryan's doing. I know he was worried about him."

An audible sigh of relief. "Hold on. I'll get him."

"This is Bill McDonough," said a deep voice that sounded very like Ryan. "You know our boy?"

Nina laughed just thinking about anyone calling Ryan a boy. He was all man. She could certainly attest to that. "I know him very well, Mr. McDonough."

"Trish said you just flew in. If you've got time for a visit, I can run right out there to the airport and pick you up."

"I'm at a hotel by the airport. Why don't I take a taxi?"

"Nothing doing. I'll be there in fifteen minutes. Which hotel?"

She told him. "I'll meet you out front," she said. "I'll be wearing a brown pantsuit, carrying a large tan shoulder bag."

"Look for a white Chevy pickup," he told her with a chuckle, "and an old gray-headed guy in a red shirt."

He sounded excited. Nina wondered if he'd still be thrilled when she asked him for a huge favor.

She looked at her watch, double-checked it with the time on the clock in the lobby and then hurried back upstairs. She had to decide what to take with her when she made her escape.

It had been three days since Nina disappeared from the hospital. Ryan knew he was in no position to storm Loren-zo's office, but he wanted to. His frustration and worry had just about reached the breaking point. No one would give him any clue as to where Nina had been sent, who was protecting her or when he could expect to find out anything. Just like witness protection back in the States.

Silence on the matter was absolute and no one in authority would see him, either at the palace or the American Embassy.

He had phoned his contacts in Savannah only to find they had been waiting to hear from him about the woman he was sending there for protection. The call to her office in La Jolla proved just as fruitless. No one there had heard from her since she'd left for Montebello. They said she had taken six weeks of vacation time and they didn't expect her back for two more.

Computer checks determined she hadn't used her plastic to pay for anything, and Ryan knew she didn't have much cash. He had checked her purse and luggage the night of the fire. Someone was looking after her every need. King's orders, of course.

Dammit, where the hell was she?

Between phone calls he had tried to immerse himself in the case to see whether he could arrive at any new conclusions.

He sat in his office now, files and evidence reports spread out across his desk along with his own scribbled notes and photos of two dead men. Desmond Caruso and Ankri Topoli, alias Jean-Paul Trignant, the man who had been hired to kill Nina. Andreas had been very cooperative when Ryan had asked for Topoli's police record. He was small potatoes, just like Ryan had figured.

The phone rang, interrupting Ryan's ruminations. He picked it up, expecting it to be Joe, who was running down the list of Topoli's known associates. "McDonough," he answered absently.

"You rang?" asked a deep voice.

Lorenzo. Ryan sat up straight and slapped down the

photo he was holding. "About every hour on the hour," Ryan snapped. "Where is she?"

"Leave that to me. You have enough to do."

Ryan took a deep breath, struggling to control his temper. "Okay, look. I agree it shouldn't be common knowledge, but my phone's not tapped. No one's listening. Tell me where the hell you took her!" Despite his attempt to rein in his anger, it was about to get away from him.

"Is there any progress on your end?" Lorenzo asked, his tone brisk and businesslike as he ignored Ryan's demand.

Ryan bit his tongue. Coming off like a raving lunatic wouldn't persuade Lorenzo to tell him anything. Probably nothing would. He might as well play it cool and hope the duke would let something slip in conversation.

With that in mind, he answered. "We've been going over Topoli's bank and phone records. He made a deposit this week. Not a fortune, but more than he was used to getting, judging by former deposits. He received two calls earlier, both from public phones here in San Sebastian. I don't think he was responsible for the fire or the break-in at Nina's apartment. He was probably hired after those incidents took place. You got anything new on that or the case?"

"My people have zeroed in on the access to the guest-house angle, both for the murder and the fire. Though you have already interviewed the guards on duty, we are taking it further, reviewing background investigations used for hiring. In essence, running them again in much greater detail."

"Include their social lives, would you?" Ryan suggested.

"Of course. If anything turns up, you'll know."

"Thanks. Now about Nina..." Ryan said. 'You've talked with her?"

The short silence was telling enough without words.

"Dammit, man, how do you know she's okay if you aren't in contact?" Ryan barked.

"I promise I will get back to you soon," Lorenzo said evasively.

Ryan slammed down the receiver. He couldn't stand this much longer. He would have to go and find her. The thought brought him up short. No, he couldn't even think about doing that. She was fine, wherever she was. No reason to think she wasn't. If *he* had this much trouble locating her, surely no one else could.

But had that head injury of hers gotten better or worse? Was she alone among strangers? Did she miss him as much as he missed her?

Ryan cursed. Deliberately, he picked up one of the files and reread it, trying with everything in him to get his full attention back where it was supposed to be.

Later in the day, he decided to go back to the apartment and grab a couple of hours' sleep. He'd spent two nights now frequenting the places where Topoli used to hang out, talking to people who had known him, especially the women. So far, none of them had any apparent connection to Desmond Caruso. Ryan was exhausted, sleep deprived and worried sick.

On the way home, he passed Pete's place and pulled over. Maybe one of Pete's many relatives could get some information for him about where Nina had gone. Suddenly he felt hungry. And hopeful.

Pete stood behind the bar, wiping it down with a towel. He looked up and grinned. "Hey, man, whazzup?"

Ryan slid onto one of the stools and made himself comfortable. "I need some info, Pete." He quickly explained about Nina's fall and her sudden disappearance from the hospital while the police were questioning him.

"Dirty pool, taking you downtown like that. You oughta sue or somethin'," Pete said. "Meantime, you want something to eat?"

Ryan nodded. "Fix me one of those grease grenades." He hesitated a second, then added, "And pour me a Guinness."

Pete's eyes rounded comically. Then he frowned. "I dunno, Mac. You been on the wagon a long time now. Just 'cause she's gone ain't no reason to—"

"Oh, for God's sake, Pete. Just give me a Guinness. I promise not to get drunk and bust up your place. Okay?"

Casting him a speculative look, Pete complied. He found one in the cooler, popped off the cap, grabbed a clean mug, tilted it and poured. Then he set it down, and the partially empty bottle beside it. "There you go. Knock yerself out."

Ryan fingered the glass handle and stared into the foaming dark liquid as he listened to Pete shout into the kitchen for the burger and fries. Years now since he'd had a drink of any kind. Was this to dull the edge of his worry? Was it to calm that jumpiness he'd felt since the moment he realized Nina was gone?

"No," he said decisively, "I just like the taste."

He was well aware of Pete watching him, pretending not to as he halfheartedly continued wiping down the bar.

Ryan took a sip, savoring the dark smoky flavor, then wiped the foam off his lips. "You think any of your folks can find out where they took her?"

Pete's eyes widened slightly. "You don't *know?*"

"Nope. Deep dark secret, apparently."

"I'll ask around," Pete told him, still keeping an eye on the beer Ryan held. "We got two cousins at the airport. You check for flight plans? Royals got to file 'em just like anybody else."

"No access except through the duke's office and he's the one keeping the lid on this. Trouble is, I can't figure out why he won't just say where she is." He took another swig of his beer.

"Maybe he wants to find out how bad you want to

know,'' Pete suggested. ''You're hung up on this chick, ain't you?''

Ryan laughed without any humor at all. ''Yeah. Looks like it.''

''Then you better go find her instead of sittin' around here guzzling stout, doncha think?''

Pete turned when Maria came out of the kitchen carrying a plate. He took it from her and plunked it down in front of Ryan. ''You eat before you go, though. That,'' he said, inclining his head toward the beer, ''sits pretty heavy on a empty stomach. You ain't been eatin', have you?''

''Not much,'' Ryan admitted. He didn't want to now, but knew Pete would worry if he didn't. So he ate. To his surprise, he enjoyed every bite and cleaned his plate. But he purposely left a third of the Guinness in the mug and also what remained in the bottle after Pete had poured it.

Half a beer. He could leave it. Ryan felt better, stronger. At least he now knew he wasn't physically addicted to alcohol, though he admitted he had needed it like his next breath at one time. A time when reality had been too painful to face.

''Once in a while we all get throwed, boy,'' Pete said. ''Don't mean we got to stay down.''

Ryan looked up, startled out of his thoughts.

''Yeah, I know 'bout your wife and kid. This whole damn island's like a friggin' beauty parlor, way the gossip flies.''

Ryan didn't mind Pete's knowing. There was more empathy there than pity. Pete had been *throwed* himself by events in 'Nam. Ryan didn't care who knew about his tragedy as long as he didn't have to discuss what had happened. He wasn't up to that yet and might never be. But it was good to realize the horror had faded enough that he could hear it mentioned in passing without sliding into dark depression for days.

At last, it had taken a place in the past where it belonged.

"Gossip may fly, but there are still a *few* secrets not making the rounds," Ryan said, more or less to himself. Like where Nina was. Like who had killed Desmond and why they wanted Nina out of the way.

Pete pursed his lips and shrugged. "What you got to ask yourself is which secret you need to uncover the most."

"You mean *first,*" Ryan said, pushing off the bar stool.

"No, I mean *most,* 'cause I don't think you got time to do both. Think about it. Longer she's gone, the more it looks like you don't give a rat's ass." Pete removed Ryan's plate and utensils, dumping them noisily into a plastic bin behind the bar. He looked pointedly at the beer bottle and the mug. "You done?"

Ryan nodded, reached for his wallet and slapped down a handful of lira. "Thanks, Pete."

"Any ol' time."

The decision turned out to be a lot more difficult than Ryan had imagined. When talking to Pete, it had seemed so obvious. Nina's whereabouts, her safety, Ryan's being with her, were paramount. No question. Nothing else came close. But on the drive home, things muddied up a little.

On the one hand, he felt relatively certain Nina was in no danger now. He could proceed with the investigation into Desmond's murder unhampered, finish it, then go looking for her. But on the other hand, Ryan instinctively knew if he didn't pursue her right away, he didn't stand a chance in hell of convincing her, after he'd finished his business here, that she meant more to him than anything else in his life.

She'd made it very clear that she wanted a man who wasn't obsessed with his job. One who put her first. Which he did. Didn't he?

God, he hated to leave things undone. Habits of a lifetime were damned hard to break. And yet, if he didn't prove to Nina that what they had found together was more precious to him than any stupid case he was working on, *he* would be undone.

"Come with me," she had said when she'd thought she was headed for Savannah.

That invitation had been a plea, Ryan realized. But it had been a plea for more than his joining her on the trip, more than their staying together as a couple. She had wanted him to confront what he had been unable to face when he'd broken with his family, his friends and his home.

In her estimation, family was everything, the core of a person's existence. He had given her the impression that it meant nothing to him.

If only he'd been able to tell her how the loss of his immediate family had disabled every feeling inside him except for grief. How he had not been able to share that with a father who didn't seem to understand the meaning of the word grief.

His dad had understood, of course, but had somehow found the secret of rebuilding what he had lost after Ryan's mother had died. And he'd done that pretty damned quickly.

The old man must have an inner strength he'd neglected to pass on. Ryan thought just maybe it was catching up to him now. Maybe too late.

Nina didn't even know what it was he had run from, but she had made the attempt to help him put his life back together. And he had refused.

Ryan pulled into his parking space, cut the engine and sat there staring into space. He knew what he had to do. And where he had to start, making things right. Not a good thing to be up against when the taste of that Guinness was still on his tongue.

Chapter 14

"Hello, Dad?"

"Ryan! Funny you should call me. I was just thinking about you." Silence fell, not even broken by the usual static.

"Good things, I hope," Ryan said, trying to put a smile in his voice. "Sorry I didn't call last weekend. I know I said I would when we talked last time, but things were busy around here. I'm on a case."

"Ah. Well, that's okay. We've been sort of busy here, too."

Ryan waited for more, for the usual effusive greeting and almost desperate attempt to engage him in conversation that always came when he called home, but there was another long pause.

"Dad? Did I catch you at a bad time? Is something wrong?"

"No, no, nothing's the matter." Ryan heard a sigh. Then an almost palpable attempt to make his words sound normal. "You want to tell me about this case you're working on, son? Might help to talk it out. You used to do that when…when you were on the force.''

Ryan sensed something lying just beneath the surface of what his father was saying. He had rarely, if ever, gone into detail about anything he worked on as a detective. His father built boats. Ryan had tried to shield him from the gruesome and sometimes dangerous things a cop went through on the job. Instead of pointing that out now, he simply said, ''Okay.''

Then, step by step, he began to relate all that had happened beginning with Desmond Caruso's death and the king assigning him to the investigation. He ended with Nina's disappearance, though he carefully said nothing about his feelings for Nina or the fact that they'd once wound up in bed together.

His account was punctuated by his father's wordless sounds of interest and understanding, the kind of replies people made over the phone so you'd know they were listening and interested. But Ryan noted there were no questions, an unusual response for any of their conversations.

''So that's it,'' Ryan said as he finished. ''I've got it to the point where I know the killer was a woman, maybe an American, and that she's most likely still here somewhere.''

''So you're close to wrapping it up then,'' his dad said. ''Well, I'm not surprised. You got stick-to-itiveness, that's for sure.''

Ryan realized he wasn't accomplishing what he had intended with the call. He was latching on to impersonal topics, putting off what he knew had to be said, hiding behind the job again. He took a breath and dived right in.

''Dad, I didn't call to talk about work. I wanted to say that I thought we should try to be a family. All of us. Put the past where it belongs. That's what I called to tell you. I know we touched on this last time we talked, but I want you to know it wasn't just an impulse and I haven't forgotten about it. I want…I want things to be the way they were with us before..." He couldn't seem to finish. He pressed his thumb and forefinger to his eyelids and bit his lip.

"Before your mom died?" his dad supplied.

"Yes. No. Before you met Trish. If she can see her way past the way I cut you—and her—out of my life. Out of our lives. Kath and...and Chrissy. They missed you those last couple of months." There, he'd said it. He had confessed one of his worst regrets, one he had never consciously put into words.

"It's okay, Ryan," his father said, his voice thick, as if he had a cold. Ryan knew he was either crying or about to. "You didn't have time to get used to my new situation before your whole life turned upside down. I understood. So did Trish. I just wish we could have helped. Done something. We were all in a bad way, if you want the truth."

Ryan cleared his throat and shifted the receiver to his other ear. "So, you think we could go on from here? Start over, maybe?"

"Oh, yeah." Ryan heard him sniff. "Oh, God, yeah! You bet! I know we can. No doubt about it."

For a long time, neither said anything. Ryan was about to say goodbye and hang up, call again in a day or so after they'd both had time to think about what they'd said to one another, when his father spoke again. "Are you doing all right, son? Sounds like this case is doing a number on you."

"I'm okay, I guess." For somebody who had just realized how he'd been throwing love away with both hands for years now. And that he had made the worst error of all within the past week. He should have told Nina how he felt. Maybe she would have come back one day.

God, he could hardly stand to think about never seeing her again, never holding her or making love to her. In his mind he could still feel her softness, breathe in her scent, hear her voice whispering his name. The emptiness without her almost made him sick.

His dad was speaking, dragging him back to the present. "You know what would be great? I mean, what could do you a world of good and fix you right up?"

"What's that?" Ryan asked.

"Fishing!"

The relief of a less emotional topic made Ryan chuckle, but he couldn't imagine what his father was talking about. "You want me to go fishing."

"Sure! Be a great idea, wouldn't it? I've still got the cabin out at Point Tipsy. Trish helped me fix it up a coupla years ago. We put in plumbing, electricity. It's a great little *hideaway* now. And if you wanted to do some surf fishing, no telling what you're liable catch out there."

Had he just imagined the way his father stressed the word *hideaway?* "What kind of fish are we talking about, Dad?"

"A finer haul than anything you'd ever find on the *West Coast.* You know, I hear nothing's biting out there now but the sharks."

Ryan's heart rate accelerated. He was afraid to hope. "Dad, if you know something I don't, just spit it out."

"Me? I know just about everything," his father said, his voice smug. "Told you that when you were around *ten* or *eleven.* If a boy don't wise up by then, I guess he never will. Problem is, you never *listen.* Nowadays I might as well be *sworn* to secrecy when it comes to giving you any wisdom."

Sworn to secrecy? Ryan was sitting on the edge of his chair now, gripping the phone so hard his hand hurt. "She's there, Dad? At the cabin?"

"She? The place is vacant right now, as far as anyone knows. The island's not deserted, of course. Got some new tenants in the old Smith cottage. Friends of mine, as a matter of fact. You remember Jip and Mackeral?"

Ryan was grinning from ear to ear. "Oh, yeah, I remember." Former cops. *Ten or eleven* were obviously dates she might be planning to leave, so Ryan figured he had at least a week. His grin faded. *If* he could bring himself to go at all, he had at least a week. Could he?

"Trish makes a great pot roast. If you get over this way one of these days, drop by, will you?"

"I'll keep that in mind, Dad."

"Those fish will be *running* pretty soon off Point Tipsy. I got just the boat for you."

Ryan didn't know what to say, so he simply said, "I love you, Dad. Thanks."

"You, too, son. Be seeing you."

Ryan cut the connection and sat there with tears in his eyes, even as he laughed. Nina was there! At Point Tipsy of all places. The relief of knowing she was all right nearly overwhelmed him.

He shook his head. The old man would never make a spy. Talk about transparent code!

Either Nina had sworn his dad not to tell him where she was, or someone in authority had. Most likely Nina herself, since Jip and Mackeral were there keeping her company. Dad had probably promised under duress not to call and had been warned not to tell if Ryan phoned him. But why? Didn't Nina want him to come?

Ryan knew he had some tall thinking to do, and the decision of a lifetime to make.

It took less than an hour to make up his mind. He called and left a message for Lorenzo, who called him back almost immediately. "You have something urgent to report?"

"I'd just as soon not discuss it over the phone," Ryan told him. "Could we meet somewhere?"

"Where are you?"

"My apartment."

"I'm on my way downtown. I'll stop by."

Ryan was glad. He didn't want to waste any time.

He had finished packing by the time Lorenzo arrived. "You have learned something important?" the duke asked without so much as a greeting.

"I was thinking maybe you had something important to tell me," Ryan replied, gesturing the duke inside. "Otherwise, you'd have ignored my call."

Lorenzo entered. When they faced one another again, the duke's jaw was working as if he was upset. "There is something you should know, but I hate like hell to tell you."

"What's that?" Ryan played dumb.

The man looked miserable. Guilty. Frustrated. He stuffed his hands into his pockets and shook his head. "We have no idea where Nina might be, Ryan. That is why I've been evasive with you. Well, the past few days, anyway. At first, before your embassy guards lost her in Savannah, I kept her destination from you to see whether your interest in her would prompt you to go after her."

"Why would you want me to?" Ryan asked. "You're the one who sent her away."

"Because you *need* someone, you fool!" Lorenzo exclaimed. "You worry me, that's why. We've been friends for two years now and it's time someone did something to... Well, I know what happened to you and I wanted to help."

"You called her, didn't you? Bringing me in on the case was your idea. Getting her over here was your idea. All of it was a setup, wasn't it?"

"Not entirely. Desmond had shown me photos of Nina and talked of her occasionally over the years. When he was killed, I wondered how she would be with no family left in the world."

"So you made sure she would come over here so you could arrange her life for her, right? And in the process, you decided to arrange mine?"

Lorenzo drew himself up to his full height, bracing defensively. "The two of you did seem to suit. She needed someone and so did you. There was interest there, don't deny it. I'd like to see you with an honest-to-God life and someone to care about, that's all. So would Pietro."

"Pete?" Ryan asked, dumbfounded to think a pub owner and a duke had gotten together and discussed his love life. "I can't believe you two—"

Lorenzo interrupted. "My uncle first suggested it, so you can't blame me entirely."

"The king?" Ryan wasn't quite as astounded as he pretended.

"Yes. Nina seemed so perfect. And I could see the sparks fly between you that first day in your office. Then when you and she...in the hotel...well, I thought it was a done thing." He threw up his arms in surrender. "But no! You refused to agree to go with her when Uncle Marcus offered you the chance. How can you expect a woman to love you if you let her go that way? I almost made the same mistake with Eliza. At least *I* came to my senses before it was too late!"

"So you thought you'd show me how absence makes the heart grow fonder? Was that it?" Ryan asked calmly.

"Yes! And now she's *really* gone! Do you understand? She has disappeared! She either ditched her escort on purpose, or she was taken. Our people have been trying to locate her since, but she seems to have vanished."

"You think someone took her?" Ryan knew better, of course.

Lorenzo heaved out a deep breath and shook his head. "No. I suppose it's possible, but I don't believe that's the case. She simply walked out of the hotel. One of her guards questioned people in the lobby who saw her leave, but they did not see what sort of vehicle took her away. They questioned the cab companies with no results. And we do know she did not go home."

"You lost her," Ryan said, his voice flat, his anger

barely concealed. The thought that someone could possibly have taken her sent chills up his spine. But she was all right, he reminded himself. She was at Point Tipsy with his father's friends.

He nodded toward the table in the dining area where he had left a stack of files. "There's all I have on the Caruso case that's not at the office or the lab. Joe Braca has duplicates of all my keys. I'd put him in charge if I were you."

"In charge?"

"Yes. My final report is right there on top. If you have any further questions Joe can't answer, you can reach me through my father. His phone and fax numbers are on the folder. I quit."

"Christ, Ryan, you're resigning? *Now?* I can't believe it!" But he looked delighted.

"Now," Ryan affirmed. He inclined his head toward the suitcases sitting to one side of the sofa.

Lorenzo followed his gaze, his eyes widening. Then suspicion dawned. "She's called you and told you where she is!"

Ryan shook his head. "I haven't spoken to Nina since I left her lying in ICU just before you sneaked her off to the airport." Damned if he'd give Lorenzo the satisfaction of knowing where she was. At least, not right away. Maybe he would call later and tell him, but for now, Ryan wanted a little payback. "You'll let me know what happens with the case?"

"Of course, gladly. You've narrowed the list of suspects considerably. It's only a matter of time now before we find this woman. She has to be on the island. As you suggested, we have been monitoring the airport and all watercraft since you interviewed Princess Samira and got the partial description." All this he said in a rush, as if not really all that interested in discussing the case. "Now, about Nina—"

"Good luck with the investigation. I hope you

find out who killed Desmond, for your sake and for Nina's," Ryan said, cutting off the question. "And thanks for everything. My regards to His Majesty." They shook hands.

"Of course. You're right to go after her, Ryan."

"I guess I don't have much choice about it," he replied. That was meant to instill a little more guilt in Lorenzo, but Ryan was telling the truth. Only it was Nina herself who left him with no alternative. She had made him love her, imprinted herself indelibly on his mind and in his heart and left him with no choice at all.

"Shall I order the rest of your things sent to your father's home?" Lorenzo asked.

Ryan looked at his two suitcases. "I'm afraid that's it."

"You travel light in the world, my friend."

"Considering all the other baggage I've been lugging around for six years, I thought it was best," Ryan admitted.

"Is there anything else I can do?" Lorenzo asked. "Anything at all?"

"No, thanks. Joe's taking care of my leases on the car and the apartment. He's picking me up. My plane leaves at two."

The duke looked concerned, regretful. "I had hoped you and Nina would find something together. But now... You *will* search for her, right?"

A horn beeped twice. *Joe.*

"You concentrate on the case," Ryan said as he passed by Lorenzo and picked up the bags. "Let me worry about Nina."

Lorenzo smiled then, a little smugly, realizing his plan had worked after all. He didn't look worried, but he wouldn't call off the search for Nina until he knew exactly where she was. Ryan decided to let him sweat it a little, phone him later—maybe from the plane—and tell him the truth.

"I will see you when I am next in Savannah," Lorenzo called as Ryan tossed the bags into the trunk of Joe's car.

Ryan threw up a hand in farewell. You had to like the guy, he thought, even if he was a royal pain in the ass sometimes.

Joe's car raced them toward the airport while Ryan said a silent farewell to this part of his life, the period of limbo that lay between abject misery and a new beginning.

How long would he have remained here, merely existing, if Nina hadn't come along and made him take a long, hard look at how he was living? Not really living at all, just going through the motions.

Would he lapse back into a similar vacuum if she had decided he wasn't worth the trouble? If he had left it too late and she had given up on him? Ryan didn't think he would.

No matter what happened between Nina and him, Ryan still had to make amends to his dad and to Trish. No way could he deny his feelings any longer. Not his feelings for his father, whom he had obviously hurt, or for the family he had lost. His mother, Kathleen and Christina. He would have to face those memories again, openly this time. And he sure knew the futility of denying what he felt for Nina.

Somehow he had to convince her of how much she meant to him.

He would tell her how wrong she had been about his not having any friends. Lorenzo sure qualified. So did Pete. Ryan himself had been the one trying to hold off on any personal involvement, but he thought he would be able to risk that now.

"You are doing the right thing," Joe said as he made the turn into the terminal.

"What? Quitting? Leaving Montebello?"

"Going after Ms. Caruso. Meeting with your father again. You will phone occasionally, let us know how things work out for you?"

"Sure will, Joe," Ryan said. "You know, too, don't you? About what happened before I came here? Why I was—you know—a little...standoffish?"

Joe glanced over at him. "Everyone knows. There are no secrets on this island, my friend. At least, not for very long." He shrugged. "The duke and I shall uncover this one that you and I have been working on together these past two weeks. You will see."

Ryan nodded. "I don't doubt it for a minute, Joe. But even if I did, I think I would still be going."

Ursula watched Nina Caruso's lover leave his apartment, carrying his bags, immediately after a visit from the duke himself. So the royals had sent McDonough packing. He looked furious about it, too.

No word of Nina Caruso had been published. Rumor said she'd died from that fall. She was no longer in the hospital. She wasn't at the hotel, and she sure wasn't up there in that apartment.

Probably safe to assume she was dead. If she had recovered and left the hospital, McDonough would have been with her.

The way seemed clear now for everything to proceed. Nina Caruso was out of the way, and dead or alive, wasn't a threat now. She obviously hadn't confided anything about Desmond's plans or contacts to the police or the royals. If so, they'd have *her* home by now. Nina Caruso must have died.

So had Jean-Paul, or rather Ankri Topoli. No wonder he used a fake name! The small notice in the papers said he had accidentally shot himself with his own gun. Now there would no longer be the chore of eliminating him. Yes, the plan could continue now without impediment. Things were working out nicely after all.

* * *

Nina needed to do something, get out and go somewhere, she thought. Cabin fever had set in the minute it had started to rain yesterday. Jip Lindsay had spent several hours teaching her to play five-card stud this afternoon.

"Not fair!" she exclaimed, slamming down her hand. "You've won all my M&M's!" She laughed and shoved all the winnings to his side of the table. "Did you cheat, Jip?"

He grinned and popped a couple of candies into his mouth. "Now what kind of gentleman would cheat a lady?"

Jip had a great face, tanned and lined, set with bright blue eyes and a large broken nose. Nina thought he must have been a truly handsome man at forty. At sixty-seven, he still looked fit. So did his friend John, though he was a bit more portly and quite bald. She thoroughly enjoyed their company but was beginning to feel guilty about taking up so much of their time.

"I think I'll go spell ol' Mackeral on watch. He's prob'ly ready for a nap and I need to stretch my legs."

Jip and his buddy, John MacKinnon—whom everyone called Mackeral—were retired cops, neighbors of the McDonoughs for years. Jip was a widower and John, long divorced. But surely they had better things to do than hang out on a virtually deserted island and baby-sit her. She was definitely imposing on Ryan's father—using his cabin— and on the old friends he had appointed to keep an eye on her.

Nina hadn't formed a concrete plan for what she would do when she left the island. She supposed she would go back to her old life in La Jolla.

Curiosity had played a large part in her decision to look up Ryan's father, she admitted to herself. It had led to the explanation of how she knew Ryan, and the whole story just spilled out of her. She had managed to leave out the news that she had slept with Ryan and eventually realized that she loved him. No reason to trouble his father with that.

Bill McDonough was the easiest man to talk to she had ever met, including her own father. However, he was enough like Ryan that he started arranging immediately for her to remain in Savannah. He was so persuasive, she'd agreed to stay for two weeks if he promised he wouldn't reveal her location to anyone who asked.

Before she knew it, she was on a fancy little powerboat, headed for the island with Bill's two best friends. At that point, she hadn't had the heart to dash their plans. This was a mission to them, like old times, so they said.

She had needed a place to stay until she could safely go home, and these men seemed to need a little excitement in their lives. But what had been amusing last week was now growing old. For all the freedom of movement she had, she might as well have gone to the safe house with the king's security people. She should have left them and the embassy guards a note or phoned later.

She followed Jip to the door. "I've decided to call tonight to see if Ryan has caught whoever was after me. You and John must be ready to go home by now."

He scoffed at that and waved away her concern. "Shoot, what are we gonna do at home? Lay around and watch TV?"

"I guess I should call anyway, let those people over there know I'm not dead or something."

"Hey, I bet Ryan's caught whoever it was by now," Jip said.

"I hope so," she replied. "I'm almost out of vacation time and ought to get back to work. Can you run me over to the coast to use the phone? It'll have to be very late. Time difference."

"Use my cell. That'd be a bitch to trace," he said helpfully. "In case anybody's still looking for you."

"Your cell phone works out here?" She had never seen him use it. He nodded.

"You've been keeping in touch with Bill?" she asked. "Has he heard anything? Has anyone asked about me?"

"Nope. Not yet," Jip said, then gave her a crafty look. "So you calling Ryan directly, are you?"

So they suspected—probably hoped—there was something between Ryan and her. Everyone wanted him to come back home, and they might think she could make that happen. She hadn't mistaken that hope in Bill's eyes and had wished she could tell him that she had tried.

"No, I won't bother him. I'll call his assistant." She switched subjects since Jip looked ready to give her advice. "I don't know how I'll ever be able to thank you and John—Bill, too—for helping me out."

He laughed. "Do one of them fancy ads for Bill's boats. The one he's got now looks like a third-grader done it."

She laughed. He was right. "Brilliant idea. Now you start thinking of what you want, Jip. If you won't let me pay you, I'm at least buying you gifts when I get home. Tell John," she called as he jogged off down the beach.

He seemed perfectly comfortable getting soaked in the downpour since he only wore khaki cutoffs and flip-flops. His snow-white hair turned gray as the rain soaked it. He threw up his hand and waved backward to let her know he'd heard her last words.

Nina smiled. She might be getting antsy for a change now, but she had enjoyed her time here in the cozy little three-room cabin. Bill had built it himself when Ryan was a boy, so Jip said. It had been their Sunday place, a getaway for Bill's one day off where he and his son could come and enjoy the beach, fish and do their father-son things together.

There were a few other cabins and cottages, but none within sight, other than the one where Jip and John were staying. There was a long wooden pier built about a half mile away, a crude marina of sorts near that, and an old ramshackle bait shop, now deserted.

The McDonough cabin perched in the dunes on sturdy pilings, out of reach of high tides. The wide front deck had an excellent ocean view. The inside sported simple hand-made wooden furniture strewn with colorful cushions printed with seashells.

The only drawback was the Ryan relics that decorated the little cabin. A crude ashtray, globs of red clay with his name and the date scratched in childish block letters on the bottom before someone had fired it. Obviously a long-ago gift for his dad.

He seemed to be everywhere she looked. The place was like a shrine to Ryan, built by a father who liked to come here and remember how close they had been once. She ached for both of them.

The photos were the worst. A shirtless, barefoot, knobby-kneed adolescent standing next to a fish almost as large as he was. A toddler picture that could only be him at around three years old, grinning over his shoulder at the camera, bare-bottomed, the foamy surf curling around little ankles.

Those and other pictures of him at various ages were hanging on the wall or sitting on tables in the main room.

More troubling was the one in the bedroom on the dresser. It was of Ryan as an adult. It was an enlarged snapshot of him, his arm around a beautiful red-haired woman who was holding a little blond girl of four or five. Both Ryan and the woman wore wedding rings.

Nina had seen another, more formal portrait of the woman and child on the mantel in Bill McDonough's living room. Right next to Bill and Trish's wedding photo and a separate picture of a younger Ryan in a police uniform. So handsome. So happy.

He had once been married, no question. And probably was a father. Nina knew she would never ask the circumstances that had made him single again, or why he never mentioned the child. Whatever had happened must have made him wary of any family connections.

If he only knew how hungry his father was to have his son back. But Nina wouldn't be the one to tell Ryan that. Surely he knew it already, and it was none of her business.

She would call tonight and see if there was still a reason for her to remain in hiding. If not, she would thank Bill McDonough for the use of his cabin and then she would leave.

Nina fully realized now that contacting Ryan's father in the first place and then staying on in Savannah had been foolish attempts to hold on to Ryan for a little longer, to know him a little better. It was time to let go now and get on with her life.

No matter what she found out tonight, it would be best if she left as soon as she could. She still had to have Desmond's ashes returned to La Jolla and interred beside Mother.

Yes, there would be plenty to do once she got back home. Maybe enough to keep her mind off Ryan most of the time. She would sell the house, get an apartment, decorate it, get a cat. Or maybe she wouldn't need a cat for company after all. *Damn.*

Nina turned and looked for the hundredth time at the photo of the grinning toddler who had Ryan's dimple. Even at that age, he wore that look of intense scrutiny, combined with a grin. The one that made him appear to know something you didn't. He had been a handsome baby who just begged hugging.

She was terribly afraid she was going to have one just like him. But she wouldn't worry about that just yet. No point in wavering between hope and dread the way she was doing. Condoms were fairly reliable. And she was only a few days late.

That peculiar feeling in her stomach when she smelled certain foods was probably because she'd been exposed to so many new dishes in Montebello and now, here, in the South. She wasn't a very good cook and neither was Jip.

No, it was still too soon to be really worried. And Ryan had been careful.

Chapter 15

Ryan sped for Point Tipsy, loving the way the *BoMarty* handled. She was a jewel in Dad's crown, that was for sure, a little sixteen-footer named for Trish's children, Bo and Martina. She had only hit the water twice before this trip, on test runs.

The squall had blown out to sea and the sun had come out. An omen, he hoped. He stood so that the wind over the plastic shield hit his face and blew his hair, wet his face with salt spray mist. Home again, he thought. *Here I am, home again.* It felt a thousand times better than he'd thought it would.

His reunion had proved as swift as it was happy. Lots of laughter, relief, forgiving hugs and no explanations or the recriminations he deserved. Just love and lots of it.

Trish had been wonderful about the whole thing, hurriedly offering him a pair of old cutoff shorts and a new, bright red T-shirt with I Love Savannah on the front. She had bought it at a Stop-N-Go on the way to the airport when they came to pick him up. ''C'mon, go change while

Bill hooks up the boat!'' she had told him, laughing. ''Time's a-wasting! That girl's probably bored out of her mind out there with those two old coots.''

No one had asked his dad questions about Nina. Who would have expected her to go to Ryan's family? The king's security people had questioned his friends at the precinct. They replied honestly that they were waiting to hear from Ryan about her.

All inquiries would have ceased by now since he had phoned Lorenzo and told him Nina had been located and was well protected. Apparently, she had called Joe yesterday and asked about the case.

Joe hadn't told her Ryan was on his way. Maybe she wouldn't have any defenses up when he got there. Just before he reached the old marina, another boat sped past going toward the mainland. Jip's white hair and Mackeral's shining bald pate identified the two occupants. Dad must have called them. Ryan waved and began to slow for his approach.

So, he and Nina would be alone. He docked, tied up the small craft and hopped out on the landing. Eagerness turned to worry as he sauntered off down the beach and around the asymmetrical point that gave Tipsy its name.

There it was, he thought, his steps halting as the cabin came into view. A movement caught his eye. And there *she* was. Nina stood on the deck. She wore yellow, a brighter dot in the midday sunshine that flooded the island. One hand shaded her eyes as she looked out over the water toward the mainland. Probably heard the engines. Jip's boat was already a speck in the distance. Ryan watched as she gave up and turned to go inside without even glancing in his direction.

He hurried then, the urgent need to see her kicking in full force. By the time he reached the path from the beach up to the cabin, he was running full tilt.

She stood in the doorway, a look of shock on her face. God, she looked so good.

"Ryan?"

Half out of breath, he took her in his arms and kissed her with a hunger he'd been suppressing since the last time he had seen her. No, since the last time he had kissed her.

He never wanted to stop. Mouths still joined, feeding the need that leaped between them every time they touched, he backed her into the cabin and toward the sofa.

"Please," she gasped, her arms locking around him as he took her down to the cushions and half covered her with his body.

He hesitated only a moment, trying to gauge what the plea meant. *Stop? Hurry? Hurry,* he decided instantly, feeling her press harder against him. He renewed the kiss, running his hands over her body, feeling nothing beneath the thin yellow beach wrap but the strings of her bikini. The vision of her in that red one teased him, aroused him further.

He pulled back, still kissing her, but only enough to rake at the wrap's ties and shove the fabric from between them. He reached around her, unclasping the top to her bathing suit as she wriggled out of the bottom.

One-handed, he stripped off his shirt and she unsnapped his cutoffs. The fevered efforts left them panting as they came together in a rush of heat, mating urgently with no preamble, no words, and no finesse.

Dimly, Ryan felt the bite of her short nails on his shoulders, his arms, his hips as he plunged again and again, harder, faster, racing toward a release, willing her to keep up.

Suddenly, she tensed, cried out and shuddered, gripping him so fiercely, he lost it completely. His mind blanked of everything but keen, almost painful pleasure centered on her. In her. In Nina. He thought it would never end, hoped it never would, and yet it was over all too soon.

They lay suspended in a haze of exhaustion for a while, content to do nothing, say nothing. Ryan finally forced himself to roll them to one side to take his weight off of her.

She drew in a slow deep breath and released it as she looked up at him and smiled. "You came," she whispered.

Ryan sighed. "You noticed."

Her laughter sounded lazy, satisfied. "Hard not to. You know what I mean. What are you doing here?"

He hugged her closer and buried his nose in the curve of her neck. "Making love to you. This is where I live now."

"Savannah? You'll be living in Savannah?"

"Right here," he clarified. "In your arms, on this sofa, in this minute. Let's not ever move."

Her hand brushed over his hair. "All right," she whispered and snuggled closer.

Ryan realized somewhere in the back of his mind that he was now out of work, had no place to call his own, no car to drive, no retirement plan and no firm commitment from the woman he loved. But he knew he had never felt so good in his entire life.

Nina woke first. It was still early afternoon. Ryan slept so soundly, she didn't even have to be all that careful not to wake him. Jet lag, she figured.

She got up, took a quick shower and dressed in a pair of shorts and shirt, one of several outfits Trish had bought for her at a local discount store.

Barefoot, hair slicked back behind her ears and wearing no makeup, she padded into the kitchen area to make coffee. While it perked, she watched Ryan sleep. He lay on his stomach, naked as a newborn. The ceiling fan above him stirred the hair on his forehead, making him frown in his sleep.

He looked younger than thirty-seven now. He needed a haircut, but she loved the sun streaks mixed in the sandy brown waves. Those wouldn't be as evident if he cut it very short.

His lean, athletic body was tanned from frequent swims in the waters off Montebello. She smiled at the marked tan lines that showed the brevity of the swimsuit he liked best. The good ol' boy gone cosmopolitan. He sure had the body for it.

She turned around and poured her coffee, deliberately denying herself the sight of him, since she was overheating. Instead, she stared out the window above the sink and watched the waves roll in. Why was he here?

As much as she had wanted him—and the ferocity of her need surprised her—Nina realized this was temporary. She had gone missing and he had worried enough to come looking for her. Or maybe Bill had called him. If she'd been smart, she would have phoned Joe Braca sooner to let them know she was all right and planned to take care of herself from now on.

"Nina?" he said, his voice gravelly with sleep. "C'mere."

She turned and saw that he had pulled on his shorts and was sitting on the sofa watching her. Somehow, she made herself smile and speak. "Coffee?"

"Sure," he growled, got up and ambled over to the counter where she stood. His arms slid around her, but she moved away, breaking his hold.

"Uh-oh," he said softly, his brow furrowed as he raked a hand through his tousled hair. "Too much, too soon, huh? Manners took a back seat, I'm afraid. I'll make it up to you, Nina."

"Have your coffee. Then we'll talk."

"Uh-huh." He looked at her, his blue-gray eyes intense. "This where we lay down ground rules?" He nodded as he stirred two spoons full of sugar into his cup. "You're right. Gotta have those rules." He took a sip, then winced. "Marriage. Gotta have that. My rule number one."

Nina crossed her arms over her chest.

"No?" he asked, then sighed and drank some more of his coffee. "Sorry, that one's not negotiable."

She leaned back against the counter and looked him squarely in the eyes. "I can't marry you, Ryan."

"Sure you can. I'll wait awhile, though, if you don't want to rush into anything." He glanced over at the sofa and smiled seductively. He did it well, too. "Don't want to rush, now do we?" he added.

She wanted to stamp her foot. "Will you be serious?"

He put down his mug and placed his hands on his hips. His head tilted slightly as if he were studying her. "I am serious, but I can see what an idiotic way that was to propose. No excuse except that I'm a little punchy."

He shrugged, then he came toward her and dropped to one knee. "Will you marry me, Nina?" he asked, looking up at her. Not smiling.

"No!" she exclaimed, stepping back. "And for goodness' sake, get up."

He did, bracing himself with one hand on the edge of the countertop. "I need to take lessons in this, don't I?"

"I would have thought you'd had practice," Nina snapped. "This isn't your first time, is it." Not a question.

Ryan stilled. "Dad told you."

"No, *Dad* didn't tell me. I saw the pictures. But that's neither here nor there. I only said it to emphasize how little I know about you, Ryan. Sure, we're good together in bed, but you know as well as I do there's more to it than that. A lot more."

"Do you love me?" he asked.

She refused to answer, but she could see he knew without her saying anything. "Beside the point."

He picked up his mug and downed the rest of his coffee. "Okay, here's what we'll do. We'll sit down over there where our explosion happened a while ago and we'll talk.

Anything you want to know about me, I'll tell you. We'll *communicate*.''

"Don't be snide. I hate that. You can be very snide." But she was warming to it. Even snide, on Ryan, had its charm.

"Snide's out," he agreed. "Sit."

She sat. He sat right next to her, their bare legs touching, the golden hairs on his tickling the smoothness of hers. Nina moved, putting space between them. She braced in one corner of the sofa and motioned for him to take the other end. "Now then, tell me. When are you leaving to go back?"

"I won't be going back," he said as he shook his head.

"The investigation's not over. I called Joe yesterday. Have you heard something from him since then? Have they caught—"

He was shaking his head again, smiling at her, but tentatively this time, as if he was unsure of her reaction. "No. The case is still open. Joe is running it, under Lorenzo's supervision. Looks good, though."

Nina couldn't believe it. "You didn't give it up," she accused.

"I did. I resigned. I'm going into the boat-building business." A lie. She could see it on his face. He relented, wearing a guilty expression as he tugged at the ragged fringe on the leg of his shorts. "Okay, I'm doing that only if there's no opening in my precinct." He looked up at her. "But I promise you, work will be secondary. No, further down on the list than that. Fifth or sixth maybe. I'll quit at five o'clock, even in the middle of a stakeout. Leave my thermos for the crooks when I take off. Scout's honor."

Nina couldn't help but laugh. "Ryan, you're hopeless."

"No, hopeful," he argued, and warned slyly, "I'll wear you down."

She huffed, crossing her arms over her breasts, hiding her response to his slow, sexy grin. This was a side of Ryan she found entirely too hard to resist. Now was not the time to cave in. He still hadn't told her about his marriage. She instinctively knew he didn't want to discuss it, but she had to ask.

"Will you tell me what happened the first time around?" she asked, venturing what she knew might end with Ryan stalking away from her.

He sobered instantly, his grin fading to a frown. "Yeah. You need to know. I was sort of hoping Dad had told you. It…it's hard for me to talk about."

Nina nodded, encouraging him to go on.

He took a deep breath and released it slowly. "Okay. Six years ago I was working day and night on a case where this guy was knocking off prostitutes. He'd killed two. The call came in that he'd popped another one.

"My partner and I met at the scene around nine that night. Took longer than we figured. We got a tip at the scene that the guy was holed up just down the hall in one of the vacant apartments. He'd gone out the window when we entered the room and was just pulling out of the alley. We chased him into the next county and finally caught him. Just like that, we caught him wearing the evidence. Blood all over him and the pros's datebook in his pocket."

"And?"

"Give me a minute," Ryan said, rubbing his hand over his face. His breathing had grown ragged. He steadied it, then nodded as if to himself. "Something happened while we were gone. This time, at my address. We were booking the perp when somebody told me. I didn't believe it." He paused, biting his bottom lip, his eyes glazed with a memory.

Nina feared what he would say so much that she held out a hand to stop him. He ignored it, or simply didn't see it.

His voice roughened. "When…when we got there…"

He stopped, cleared his throat. "Half my house was gone. Just…gone."

Nina held her breath. He wasn't through.

"Sometimes when I worked late, Chrissy would sneak in and bunk down with Kath in our bed. She was only five. Scared of the dark a little. That night Kath went to her room for some reason. Otherwise, the blast—" He fell silent, made a movement with his hand, then fisted it and pounded once on his leg.

Nina couldn't speak. It was a little like watching a train wreck. You knew what was about to happen, but couldn't stop it. No way to stop it.

His chest heaved and he made an attempt to speak clearly, concisely. "The bomb had been planted earlier. Timed device. Nothing sophisticated, but certainly effective. Our bedroom was completely gone, bathroom, the den, most of the kitchen." He paused, then looked at her. "In Chrissy's room…the outer wall fell in. The brick wall. Death was instant."

"Oh, God!" Nina reached out, but he shied away.

"Not yet. Hear it all. I held it together that night, did what I had to do." Ryan pinched his lips together for a full minute, thinking, before he spoke again. "It wasn't until the next afternoon that I went off the deep end. I had to go to the morgue to…see them. Sam had to drag me out of there. I don't remember much about the rest of that day."

"How awful, Ryan," she whispered. Words seemed inadequate.

"Later, I must have seemed better, all right maybe. There were questions to answer, stuff to take care of. The captain put me on leave. Suspension, I guess. I had too much time to think. Imagine what it was like for them. If they weren't asleep."

"Don't, Ryan," she pleaded.

"It got to be too much. Nightmares hit," Ryan said, calmer now that he was past the crucial point in the telling.

"I couldn't sleep, so I drank. I honestly don't remember anything that happened for nearly a year. Must have functioned on some level, I guess. Helluva blackout."

"Amnesia," Nina guessed. Hoped.

"Nothing as pretty as that. I was drunk. I woke up one morning in a holding cell in some podunk town in Mississippi with nothing to drink. By the time they let me out, I had realized I was killing myself. How I'd stayed alive that long, I'll never know."

"What then?" Nina asked, certain she had heard the worst. Nothing could be worse than the tragedy he had related. "What did you do?"

His shoulders straightened. "Got myself together, cleaned up. Went home and visited their graves. Spoke briefly with Dad, then Sam. After that, I knew I couldn't stay there. A friend asked me to go to Amsterdam on a courier job. I did runs like that for almost three years, stayed out of the country as much as I could, well away from Georgia where the memories were. Then I met Max Ryker, Lorenzo's brother. We got to talking. He said he'd give me a recommendation if I wanted to settle in Montebello. The rest is history."

He looked at her, his eyes weary and red rimmed, though he hadn't wept. Not one tear. "Any questions?"

Then he smiled, a sad smile. "Of course, you have questions. To answer the first one, yes, I loved Kathleen, but I do know she's gone now. I've let her go, and what I felt for her doesn't affect my loving you at all. In fact, I believe I know more about love now than I did then."

He went on without pausing. "Chrissy was my heart. I don't think I'll ever get over her. You might as well know up front, Nina, I won't have any more children."

Nina's intake of breath was audible in the silence after that statement.

Ryan's gaze intensified, dropping briefly to her flat stomach, then reconnecting. She remained silent, probably looking guilty as hell.

"You're not," he said softly. "You can't be."

She could see a muscle working in his jaw as he clenched it. A vein throbbed in his temple. She couldn't look at his eyes.

"We were careful," he insisted. "You're mistaken."

Nina couldn't bear seeing him this upset. This quietly upset, as if he couldn't imagine anything worse than the prospect of having another child. And she understood.

"I expect you're right," she said. "At any rate, it's not going to be a problem for you. Or even for me, if it's true," she added quickly. "You don't have to be involved."

"Are you crazy?" he asked, angry now. "I *am* involved! Whether you're pregnant or not, I am so *totally* involved with you. I can't live without you, Nina!"

"Sure you can!" she argued. "You don't even have to know whether I'm pregnant or not. Look, get me off this island and I'll be gone. You can pretend we never met."

He was up now, pacing erratically. "Wait right here!" he ordered, pointing at the floor as he slammed out the front door.

Well, she didn't have much choice about that. She had seen Jip and Mackeral taking off in their boat earlier, and Ryan was probably headed straight for his. Unless there was someone else here at Point Tipsy that she didn't know about yet, she was stuck *waiting right here* until somebody came for her.

Nina knew better than to sit and cry. It wouldn't help a thing. But she did it anyway. She curled up on the sofa where she had made love to him and cried for Ryan, for his beautiful wife and the sweet little girl with the dimples.

She wept for Bill and Trish, and for her own parents while she was at it. Even Desmond. Last of all she allowed a few tears for herself and the baby she might be carrying. Poor little thing whose parents were afraid of it.

Eventually, she had cried herself out and decided it was time to be an adult again. She washed her face and downed a glass of juice to rehydrate. When she had herself together, she went looking for Ryan. He had been alone too long.

She found him down the beach, building a sand castle. For a long time, she crouched there in the sand nearby and watched him work. Finally, she risked speaking. "You're building it too close to the water. High tide might wash it away."

"I can build another one," he said, making a window in one tower with his index finger.

"It wouldn't be the same," she told him. "The new one would be altogether different."

"I know. Even better maybe. And I would have learned not to build so close to danger."

"You think we could build something together, Ryan?"

He smiled and looked out to sea, sitting back on his heels and dusting the sand from his hands. "Yeah. I know we can. I haven't given you much reason to think so today, but I will."

"You need me, Ryan. And I need you. I do love you, you know."

"I hoped," he said, meeting her eyes with his steady blue-gray gaze. "Because I certainly do love you."

She hesitated, watching him closely. "And a baby, if there is one?"

He got up and came over to sit beside her on the sand, picking up a handful and letting it sift slowly through his fingers. "I've been sitting out here for three hours now thinking about Chrissy. She was a happy kid, Nina. I think I did a good job as a father. If you don't count that one night when a bastard I had arrested got out of prison and decided to take his revenge, I don't have any regrets about the kind of life I gave her."

He looked up again. "I promise you won't ever have cause to worry about anything like that happening. I won't go back to the job. I'll work with Dad or do something else. Something further back from danger."

"No, Ryan. You were born to do what you do. I can't imagine your doing anything else. Did they catch the man?" Nina asked. She didn't have to specify which man.

"Yeah, I got him," Ryan said. "I knew who he was and where he might be. That same night after I saw what was left of my house, heard what was left of Kath and Chrissy, I found him. He was establishing his alibi at the time."

"You arrested him?" Nina asked tentatively.

"No, I shot him. I identified myself. He ran. I knew he would. I don't think it would have mattered if he hadn't. Lucky for me he had a gun in his hand at the time. And no, I didn't put one there." Ryan's eyes were as steady as his voice. "It doesn't haunt me. I was justified."

"Yes, you were. Let's go back to the cabin now," Nina suggested as she stood. "You could use some rest and so could I."

He joined her and reached down to take her hand, lacing his fingers through hers as they walked. "Nina?"

"Yes?"

"I'm sorry you had to hear all that, but I think I can discuss it now without getting so wound up. It's just that today was the first time I've actually talked about it to anyone since it happened. I feel better, but now you're shook up. That can't be good for you in your condition. If there is a condition."

She squeezed his hand, returning his bittersweet smile. "Don't worry. I'll have some oatmeal and I'll be just fine."

He actually laughed. "What am I gonna do about your eating habits? I'll bet your cholesterol is minus zero!"

"What if I make us hamburgers just like Pete's?" she asked, trying to sound cheerful.

He rolled his eyes and groaned, his good humor either restored or pretended. Either way, Nina knew he would be all right now.

What she wasn't sure about was whether she should marry him. She had known all along Ryan had baggage. She just hadn't realized how heavy it was. She glanced up at him. He did look relieved. After that long flight, their rather vigorous lovemaking and only enough sleep to muddle the mind, he hadn't needed to rehash the worst tragedy of his life.

She would have to wait and see. This love of theirs, powerful as it seemed, was too new to trust completely.

Ryan sat at the table slicing potatoes into strips while he watched Nina fry the burgers. He liked the way they worked in tandem. Hell, they loved in tandem. They would be better than good together. He also knew she needed some space, some time to think. He had tried very hard to stay calm while telling her about Kath and Chrissy, but it had been harder than he'd thought it would be. It turned out to be something of a catharsis for him. He realized now that he should have told someone else first.

Amazing how much it had helped, just getting it all out there. It had upset her. She had cried. He knew Nina well enough to know those tears had been for his family and for him.

"You're a generous woman," he said, dropping the last pieces of potato on the plate and standing up to join her at the stove.

"I know," she replied. "Otherwise I would be stirring in raisins and cinnamon right about now." She shoveled the meat patties onto a plate with the spatula.

He added oil to the pan and waited for it to heat. "Thank you."

"You're welcome." She busied herself arranging the hamburgers on buns, adding the condiments to both. "Maybe I should tell you I plan to sleep on the sofa tonight."

Ryan shrugged. "It's a little narrow unless we sleep

stacked up, but I don't mind. You can have the top this time.''

She turned to him and placed a hand on his forearm. ''Give me some time to think, Ryan.''

''Sleep with me. Just let me hold you while you think, hmm? We don't have to make love.''

Reluctantly, she nodded. He knew he shouldn't push, but he just didn't think he could be apart from her tonight after all they had said and done today.

The next morning, Ryan woke up feeling better than he had in years. Sunlight streamed through the window and the September breeze cooled his skin where the sheet had slipped away.

Nina lay curled next to him, her dark hair silky against his shoulder. He drew the covers over her bare arm and watched her sleep, breathed in the sweet scent of her and felt the soft rise and fall of her breasts against his body.

The silver frame on the dresser caught his eye and he couldn't help the small jolt at seeing the unexpected. Dad must have put the picture there, or maybe Trish had when she'd decorated the place.

Ryan stared at the photo for a long time, letting the memories flood back. Good memories. None of them involved Point Tipsy. Fair as most redheads, Kath always avoided the beach. And she hadn't liked boats at all.

''I didn't move it,'' Nina said softly, awake now and watching him. ''I left it there last night on purpose. To see your reaction,'' she admitted, looking a little ashamed of herself.

Ryan smiled down at her. ''You don't feel like you're competing with ghosts, do you?''

She winced. ''A little, maybe. Not that you should forget them. That wouldn't be right, either.''

''Couldn't if I wanted to,'' he admitted. ''But they were part of another life, Nina. I was a different man then, I think. I can't feel anything of the old one in here anywhere now, and that's probably just as well.''

He got up and put the picture away, touching the two faces with a fingertip and smiling back at them before he closed the drawer and turned away. They would always be there in a part of his heart and mind, but that was all right. The goodbye had been said and he knew they would wish him well in what was left of his life. He would have wished the same for them.

Nina was watching him, but looked away when he turned.

"Ready for breakfast?" he asked. "I'm starved."

"No," she said. "What I'd really like to do is go over to the mainland and find a pharmacy."

He couldn't contain a grin and by God, it felt genuine. "Pregnancy kit, huh?"

She nodded. "I can't stand not knowing. You must be fairly curious to find out yourself."

"It might be too soon to know. Suppose you weren't pregnant before and it happened yesterday?"

"Omigod! We didn't use anything! I was so…I didn't even think about it then!"

"Because you were fairly sure you already were, right?"

She didn't have to answer, it was written all over her face. "You didn't think of it, either," she accused.

He smiled. "Is that what you'd call a Freudian slip?"

"No, I wouldn't. You certainly can't blame Freud for it."

"Me? I'd like a boy. Fishing buddy," he told her. "But if you insist on a girl, I think I can remember how to screw Barbie heads back on."

Nina laughed. "You're okay with it? You're sure?"

"I'm okay with it." He leaned down, gave her a lingering kiss, and tugged the sheet away. "So get up already. After you turn the little stick pink and I pick out the teddy bear, we have a wedding to plan."

Nina slipped off her T-shirt and held out her arms. "Not before I get the proposal I deserve. Come here, Mac."

"Uh-oh, she's calling me *Mac,* a sure sign of displeasure. You *had* a proposal, you greedy little beach bum," he argued. "Didn't I already get down on one knee? Did I dream that?"

"Well, it didn't exactly match *my* dream," she told him as he lowered himself over her and nuzzled her neck. "What I had in mind definitely didn't involve your knee. Are you okay with this?"

"Not yet, but I think I will be in a minute." He slipped off his shorts and brushed his body against hers, teasing, seducing, persuading, and then loving her for all he was worth.

"So, Nina Caruso," he growled, "will you marry me now?"

"The only word I can think of is *yes,*" she said with a sigh of satisfaction. "See? It's all in the way you put the question."

"Since you're only *thinking* about a yes, maybe I'd better ask you again." He grinned and nibbled her earlobe.

"I'm okay with that," she murmured as she snuggled even closer. "Ask away."

* * * * *

Don't miss

SARAH'S KNIGHT

*by Mary McBride (Intimate Moments #1178),
available next month when*

ROMANCING THE CROWN

continues!

Turn the page for a sneak preview....

Chapter 1

With each step down the palace stairs, Sarah cursed somebody else. She cursed her father for sending her to this Mediterranean monarchy in the first place. She cursed King Marcus, too, for asking her to come. She added another little expletive for Lady Satherwaite, who'd been in cahoots with the king.

Last but hardly least, she cursed Sir Dominick Chiara. Roundly. Soundly. Up one side and down the other of his elegant black tuxedo. How dare he have those gooey brown eyes, so dark they were nearly black? Not chocolate like normal brown eyes, but lovely, luscious licorice. How dare he wear a five-o'clock shadow so sexily when most men with even a suggestion of stubble on their jaws just looked like bums? The son of a pirate, indeed! The bluebeard!

God bless it. How dare the man kiss her hand and send a jolt of pure electricity through her when she had deliberately unplugged herself from those sorts of attractions? And he hadn't zapped her just once, but twice—first as a lowly plumber, then as a certified knight. Or a duke or a baron or an earl. Whatever the hell the Sir stood for.

Sir…as in surprised!

As in surreal.

As in he certainly wasn't what she'd expected little Leo's father to be, although why she had assumed Sir Dominick Chiara was a withered and doddering old codger was beyond her recollection right now.

Just ahead of her, she saw a stone bench beside another one of the palace's many fountains. This one appeared to be a chubby marble cupid with his bow tightly drawn and his arrow aimed directly at the moon. Maybe if she sat for a moment she could get her bearings.

Plopping on the bench, Sarah smoothed out and arranged the vast satin yardage of her skirt in front of her. In the moonlight, its color was less a vivid red than a rich and wine-drenched burgundy. She reached down and edged back the hemline in order to peek at her toes in the silver sandals. Their thin, metallic leather straps glittered almost magically.

"Weren't you supposed to lose one of those slippers on the palace stairs, Cinderella?"

Much to Sarah's amazement, she recognized Sir Dominick Chiara's voice. It was a deep, rich baritone, just touched by an Italian accent, tinged by some kind of private amusement. Solid. Sure. Sexy. It sent a little cascade of chills down her spine.

"If Cinderella's shoes had been this tight, her fairy tale would have ended at midnight," she answered, slipping off one of the sandals and reaching down to rub her foot.

"Well, then, thank heaven for loose shoes."

"Mmm," Sarah murmured. "None of this was my idea, Sir Dominick. Your aunt was the one playing fairy godmother tonight."

"Doesn't surprise me," he said with a chuckle. "May I join you?"

Sarah moved her satin skirt to make room for him on the little bench. His shoulder was warm against her bare arm. Moonlight glanced off the tips of his polished shoes while a faint breeze wafted his aftershave in her direction. He smelled divine. Citrus and sandalwood and something very intensely male. She almost didn't want to speak, but rather just sit here inhaling him.

Still, Sarah had never been known for her ability to maintain silence. Especially when she was nervous. Her mind tended to race. It was going about ninety miles an hour at the moment. In circles.

"How did you win it?" she asked.

"Excuse me?"

"Your bronze medal."

"Oh. That." He pointed toward the fountain that was gently splashing in front of their bench. "Just like our friend over there," he said.

Sarah blinked and then stared at the pudgy marble statue. "You won a medal for playing Cupid?"

"Archery, Miss Hunter." He laughed softly. "It's an ancient and much-revered sport in Montebello, something every schoolboy learns as soon as he's tall enough to hold a bow."

Playing Cupid! She felt like slapping herself up the side of her head. How stupid could she be? "Archery. Of course. That will be nice for you and Leo," she said as her mind went skipping ahead again.

"What will be nice?"

"You'll teach him to use a bow and arrow, won't you, when he's tall enough?"

"Perhaps."

His voice drifted off a bit sadly, reminding Sarah of the reason she was in Montebello in the first place. She wasn't Cinderella, after all, here to linger in the moonlight with Prince Charming. She was a psychotherapist and this man's son was her patient.

She wondered why Dr. Chiara had been so reluctant in getting help for the child. His concern for the boy was evident in the tone of his voice. She tilted her head in his direction and witnessed the dark distress on his handsome face. She made herself focus on the distress. Not the sculpture of his nose or the strong line of his jaw. Not the way the moonlight picked out silver threads at his temples. Especially not the obsidian shine of his black eyes.

"Leo will speak again," she said. "I'm sure of it. And I don't think it will take long. I have every confidence that I can help your son, Dr. Chiara."

"Really?" There was a dubious note in his voice, and then he sighed with just a hint of indulgence. "How long have you been in the nanny business, Miss Hunter?"

The nanny business. Sarah shook her head. This really wasn't going to work.

"Well, that's just it. I'm not exactly in the nanny business, Sir Dominick." She drew in a breath, a deep one to fuel her confession. "I'm supposed to pretend to be a nanny so you won't throw me out of the house before I've been able to work with your son. This was the king's idea. And Lady Satherwaite, too."

He merely gazed at her, fixed her with those ebony eyes, while Sarah gulped in more air and continued.

"The king and your aunt were frustrated, I believe, by what they perceived as your lack of action, and they felt they had to do something before Leo's condition became worse. So the king prevailed upon my father, his longtime friend, and my father prevailed upon me."

Sir Dominick was staring at her now, hard, terribly silent, a rather bemused expression on his face. Sarah took another deep breath and pressed on.

"Well, actually, my father did more than prevail. He sort of kidnapped me and tossed me on a royal jet, I think it was yesterday, but, you know, my mind's sort of fried at this point, so it could have been the day before. And, well…''

She threw up her hands, then let them drop in her lap. There was really nothing more to say except…

''Here I am.''

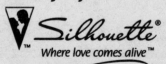

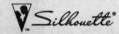

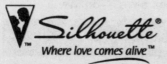

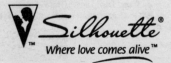

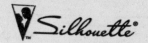

COMING NEXT MONTH